300

THE FIFTH RULE

THE FIFTH RULE

BY

DON AKER

HarperTrophyCanada™

Published by Harper*Trophy*Canada™,
an imprint of HarperCollins Publishers Ltd.

First Edition

HarperCollins books may be published for educational, business, or sales
promotional use through our Special Markets Department.

Harper Collins Publishers Ltd
2 Bloor Street East, 20th Floor
Toronto, Ontario, Canada
M4W 1A8

www.harpercollins.ca

Library and Archives Canada Cataloguing in Publication
Aker, Don, 1955–
The fifth rule / Don Aker.

ISBN 978-1-55468-863-0

I. Title.
PS8551.K46F54 2011   jC813'.54   C2010-907170-0

Printed in the United States
HC 9 8 7 6 5 4 3 2 1

For Becky Lodwick, Michelle Ash, and Nadia McLean-Gagnon,
three amazing teachers,
and for the students at Lindsay Collegiate and Vocational Institute,
who made me feel like a rock star.

THE FIFTH RULE

CHAPTER 1

THE TWO GOONS AT THE DOOR ARE NO TALLER THAN REEF, BUT EACH outweighs him by at least forty pounds. Eastern European body-builder types: all steroids and supplements, necks nearly as thick as Reef's thigh, faces like potatoes. And the guns they carry would make a gangbanger blush.

"Your boss here?" asks Reef. He was already patted down at the gate, but he's getting the same treatment inside.

The goons say nothing, just finish searching him and then return to either side of the door, where they remain, impassive mountains of muscle.

Reef waits, staring up at the security camera like the one he saw mounted above the gate outside. He wonders about the person on the other end of those cameras, wonders what it must be like to spend all day scrutinizing everyone who enters and leaves. While he was standing on the street waiting to be let in, Reef could feel someone's eyes studying him closely and, at one point, he even thought he heard the click of a camera nearby. But that, he knew, was just nerves. He isn't important enough to rate a picture.

He is, however, important enough to rate a meeting with Alexi Sukorov, the Russian "businessman" who immigrated to Calgary ten years ago and immediately got involved in a wide range of "ventures" that, according to newspaper articles, have attracted the attention of both the Calgary Police Service and the RCMP. No wrongdoing has ever been proven—even a thug like Sukorov knows how to be careful, which the multiple cameras and pat-downs prove—but word on the street is that Sukorov is heavily involved in drugs and prostitution and has recently branched out into smuggling young girls from Ukraine. It's drugs, though, that bring Reef here this evening.

The door swings open and another goon—bigger and, surprisingly, even uglier than the other two—beckons Reef inside, then remains standing at the door. Everything in the spacious room is the colour of sand—walls, furnishings, draperies, floor coverings, even the artwork that hangs at eye level—making it look oddly like a rectangular desert.

"Good evening, Mr. Kennedy," a voice says, and Reef turns to see a smiling Sukorov enter through another door. Carrying a file folder, Sukorov wears a suit nearly the colour of the room, along with his trademark gold earrings, gold chains, gold cufflinks, and gold watch. Reef can't help thinking for a moment about everything he could buy with that gold.

"My apologies for keeping you waiting so long," Sukorov continues, sitting down on a loveseat that appears to be as much unusual art form as it is furniture. "I make it a practice to check out my visitors thoroughly before I entertain them, and your information was, if you will, a little more challenging to retrieve. The advantage of youth," he grins, clearly referring to Reef's criminal record sealed under the Youth Criminal Justice Act. Apparently, though, not sealed sufficiently to keep one of

Sukorov's computer jockeys from hacking into it. "Please," he says, gesturing toward an identical loveseat opposite him. "Do sit down."

Reef sits, surprised by both Sukorov's polished manner and his perfect English, which is completely free of accent. For a weird moment, this encounter feels more like a job interview than what it really is—a confrontation.

As though Sukorov has read his mind, he asks, "Do you seek employment? I always have openings for someone with your, if you will, background." He taps the folder in his hand and smiles broadly, and Reef can see the guy even has gold teeth. Lots of them.

Reef shakes his head. "Thanks, but I already got a job."

"Yes, I see that," says Sukorov, opening the folder. "In construction. I assume it affords you entrance into buildings whose access you require. A clever cover, to be sure."

Reef feels heat in his face. "It ain't a cover. It's my job."

"Ah," says Sukorov, "then you're looking for something more lucrative. I applaud your initiative."

More than anything right now, Reef wants to tell him he can stick initiative up his ass, but he has to be careful. What was it Nan used to say? *You'll catch more flies with honey than with vinegar.* "I need somethin' from you, Mr. Sukorov, but it ain't a job."

"And what would that be?"

Reef takes a deep breath. "I need you to stay away from the street kids who hang out at Safe Haven Unitarian Church on Eighth Avenue Southeast."

Sukorov stares blankly at him for a moment, then throws his head back and laughs, the sound bizarrely out of place in that monochromatic room with armed muscle on either side of the door. "Seriously," he says when he finishes, "what is it you need?"

Reef frowns. "Stay away from the kids at Safe Haven Unitarian."

It's as though a chilling draft has swept through the room. Sukorov looks at him for a moment without expression, then drops the folder onto the loveseat, the gesture one of obvious finality. "You're aware of my—" He pauses, steepling his fingers together. "—resources?"

Reef nods.

"Then you also know what I'm capable of."

"I can guess."

Sukorov shakes his head, clearly amazed. "And still you come to me with this ridiculous request."

It's Reef's turn to shake his head. "It ain't a request."

The goon at the doorway steps forward, but Sukorov holds up his hand and the mountain moves no farther. "Your balls are as impressive as your background, Mr. Kennedy. I wish you'd reconsider my offer of employment. A person with your courage would be a great asset to my organization."

Now it's Reef who wants to laugh. *Organization. Next thing you know, the guy'll be callin' himself an entrepreneur.* "No, thanks. I like the job I got."

"Explain for me, if you will, your connection to these street people," Sukorov gestures extravagantly. "As a matter of interest."

As a matter of interest. Right. Although Reef knows that Sukorov has zero interest in his story, he wishes he could just lay all his cards on the table, wishes Sukorov actually cared enough to listen to how he ended up moving from Halifax to Calgary last year. He'd tell him how Frank Colville had gotten him a job working for Wayne McLaren, a buddy of his who has his own construction company out here. He'd tell him how he likes the work, likes how it tests his strength every day, how it's packed even more muscle onto his tall, powerfully built frame. And how it tests his skills, too, makes him think of better, faster ways to do the things required of him.

He wishes he could tell Sukorov how, although he liked the work and the growing balance in his bank account from the beginning, he hadn't felt content in his first weeks out here. The guys on his construction crew are great, but the ones who aren't married are into the bar-and-brawl scene, and he was looking for more than that, looking for something that would help ease the ache he still feels whenever he lets his mind drift back to what happened two years ago in Nova Scotia. It was Frank who suggested he try filling his free time with the kind of work he'd done in Halifax the year before.

So on one of his days off, Reef contacted the Calgary Police Service and spoke to a community liaison person, Rashid Buhagiar, about his past trouble with the law and his court-ordered service with youth groups. When he asked if there were organizations in Calgary that might have a similar use for him, Rashid put him in contact with several, and it wasn't long before Reef was giving talks to at-risk youths like he'd done back east. Rashid also directed him to Constable Jacob Paul, a First Nations policeman who, in his spare time, spearheaded an outreach program for teenagers on Calgary's streets, many of them Aboriginals, too. The cop arranged to meet Reef one evening at the Unitarian church he used for gatherings, and despite the early hour—seven o'clock—street kids were pouring out of the building on the dead run just as Reef arrived. He'd gone inside to find the constable alone and wrapping up a stab wound in his arm he'd received when he tried to break up a fight over food. It was then that Reef realized giving talks to teenagers in schools and correctional centres was a world apart from the work this policeman was doing in his spare time and, as he drove the cop in his van to an emergency room for stitches, Reef doubted he'd be returning to that church basement any time soon.

But he did.

And he doesn't regret it, although he has every reason to. Working with the St'uds—the name one of the Safe Haven kids gave the "street buds"—is routinely frustrating and thankless, and it's also cost him some of the cash he's saved. Funding for outreach programs is always in jeopardy, and Jacob often pays for supplies with little expectation that he'll ever be reimbursed. And despite Jacob's protests, Reef has begun doing the same. Of course, none of the St'uds know this. The kids have no problem stealing whatever they need or helping themselves to the food and clothing Jacob and Reef manage to round up each week from strangers, but many of them, like Wheezer and Flap, refuse to take charity from people they know. So it's better having them think the money filters down from some anonymous bureaucrat who rides a government desk.

None of which Sukorov would understand, of course. "I volunteer with those kids," Reef says simply in response to the Russian's question.

"Admirable, I'm sure," Sukorov comments, making no attempt to disguise his sarcasm.

"A couple 'a your guys have been comin' around," continues Reef, "offerin' them money to courier for you." Bone was the first to bring it to Jacob's and Reef's attention. The kid had bragged about it earlier in the week at one of their basement drop-ins, telling everyone he wouldn't be putting up with assholes like them much longer because, unlike said assholes, he had "prospects." It had taken a while for Jacob to coax the story out of him, but eventually Bone had shared privately how Sukorov's goons approached him at Olympic Plaza, offered him some easy money for "deliverin' a sealed package, no questions asked." And they offered him even more to hook them up with others who might be interested in making some easy money, too.

Sukorov smiles. "That's the beauty of this country," he says. "Absolute freedom of choice."

Yeah, thinks Reef, *like those kids* chose *parents who drink or snort or shoot up their paycheques before there's food on the table, forcing them to find it themselves however they can. Like they* chose *communities where survival depends more on your muscle than your mind. Like they* chose *poverty and the probability of dying young.* He feels the heat in his face again and struggles to keep his voice even. "There's lots 'a other people who can do what you want."

"But surely you, of all people, understand the advantage of youth," Sukorov says, smiling as he repeats that phrase.

Reef understands that advantage only too well. It was, after all, his own youth that kept him out of prison after nearly killing a girl.

And it is youth that he wants to protect now. "Those kids are off limits," he says.

Sukorov's smile vanishes. He looks down at his gold watch—a Rolex, Reef sees now—and casually wipes a speck from its impressive band before he speaks. "You are a fly to me, Mr. Kennedy. I swat flies. Daily."

"Just so you know," says Reef, "I ain't your average pest problem."

"Really?" Sukorov responds, glancing at the goon by the door, and Reef knows their meeting is quickly coming to an end.

"I wrote a letter explainin' I was comin' here," says Reef, "and I gave it to a friend who'll deliver it to the authorities if I suddenly turn up missin'."

Sukorov smirks. "You would be surprised to know how many policemen work for me," he says.

Reef nods. "Probably. But one person who *don't* work for you is the Crown attorney. There's been lots in the news about how he's tried to bring you down, so I'm pretty sure he'd be interested in both my letter and my sudden disappearance."

Sukorov's smirk disappears. "You mess with wrong person." This is the first time he's spoken anything but perfect English, his accent now thick and guttural. The man is clearly agitated.

"You took the words right outta my mouth," says Reef. *Just not with that accent.*

Sukorov stares at him for a long moment. Then, his perfect English returning, he says, "I have yet to hear why I should curtail my—" He pauses, seeming to grope for a word. "—recruitment."

"I was at the plaza the last time your guys showed up. I videoed the whole thing." Reef grins. "Amazin' how great the picture 'n' audio are. Even with your guys' accents, your name is crystal clear. Both times they said it."

Sukorov's face is impassive, but his eyes give him away. Reef knows what hatred looks like. "I wish to see this video," he says, his voice completely without inflection. He could just as easily be ordering eggs over easy.

"You think I'm an idiot?" asks Reef. "I'm not leadin' your muscle to any of the copies I've hidden. And just so you know? They're time-sensitive. If I don't check in every few days, all of 'em go straight to the Crown attorney." Reef is amazed at the intricacy of his own lies, each one more outrageous than the last. *Watchin' all those spy movies with Owen at North Hills must be payin' off*, he thinks. He can only hope that Sukorov mistakes this Hail Mary pass for something close to the truth. He had no time to do any of the things he's just claimed. Not only is there no recording, there is no letter to the Crown attorney. Worse, no one even knows he's here, not even Jacob. Because his friend is a policeman, Reef wants him to have no connection whatsoever with Sukorov, even one as tenuous as this.

Sukorov's eyes grow more menacing. "You are playing a dangerous game, Mr. Kennedy."

Reef doesn't flinch. "No games. You keep away from those kids and you got nothin' to worry about. You'll never hear from me again."

The Russian stares at him long and hard as though sizing him up, preparing a ledger in his mind balancing the benefits those street kids offer against the hassle this dark-haired nineteen-year-old is promising him. Reef feels beads of sweat form on his brow, feels his palms grow clammy and his heart race in that testosterone-filled room, but he gives no outward sign of his anxiety, merely sits waiting for Sukorov to respond.

Finally, the smile returns, although there is no warmth in it. "As you say, there are others in the city who can provide the services I require," he says as though tossing a bone to a dog. "I shall ask my associates to look elsewhere."

Reef releases the breath he's been holding. "Thanks," he says, then gets up to leave.

Sukorov's voice stops him. "If you know anything about me at all, Mr. Kennedy," says the Russian, "you know that I have overcome much in my lifetime to get to where I am. Experience has taught me that winning is a completely arbitrary concept. The only thing that truly matters is the last man standing."

There is no ignoring the implication. Reef nods, then follows the goon out.

Twice on the way back to his apartment, Reef catches himself laughing aloud, much to the suspicion of those seated near him on the bus. It's the release of tension, he knows, a physical reaction to the emotional strain of bluffing Alexi Sukorov. Reef has never kept a poker face for so long, nor with such high stakes on the table—his own life. Not that he can celebrate what's just happened. Sukorov isn't stupid, just careful. He may not—in fact, probably *does* not—believe the story Reef told him, but he's erring on the side of caution for the moment. Reef has done little more than buy some time, but that's enough for now. Why look a gift horse in the mouth?

As the bus approaches his stop, Reef wishes there were someone in the city he could talk to about this evening, someone who would understand why he did what he's done and why even this small victory is a triumph nonetheless. But there is no one in Calgary he can share this with. Certainly not Jacob. If any of this goes south, his friend must have complete deniability.

Reef thinks of the guys on his construction crew. He likes all of them, and they seem to like him despite the fact that he spelled out his past for everyone his first day on the job. He hadn't intended to make people uncomfortable; he just didn't want there to be any secrets. Calgary was his new beginning, and he didn't want to screw it up by having people think Reef Kennedy was anyone but who he was. They could take him or leave him—it was up to them. Fortunately, everyone on his crew seems to have accepted that the person working with them now is nothing like the person he'd been only two years ago.

Walking into his apartment building, Reef heads for the stairs thinking about a couple of the guys he works with—Devon

Connell and Steve Pike, who often call and invite him to shoot some pool or just hang out. He wishes he could tell them about tonight, but they'd had a hard enough time understanding why he volunteered with a bunch of street kids in the first place. They'd be hard pressed to understand why he'd get involved in a pissing contest involving those same kids, especially a pissing contest with the likes of Sukorov.

Reef knows, of course, whom he'll tell—the one person who has always understood everything. He's probably asleep by now, but he's never once complained when Reef calls despite the fact that, because of the three-hour time difference, he's usually in bed. Reef can always tell Frank is glad to hear his voice no matter what time it is.

Unlocking his door, Reef enters his apartment and tosses his keys on the scarred cast-off that does double duty as dining table and desk, thinking for the umpteenth time how the place looks exactly the way it did the day he moved in—early Salvation Army with a dash of bargain basement for good measure. But he does little more than sleep here, so what's the point of trying to make it anything more than what it is?

He's on his way to the refrigerator for a glass of orange juice when he notices the red light blinking on his land line's answering machine. He often forgets to check the thing because everyone he knows in Calgary calls his cellphone, which has its own voice-mail. He sees he has eleven messages and briefly wonders how long they've been waiting for him, then presses the Play button, glancing at the clock on the microwave.

9:04.

CHAPTER 2

LEEZA HEMMING OPENS HER EYES.

Lying in her bedroom in Halifax, Nova Scotia, she listens for whatever noise or movement in the darkened house has woken her. Nothing. There is only the swish of a car passing by her parents' Connaught Avenue home, a late-night sound she has lived with for most of her nineteen years—nothing that would thrust her into the wide-eyed wakefulness she feels now, a sudden surge of sorrow like snow inside her body, drifting against the lining of her chest.

Watching the beam from the car's headlights slide across the ceiling, she wonders if it was a dream that woke her. She is no stranger to unsettled slumber, having lived through a nightmare two years ago that haunted both her sleeping and waking hours. But that period of her life is over and her memory of it no longer brings the pain it once did. Sure, a melancholy every now and then—when she allows it—a sense of loss that still tugs at her, but the pain is behind her, like that car cruising south on Connaught. That's what she's told herself for two years anyway.

And she tells herself now it isn't a dream that woke her.

She thinks of Ellen and wonders if the dead can make this happen, bring grief in hard waves after all this time. But she knows Ellen would never do such a thing, wouldn't reach from the grave and wake her just to have her choke back sobs in the dark. Her sister was many things: determined, driven, infuriatingly single-minded sometimes, but also sensitive and kind and fiercely loyal. Yes, they'd fought—what sisters didn't?—but they were best friends, had loved each other unconditionally, always had each other's backs. Until the end.

No, Ellen hasn't done this.

Wiping away tears with the back of her hand, Leeza considers the leftover macaroni she ate because her parents were out and she was too busy to make herself a decent supper. It smelled funny when she'd sniffed under the Saran Wrap, had even thought about throwing it out, but she'd heated it up and eaten it while reading the last novel in the course she's taking at Dalhousie University this summer. Yes, she decides now, it's the macaroni working its way through her, playing havoc with her body and her emotions. *That's what this is,* she tells herself again, suspecting she's in for a long, difficult night.

Reaching for a tissue in the drawer of her nightstand, she looks at her bedside clock, its red numbers floating in the darkness.

12:04.

And she can't shake the feeling that this is more than macaroni, that something in her universe has shifted somehow.

CHAPTER 3

STANDING AT THE PULPIT, REEF LOOKS OUT ACROSS THE PACKED church, avoiding eye contact with the people sitting before him as he struggles to keep his emotions in check. He doesn't want to break down, doesn't want to humiliate himself and, worse, lose this opportunity to honour the man who was like a father to him. No. *Better* than a father—his own, anyway. A lemon-sized lump crowds his throat and he coughs into his fist, fighting back the tears that have threatened since the funeral began. Despite the hundreds of people sitting before him, the silence in the church is deafening.

Someone else coughs loudly near the back and he glances in that direction, hoping to see Bigger and Jink sitting in the crowd. But they aren't, of course. Funerals aren't their thing. Then again, funerals aren't *his* thing, either; the last one he attended was his grandmother's when he was nine.

He looks down at the words he spent the whole flight from Calgary trying to put on paper, trying to sum up the man lying in the closed casket before him, trying to convey the impact the man has had on so many lives. But the words seem meaningless now. He folds up the paper and slips it inside his suit jacket, takes a deep breath, and begins. "My name is Reef Kennedy. Frank Colville saved my life."

He waits a moment before continuing. "And not just mine. He saved the lives of lots 'a guys just like me, guys who made so many mistakes and went down so many wrong roads that they thought there was no turnin' back and no way to go forward. Guys who thought there was no place for them anywhere. Luckily, for some of us there *was* a place. It's called North Hills Group Home, and it was Frank's fortress against a world that's only too ready to turn its back on guys like me. And guys like him, too."

Reef briefly summarizes the wrong turns that Frank made in his own life, his arrests for disturbing the peace, breaking and entering, assault and battery, his drug conviction that led to five years in Dorchester Penitentiary. "Some 'a you," says Reef, "may be wonderin' why I'd bring these things up when we're here to pay Frank Colville our respects." A gentle rustling in the church confirms this. "It's because 'a that part 'a Frank's life that he understood guys like me and all the people who ended up in his care, understood what we needed most."

Because he's not reading his paper, Reef is able to look at the people before him as he speaks, and he recognizes faces: the mayor of Halifax, other government officials, several journalists, even a few TV personalities. The circumstances of Frank's death have made his funeral a media event, a fact underscored by the numerous vans lining the street outside the church, logos from various news networks emblazoned on their sides.

But these aren't the people that Reef focuses on. His eyes quickly slide over them, lingering instead on familiar faces he hasn't seen in more than a year. Greg Matheson, the social worker who first took him to North Hills. Four of the guys who lived at the group home while he was there—Owen White, Jimmy Franz, Keith Benjamin, and Gordy Towers. And there are other familiar faces, too, like Shelly Simpson from the Halifax Rehabilitation Centre and Tom Phelps from Victoria General Hospital, where Reef eventually finished his volunteer hours.

There is, of course, one person he was longing to see more than any other. Not that he expected to, but he'd been wishing anyway, hoping that maybe after all this time Leeza might have forgiven him. But he can see by her absence how foolish that hope had been. Two years wasn't nearly long enough for what he'd done to her.

Grimacing at the memory, Reef continues, "When I first met Frank Colville, I'd done a terrible thing." He pauses. He has told this story countless times to groups of young people, but it never gets easier. He hadn't planned to tell it today, but he knows this is the best way to honour the man in the casket, to have people understand the miracles that Frank performed, taking ruined lives and making them whole again. "Before then," Reef says, "I did drugs, trashed property, stole anything that wasn't nailed down, mugged people, beat the sh—" He catches himself, remembering all the times Frank worked with him on his language. "—beat the crap outta anyone who as much as looked at me the wrong way. I was bad news. But even all that don't compare to what I did just before a judge sent me to North Hills."

Reef looks down at Greg Matheson, who smiles encouragement. "Some 'a you may remember seein' in the news a couple years ago a story about a seventeen-year-old who threw a rock off an overpass into traffic. It caused an accident that nearly killed one 'a the drivers. She ended up in a coma for three weeks and then went through months of painful surgeries 'n' rehabilitation learnin' to walk again, learnin' to do all the things the rest of us take for granted every day." He takes a deep breath. "I was the guy who threw that rock."

There is sudden movement in the church, a drawing back, a shaking of heads, an exchanging of looks and murmured words. Reef lets the seconds pass until a hushed silence again fills the space. "That's the person who showed up on Frank Colville's doorstep," he tells them. "Mad at the world, aware 'a nobody else's troubles but my own, convinced that the huge tree of a man who welcomed me was just one more obstacle I needed to get around. As if he didn't already know the games guys like me played." Reef shakes his head sadly. "And despite what I'd done, what any of us had done to end up at North Hills, Frank Colville accepted each of us for who we were. More important, he saw in us so much more. And he helped us see it, too."

Tears well up again and he struggles to hold them back as he continues to speak, his voice a ragged echo in the church. "Frank had five rules: respect yourself, respect others, be accountable, honour your commitments, and do the right thing. He taught us by example how to live them. But even more important than those rules was somethin' Frank showed us every single day— that we could be loved."

Reef sobs suddenly, a harsh choking sound that the microphone amplifies throughout the huge space. But his isn't the only sobbing heard in the church. Reef looks down and sees Jimmy with his face buried in his hands, Matheson's arm around his shoulders, while Owen and Gordy wipe at their own tears. Keith stares hard at the back of the person in front of him and Reef can see the muscles of his jaws clench again and again. And in the rows behind them he sees other young men struggling with emotion.

Clearing his throat, Reef drags the back of his hand across his eyes, then grips the podium, drawing strength from the smooth hardness of the polished wood he knows Frank would have admired. "Even when we fought him," he continues, "even when we did all we could to prove we didn't need him or anybody else, Frank loved us. That was his greatest gift to everyone at North Hills." He swallows thickly. Swallows again. "Which is why I know Frank wouldn't want us to condemn the person responsible for his death."

There is another rustling murmur in the church, and Reef sees on the faces of the mourners gathered before him that they're thinking of the stories that headlined the news following Frank's death, stories Reef read on the plane from Calgary: "Joyriding Teen Causes Fatal Crash," and "Young Offender Kills Respected Youth Worker." The irony of that last headline was not wasted on the hundreds of people who once again wrote letters to their Members of Parliament decrying the country's stance on youth crime and calling for stiffer penalties for young offenders. In fact, Reef now recognizes another face in the church—Roland Decker, one of the most outspoken critics of the current legislation. Frank mentioned him once and Reef had Googled him afterwards, read how the man is running for election on a "no coddling young criminals" platform and promising to revamp the Youth Criminal Justice Act. Lots of websites posted by right-wing hard liners called the man "visionary" and "committed to the common good," but others were less flattering, offering descriptions ranging from "myopic" to "ruthlessly opportunistic." Regardless of which view is more accurate, Reef suspects Decker will be eager to put the media to use when the funeral is over.

Reef takes a long, shuddering breath before continuing. "The moment I heard about the accident, about the car that rammed into Frank's pickup, I wanted to kill the kid who'd stolen it and tried to outrun those police. I wanted to kill him," he repeats slowly. "Probably not the kind 'a thing a guy should say in a church, but that's how I felt. And I'll bet that a lot 'a people felt the same way." He looks down at the burnished mahogany casket at the foot of the pulpit. "But knowing Frank Colville the way I do—" He stops, clears his throat again. "—the way I *did*, I can tell you that's the last thing he would've wanted. If Frank could be here today, he'd be holdin' out his hand to that kid, the way he did to me. If it weren't for Frank Colville, I'd be sittin' in a prison cell or lyin' in a gutter somewhere. Or worse." His voice catches and again he struggles to keep from breaking down. "That was the kind 'a man he was. The world is so much less without him."

"Frank would've been so proud of you today," Greg Matheson says, his voice husky as he hugs Reef to him. He and the four guys standing beside him have waited until now to greet Reef, have hung back while many of the other mourners shook his hand, explained their connections to Frank, shared their own stories of the remarkable man. One of them, Frank's sister from Fredericton, sobbed into Reef's jacket as she'd thanked him for his eulogy, just as Matheson is doing now. "If you could've heard the way he talked about you, how pleased he was—" Matheson's voice breaks and he pulls away, making a sudden production of adjusting his tie.

Reef puts his hand on Matheson's shoulder. "Thanks, Greg. Means a lot to hear you say that." He turns to the group around him in the emptying church. "Jeez, it's great to see you guys."

Owen slaps Reef on the back. "You, too, man. Too bad it took somethin' like this to get your ass back here, though."

Reef nods. "Any 'a you still at North Hills when it happened?"

They all shake their heads. "Whole new bunch there now," explains Gordy.

"So you all turned citizen," says Reef, a comment that elicits a chuckle from each of them. "Turned citizen" was a favourite phrase of Alex Praeger, a flamboyant gay teenager who was the first of their group to leave North Hills and return to his family. Reef is suddenly surprised not to see him there, too. "Hey, where—?"

"Last I heard," says Matheson, as if reading his thoughts, "Alex left for Toronto as soon as he graduated. Things hadn't improved much at home."

Reef nods. He saw Alex only once after he'd moved out of North Hills, and he sensed at the time that things weren't good. Not that Alex said anything—he'd cranked up his Hollywood diva routine five notches and entertained the entire food court at the Halifax Shopping Centre with his antics—but Reef had felt uneasy when they'd said goodbye for the last time.

"What'll happen to the guys who are at North Hills now?" asks Reef.

"They've got caseworkers staying there temporarily," Matheson explains. "We should know in a couple days what it'll look like when the dust settles."

Owen shrugs. "Won't be the same without Frank there."

All of them nod emphatically.

"That was some speech," says Keith.

Reef shrugs off the compliment. The afternoon is still too raw, the risk of breaking down in front of his friends still too great, so he changes the subject. "You look good, man," he says, and it's the truth. Keith has lost a lot of the extra weight he was carrying when he was at North Hills, and his acne is almost gone, too.

"He's got a girl," explains Jimmy Franz.

"And *you*," says Reef, turning to the sixteen-year-old. "You grew a foot!"

Jimmy grins. "Who'd 'a thought all that stuff you hear about healthy eatin' is true?"

Gordy, once the tallest of the North Hills gang but now an inch shorter than Reef, jabs him in the ribs. "Healthy my ass. He was scarfin' down a corn dog when we picked him up."

All of them laugh and Reef looks around the group, pleased that, despite the year they've spent apart, they're still comfortable with each other. Besides Bigger and Jink, they are the closest thing to family he has.

"Keith's right," says Owen, his voice taking on a sober tone. "That was some eulogy."

Seeing the last mourners leave the church, Reef nods, draws a breath. "Thanks, man. I wrote somethin' else but, when I got up there, it just didn't seem right. It wasn't Frank."

"Still hard to believe he's gone," offers Jimmy, and they all nod absently, momentarily lost in their own remembrances of the man.

"You back for good?" asks Owen.

Reef shakes his head. "Flyin' back to Calgary tomorrow."

"Where're you stayin'?"

"Booked a room downtown."

Matheson shakes his head. "Cancel it. You can stay with me," and he gives Reef the address.

"I appreciate the offer, Greg, but your family doesn't need me bargin' in on 'em."

"No discussion," says Matheson. "It's the least I can do after you flew all this way to speak at his funeral."

As if on cue, the funeral director and an assistant roll the wheeled platform carrying the casket down the aisle, and all six turn toward it as it passes, watch through the open doorway as other men in black suits lift the casket and carry it down the steps, then load it into a waiting hearse. He knows from speaking briefly with the funeral director earlier that the crematorium is the hearse's next stop and that Frank's sister will be taking his ashes home with her. "You heard he asked to be cremated?"

Matheson smiles. "Leave it to Frank not wanting that mahogany to go into the ground."

This brings grins to the five faces before him. "Remember all the times I had to polish that damn pineapple?" asks Gordy.

"*You?*" the others chorus. This sparks another round of recollections as all five recount times they broke one of Frank's five rules and, as punishment, had to polish his beloved hand-carved oak newel post. Frank had found it in a Lunenburg antiques shop, his only extravagance when he'd restored the rambling two-and-a-half-storey Victorian house that became North Hills, and multiple infractions by residents had resulted in the newel post's continued high gloss.

"So," says Matheson when their laughter subsides, "you're staying with me, right?"

"If you're sure it's okay with your wife."

"More than okay. She's looking forward to finally meeting the guy she's heard me talk so much about. So are my girls."

Reef nods. "I'd like that."

Matheson's tone is suddenly more serious. "After that eulogy, you know there'll be a mob outside waiting for you," he says.

"You're not a minor anymore, and those news people will be waiting to pounce. You want to come home with me now?"

Reef shakes his head. "Might as well deal with it here. They won't give up 'til they get their story, and you don't want 'em camped outside your house. Besides," he adds, "Decker's probably puttin' on a show out there, and Frank wouldn't want that guy gettin' the last word today."

"We can wait for you if you want," offers Owen.

"Thanks, but this could take a while. Besides, there's some things I wanna do before I go back."

"Okay," says Matheson. "You got a bag?"

Reef nods. "I came straight here from the airport."

"Why don't you give it to me? That way you won't have to lug it around all afternoon."

"Thanks, Greg," says Reef. He climbs the steps to the pulpit two at a time and disappears through a door to the left, then returns moments later carrying a backpack that he hands to Matheson. "I don't know when I'll be—"

"Take all the time you need."

"You'll probably get there before Greg does anyway," observes Jimmy dryly. "You can guess what he's drivin,' right?"

"Don't tell me you still have that old Escort," says Reef, remembering the day Matheson first drove him to North Hills. The ancient Ford had sputtered and belched blue smoke the whole way.

"Hey!" responds Matheson. "That car's a classic. Besides, I did some bodywork on her and had the motor replaced since you saw her last. The old girl's got some good years left in her yet."

"And you rode here with him?" Reef asks the others. When they nod, he shakes his head. "Guts." Even Matheson laughs at that.

The others say their goodbyes, clapping him on the back and making him promise to stay longer the next time he returns from Calgary. Reef watches them leave, then loosens his tie and makes his way down the aisle toward the exit.

He dreads what's waiting for him beyond those doors.

CHAPTER 4

"SO WHADDYA HAVE LEFT TO DO?"

Leeza yawns into the phone. As she'd predicted, she hadn't gotten much sleep after waking up last night. "Two papers, a presentation, and a final exam."

On the other end of the line, Brett Hollister whistles. "I thought summer courses were supposed to be *easier.*"

"Some of them might be, but this one isn't," says Leeza, stifling another yawn. "I've written a midterm and two papers already, one of them a fifteen-page research assignment. This prof doesn't let up."

"That'll teach you to try getting ahead of the game," says the young woman. "Why didn't you just take the summer off?"

"You know why," Leeza breathes into the phone—her mother is working in the next room and might be listening. She changes the subject. "And speaking of knowing things, you didn't call just to talk about my course, did you?"

There is a moment of silence before Brett replies, "Am I that easy to read?"

"I haven't heard from you in a couple weeks and then you pick today to phone. Like a *four*-year-old couldn't see through that."

There is another brief silence. "Well, anyway, I was just wondering whether, you know, whether you'd seen the news about—"

"Yeah," says Leeza. She gets up from the island in the kitchen where she has spread course materials, reference books, file folders, and pages printed from the Internet, then walks to the patio door and steps out onto the deck. Out of her mother's earshot. "I saw it."

"So did you go?"

"No."

"Why not?"

"I never even met the guy. Why would I go to his funeral?"

"You *know* why," says Brett. "A person doesn't need to take a university course to figure *that* out."

Leeza looks across the groomed backyard and watches as a hummingbird helicopters beside the feeder her mother refilled this morning. The tiny creature seems to hang in the air, like the comment Brett just made.

"Leeza? You still there?"

"I'm here."

"It's been two years, girl. You should see him."

"What makes you think I *want* to see him?" asks Leeza. Her eyes follow the hummingbird as it darts back and forth in the afternoon heat, but her mind is elsewhere. In a room at the Halifax Rehabilitation Centre, a dark-haired teenager standing beside her bed, pleading: *I'm so sorry. You gotta believe me.*

"I don't care whether you *want* to or not. You *need* to see him if you're gonna put all this behind you once and for all."

"I put it behind me a long time ago," says Leeza. "Two *years* ago."

"That's crap and you know it."

Leeza is tempted to hang up the phone, but she's sure it will only ring seconds later if she does. Brett isn't easily dissuaded once she sets her mind on something—having shared a hospital room with her for several months, Leeza is well aware of her bulldog tenacity. She tries another manoeuvre. "Speaking of crap, how's work?"

In the past, Brett has been known to complain at great length about her job at Brookdale's Home Hardware, but she neatly side-steps the diversion this time. "I'm off for the next couple days," she says, and then goes straight for the jugular. "You back to swimming yet?"

Leeza sighs. "I've been busy—"

"Yeah, and it has nothing to do with those scars on your legs, right?" When Leeza doesn't respond, Brett continues, "Dating anyone?"

Leeza opens her mouth, then closes it.

"Yeah," says Brett, her voice flat with understatement. "You put it behind you a long time ago."

Leeza makes no effort to disguise the anger in her voice as she remarks, "All of us aren't as resilient as you are."

"Hell, Leeza, you make me sound like I'm made of rubber. You think I *bounced* when that parachute didn't open? All the afterwards stuff was hard for me, too, you know."

"Yeah, but you already had Sam," Leeza says softly, referring to Brett's husband. The two had been engaged before Brett's skydiving accident, and they'd married shortly after Brett was released from rehab.

There is a pause on the other end of the line. "Knowing Sam before was harder in some ways, Leeza."

"How?"

"Because he already knew my body. It wasn't easy letting him see what I looked like after those doctors put me back together again. It was hard on Sam, too, at first." She hesitates for a moment and, when she resumes speaking, her voice is subdued. "It *still* is sometimes."

This surprises Leeza. Sam was so supportive of Brett at rehab, making that two-hour drive from the Annapolis Valley as often as he could to see her, doting on her the whole time he was there. "I'm sorry, Brett. Really."

"This isn't about me, Leeza. I'm telling you this so you'll know there's no calendar that says we're over it because a certain amount of time has passed. I don't know if we're ever completely over it. We just get through it, put one foot in front of the other and keep going forward. At least," she says, "that's what I try to do."

Leeza marvels at what she is hearing. At rehab, Brett was the patient who kept everyone laughing as she teased, cracked jokes, organized unsanctioned wheelchair races, and short-sheeted beds when other patients were at physio on the second floor. She would go to any lengths to force a smile from people who, like her, were living with constant pain, and it was partially because of Brett that Leeza was finally able to emerge from the funk she wallowed in for weeks after waking from the coma.

The other reason, of course, was Reef Kennedy, the good-looking guy who volunteered day after day at the rehab, taking her for long walks, teaching her how to play poker, showing her that she could be strong, that it was okay to laugh again, to live again. Even begin to love again.

It was only later that she learned he was the same guy who'd stood on the Park Street overpass and thrown the rock that had shattered her windshield.

And then shattered her a second time months later in her room at rehab.

No. She isn't being completely honest about that. To be fair, she learned later that he had no idea who she was when he began his court-ordered volunteer work, part of the sentence he received for causing the accident. And she'd had no idea who *he* was since the rock-thrower was a seventeen-year-old young offender whose identity was banned from publication. It was her mother who, upon finally meeting the guy Leeza had talked about so much, recognized him as Chad Kennedy from the court hearing she'd attended, then ordered him out of Leeza's room and her life.

Against her mother's demand, Reef came to see Leeza one more time, tried to tell her how sorry he was, that he was no longer the same person who'd thrown that rock. *A person can change*, he'd told her, his face a portrait of anguish. That was before her mother had arrived and thrown him out for the last time, then petitioned the court for the injunction that prevented him from seeing or contacting Leeza again.

Leeza knows now that she has not put one foot in front of the other. Unlike Brett, she has not moved forward. Even two years later, she's still the person whose left side twinges whenever she sits in one position for too long, whose pelvis and left leg bear the scars of her surgeries and the external fixators that kept her broken bones aligned while they healed, whose nightmares still jolt her from sleep sometimes, a scream frozen in her throat as she claws her way to consciousness. She is still the person who finds it impossible to trust any of the young men at Dalhousie University who show interest in her before she shuts them down.

"Leeza?"

Brett's voice reorients her, brings her back to the here and now. "It's too late, anyway," Leeza tells her.

"Why do you say that?"

"Even if he was at the funeral—"

"He was there," Brett says firmly.

"How can you be so sure?"

"Don't you remember how Reef talked about the guy? How he complained all the time about his rules? How the guy was such a pain in the ass?"

"My point exactly."

"No," says Brett, "you're *missing* the point. He talked about him all the time, Leeza. You could see how the guy was such a big part of his life. After all those foster homes Reef lived in, here was a guy who actually gave a shit about him."

Leeza knew Brett was right long before she said it. Just as she knew Reef would be at that funeral the moment she saw the news about Colville's death.

Then, as if reading her mind, Brett says, "You *knew* he'd be there, didn't you?"

Leeza's silence speaks for her.

"What are you afraid of?" asks Brett.

"I'm not afraid of anything."

There is dead air on the line for a moment. "Keep telling yourself that, kiddo. Who knows? One of these days you might actually start believing it." Then there is only a dial tone.

Leeza clicks the phone off, then stands watching as the hummingbird zigzags around the feeder one more time before darting away for good.

CHAPTER 5

"MR. KENNEDY! OVER HERE!"

"Reef! Can I have a word?"

These and other voices come at him from all directions, and Reef hesitates at the top of the church steps. He knew it would be crazy outside, but not *this* crazy. Cameras are rolling, several mics are extended on booms, sound people wearing headphones are checking voice levels on the equipment they carry. Apparently, even after two years, Reef is still very much news. And why not? He's just spoken publicly about the crime he committed and, since he's now an adult, the media no longer need to protect his identity. He can almost see them salivating in the July heat.

He waits until the hearse pulls out of the churchyard, says a final silent goodbye to Frank, then removes his suit jacket, takes a deep breath, and makes his way down the steps.

"Reef! Channel Nine viewers would like to know—"

"Mr. Kennedy! What do you have to say about—"

Reef holds up one arm and, while the pandemonium does not cease entirely, a kind of order settles over the gathering. "If you have questions," he says loudly, "I'll try to answer 'em one at a time. But I can't do that if I can't *hear* 'em."

Immediately, a hush falls over the crowd of news people and hands shoot into the air. Reef suppresses a smile. *Sooner or later*, he thinks, *everyone ends up behavin' like they're in a classroom.* But all the classrooms he's spoken in during the past two years have not prepared him for this. His thoughts return to Frank, and he wishes for the hundredth time today that he were here.

"Yes?" asks Reef, nodding toward a good-looking woman wearing a blue suit and holding a microphone.

"You admitted in your eulogy that you were the person who—"

"*Admitted* makes me sound like I was *hidin'* it. Durin' the past two years, I've spoken to hundreds 'a people about what I did."

"Yes, but this is the first time you've revealed it to the media."

Reef feels himself grow warm, something that has nothing to do with the summer sun overhead. "I was payin' my respects to Frank Colville. You people just happened to be there."

The woman in the blue suit seems annoyed. "Isn't it true that Judge Hilary Thomas *ordered* you to give those talks as part of your sentence?"

Reef nods. "I'd like to take this opportunity to publicly thank Judge Thomas for her ruling. Another judge might've bowed to public pressure and sent me back to Riverview," he says, referring to the correctional institute where he spent time when he was sixteen. "Instead, she sent me to North Hills." Other reporters raise their hands, but Reef ignores them. "Yeah, Judge Thomas ordered me to give a certain number 'a presentations to schools and youth groups. I finished those midway through my last year at school, and I've given five times that many since then. Those aren't court-ordered. I do 'em because I want to. If I can keep just one other person from makin' the kinds 'a mistakes I did—"

"Reef!" interrupts another reporter, a short man whose surprisingly deep voice carries above the crowd. "I hear you spent some time with the girl you almost killed in that car accident. Is that true?" This information sparks murmurs among the other reporters, and several hands begin waving again.

Reef momentarily says nothing, his only movement a nearly imperceptible flicker of muscle in his right jaw. Finally, "I'm not talkin' about—"

"I have here," says the same reporter, holding up a piece of paper, "a copy of the court order her mother requested to prevent you from seeing the girl again. Doesn't sound like you changed much if a judge had to issue an injunction to keep you away from her."

The murmurs swell. Other reporters begin shouting questions.

Reef gives the short man a hard stare. "Look, I said I'm not talkin' about—"

"It's easy to see why you wouldn't want to talk about it," calls another man standing behind the reporter. Reef can't see his face amid the throng, but he can hear the scorn in his voice as he continues. "Hard for a guy to keep his nose clean when he's gotten into as much trouble as *you* have. You tell everyone you've turned over a new leaf, but it's all an act, isn't it? After all, you're the poster boy for the bleeding hearts who want to prevent people like me from enacting legislation that will finally get tough on youth crime." As he speaks, the man steps into view, but even before seeing his face, Reef knows who's speaking: Roland Decker.

Decker and the short reporter have sandbagged him.

Now all of the media people are shouting questions at Reef, some of them scribbling furiously on notepads as they call his name.

Reef feels his face burn, and his hands form fists before he's even aware they're doing it. He reaches inside his pants pocket, grips the smooth round stone he found two summers ago at Crystal Crescent Beach, where he'd gone with Bigger, Jink, and Scar. It was the first stone he'd found since his grandmother died that he hadn't thrown in anger. Holding it tightly in his hand now, he tries to remain cool, tries not to give in to the mounting fury that threatens to unleash itself in that churchyard. He breathes evenly through his mouth, waits for silence.

Finally, it comes.

"I have one last comment to make," he says as microphones are thrust at him. "Two years ago, I almost killed an innocent girl. I gotta carry that with me for the rest 'a my life. There isn't a day that I don't think of her, don't wish I could take back the terrible thing I did to her. I also don't want to cause her any more unhappiness, so I got nothin' to say about her. She deserves to be left alone." Although several of the reporters try to interrupt him, he presses on, glaring at Decker. "Today isn't a day for campaignin'. And it isn't a day for invadin' someone's privacy, either. What today is about," he says, "is honourin' Frank Colville, a man who made a difference."

Despite the shotgun-spray of questions from the group, Reef abruptly turns and walks away. Many of them follow, still yelling his name, but he strides purposefully across the parking lot toward the street. He had intended to call a taxi, but he doesn't want to wait here a moment longer, wants more than anything to put as much distance as he can between him and those reporters. He has to force himself not to break into a run.

Just then, a battered Buick Century roars across the parking lot, scattering loose pebbles in its exhaust-filled wake, and it slides to a halt beside him, its rear passenger door flinging open. "Get in!" the driver barks.

Reef's astonished expression morphs into a wide grin. He climbs in and the car roars off.

CHAPTER 6

"WHO WAS THAT ON THE PHONE?" DIANE MORRISON ASKS THROUGH the screen in the patio door.

Leeza turns to her mother. "Brett," she replies.

"It's been a while since I've heard you mention her," says Diane, sliding the door open and stepping onto the deck. "How is she?"

"Fine," says Leeza.

"What's she doing these days?"

"Same as always. Working at Home Hardware. And making Sam miserable." She intends the latter as a joke, but she can tell the grin on her mother's face is artificial, as though she's thinking about something else.

"So what did she call about?"

Leeza feels herself growing annoyed. "To say hi," she fibs. "She just called to say hi."

Her mother seems about to say something more, then shrugs. "You hungry?" she asks. "Anything in particular you'd like for dinner this evening?"

Leeza shakes her head. "Whatever you want to make is fine with me."

Diane glances at her watch. "I'm a little behind on this next set of designs, so I might ask Jack to pick up something on his way home from work. Or," her mother adds, "if you'd like, we could eat out."

"Takeout's okay with me," says Leeza. "I have a lot of work to finish before class tomorrow."

Her mother nods. "You work too hard, sweetheart," she says, laying her hand on Leeza's shoulder. "You should take a break. Go for a run or something." Then her face darkens. "If you *do*, though, you should keep an eye out for shady characters. I saw in the paper there was another mugging yesterday, this one only a few blocks from here. In broad *daylight*, no less! Two thugs bold as brass." She shakes her head. "Halifax used to be a safe city. There's a man named Roland Decker who's trying to put those kinds of people where they belong . . ."

Leeza is only half listening. There is nothing she'd like more than to go for a run, to hear her feet pound pavement while home recedes rapidly behind her, but the humidity gives the afternoon heat a wool-blanket feel and she doesn't want to put on her sweatpants. She has not worn shorts in public for two years. "I'll just lie here in the sun for a few minutes," she says when her mother finishes, lowering herself onto one of the loungers scattered on the deck.

"The UV index is high today, dear. You should put on a hat and some sunscreen first."

You should. Leeza forces her jaws to unclench. "I'm not going to be here long. Ten minutes." She settles back into the brightly patterned cushions, closes her eyes to avoid seeing her mother's anxious expression.

"I'll set the timer on the microwave," Diane offers. "You should come inside when it goes off."

You should. "Mm," Leeza replies through clenched teeth, listening for her mother's footsteps to retreat into the house. Finally, they do.

For the next few moments, Leeza allows herself to wallow, waves of self-pity rippling over her as she wishes for the thousandth time that she'd moved out of the house when she'd begun university last September. From an economic standpoint, it didn't make sense since the Dalhousie campus is a short bus ride from her house and, in fact, she often walks home from class. After sitting for hours in a lecture hall, she enjoys the exercise that eases the stiffness in her legs. She also welcomes the extra moments of peace that walking brings her, peace that is usually interrupted by cross-examination the moment she enters the house and crosses her mother's radar.

She knows now that she should have applied to universities outside the province, or at least beyond the city, but she appreciated the support of her mother and stepfather when she eventually returned to high school after the accident. She knows now that she relied too heavily on them, allowed their support to erode her confidence. Before graduating, she'd applied only to Dalhousie, despite having a high-school transcript that would have gotten her into any university she'd wanted—top marks being the single benefit of her reluctance to party or even date during her senior year. She now regrets not having applied to universities out west. Her acceptance there would have put a continent between her and her mother.

That thought brings a sudden groundswell of guilt—her mother would be devastated if she knew how smothered Leeza has felt. Diane's overprotectiveness is, after all, understandable.

Two years ago, in the span of a few months, one of her girls died from cancer and she nearly lost the other in a senseless accident. What mother wouldn't have reacted the same way, doing everything in her power to keep her remaining daughter safe? It was that single-minded desire to protect Leeza that drove her to get the restraining order preventing Reef from seeing or contacting her daughter. It was that same desire that made her ask Leeza about her day each time she returned to the house, tell Leeza to call if she was going to be even a few minutes late, and insist that Leeza wear a hat and sunscreen.

The microwave in the kitchen suddenly chirps, and Leeza glances at her watch to see that her mother programmed the timer for only three minutes. As if seven more in the sun would kill her. Leeza wants to ignore it, wants to lie here for seven more minutes without moving, let the sun beat down on her, broil her. But she knows if she does her mother will only come to the door with hat and sunscreen in hand. Besides, Leeza has a lot of work to do for the course that she is taking simply because it gives her an excuse to be out of the house. There was no need for her to get a job this summer—with her sister no longer alive, there is more than enough money in their education fund to cover all of Leeza's university costs—so lectures, assignments, and midterms are the price she pays for time she doesn't have to account for.

Sighing, Leeza swings her feet over the side of the lounger and gets up, her jeans already sticking to the backs of her legs. She longs to pull them off, replace them with a pair of light cotton shorts that she wears only at home, but she hates the expressions—even fleeting—that cascade across her mother's face when she sees the scars on Leeza's legs: pity, followed by anger and disgust at the person responsible for them.

Leeza thinks again of her conversation with Brett, thinks again of the two years that have passed since she last saw Reef Kennedy. She assumed a long time ago that he must have moved away—Halifax is such a small city that it's unlikely so much time could have gone by without their paths crossing somewhere. But she's sure he has returned for the funeral. *You could see how the guy was such a big part of his life.*

It's no secret that Brett had liked Reef a lot. She had met him the first day he volunteered at the rehab and suggested to Carly Reynolds, the nurse in charge of the musculoskeletal unit, that he should spend time with her roommate. Leeza had continued to spiral more deeply into depression each day she spent there, and Brett thought a good-looking guy her age might be a help-ful distraction for her. He turned out to be far more than that, though. He was the person who pulled her out of the pit she'd been digging for herself since the accident. Even *before* the accident, really. Since Ellen died.

Leeza hadn't known why Reef was volunteering at the cen-tre and had just assumed it was something North Hills residents did. And although he'd asked her what had brought *her* there, she hadn't told him about the accident because she'd done noth-ing but dwell on it since waking from her coma and seeing the wreck her body had become. It felt good to finally stop obsessing about it and get on with the business of healing, the business of living again. She has wondered many times since then what might have happened had she known in the beginning who that volunteer really was.

But, of course, the Reef she came to know wasn't the same person who threw the rock that nearly killed her. Brett had found out from someone at North Hills how Reef had never known his father, a teenager not much older than him, and how his mother had died when he was born. How Reef had been raised in poverty by his mother's parents, moving repeatedly from one rundown tenement to the next. How his alcoholic grandfather cursed Reef's existence every day until a stroke killed him. How his grandmother, the only person in Reef's life who'd loved him unconditionally, had died from cancer when he was only nine years old. How he'd been shunted from one foster home to another in the years that followed. *That* was the young man who'd stood on the Park Street overpass and hurled the rock in anger into Leeza's windshield.

Leeza thinks now of the Reef she came to know, the first person she'd met outside her family who knew exactly what it was like to lose someone you loved to cancer. Her friends from school hadn't known what to say to her, avoided mentioning Ellen in conversation, and some even began to avoid Leeza as she floundered in her loss. And when she ended up in rehab after the accident, even her closest friends eventually stopped coming to see her. Not that she blamed them—what normal teenager would *want* to spend time in Gimp City? Leeza now spoke a different language than her friends did: where their vocabulary included dates and dances and parties and hook-ups, hers consisted of pain and morphine and physio and more pain.

But then she'd met Reef. Leeza remembers him listening intently the day she told him about Ellen and the disease that killed her, remembers how his deep voice grew hoarse as he spoke about his own loss. She remembers how he came to visit her again and again, how his shyness began to fade in the days and weeks that followed, how he looked at her each time they were together, how he seemed to study her face as they talked.

And she'd studied his, admiring his strong features that seemed carved from stone. She'd admired the rest of him, too: black curls that immediately rearranged themselves if he dragged a hand through his hair, biceps that bunched into base-balls whenever he helped her from her wheelchair to her bed, broad shoulders that seemed to fill the doorway each time he appeared.

Standing on the deck, Leeza flushes as she realizes the warmth she's feeling now has little to do with the sun on her skin. It's a warmth she hasn't felt in a very long time. Two years.

What are you afraid of? Brett had asked her.

I'm not afraid of anything, she'd lied.

Sudden movement draws her eyes to the birdfeeder and she sees that the hummingbird has returned, its ruby throat like a bright jewel in the backyard. Watching him hover before her, she wonders how long he'll stay, then turns and goes back into the house.

CHAPTER 7

"*TOOK* YOU LONG ENOUGH, ASSHOLE!"

"Yeah, you sonuvabitch. I could feel my *hair* growin'."

Reef grins at Jink and Bigger sitting in the front seat as the Buick roars down the street. "Man, I missed you guys," he says.

Bigger reaches over the seat, punching him playfully with a fist the size of a cantaloupe. "Us, too, buddy. Been *way* too long."

"Quite a scene back there," says Jink.

Still seething from Decker's accusations, Reef doesn't want to talk about what happened in the churchyard. Instead, he spends the next few minutes catching up on news about friends still in the area and friends who've moved away.

"Ever hear from Scar?" asks Jink.

"E-mails me every once in a while," says Reef. "You?"

"Christmas cards, shit like that," says Bigger. "She signs them *Scarlet* now," he adds.

Scar had been involved with Reef for a while before he ended up at North Hills. Besides being a reluctant mule for her drug-pusher dad, she was also a brilliant student who'd graduated from school ahead of her classmates. With the help of a supportive teacher, she received a scholarship from Queen's University in Kingston, Ontario, where she's been ever since.

"What's the deal with the chickens?" Bigger queries.

"Chickens?" asks Reef, puzzled.

"Yeah," says Jink. "She wrote on her last card that she was doin' something with coops. I thought she was takin' a business degree."

Reef swallows an impulse to laugh. "Not *coops*, guys. She's in a *co-op* program. She takes courses for part of the year and then works the rest of the time for a company usin' what she's learned."

"Chickens," mutters Bigger, clearly embarrassed.

Reef quickly changes the subject. "Nice wheels," he tells Jink, who steers with one hand, the other hanging off the dented side mirror. The wind rushing through the open window swirls dust around Reef's face, along with what looks like slivers of stuffing escaping from torn seat cushions. The dashboard to the right of the instrument panel has a gaping crack in it, and multiple gashes in the upholstery overhead expose rusted metal. The car has certainly seen better days. Better *years*, in fact.

"Got her at an auction," says Jink. "Three hundred bucks. She's been in a couple accidents—"

"No, *seriously?*" jokes Reef, imagining the blow that cracked the dash. Did a *face* do that?

Jink ignores the comment. "She runs good. Leaks a little oil, but she's got plenty 'a power. She'll do one-eighty easy."

"And shimmies like a whore's vibrator," Bigger drawls.

"Yeah, there's a problem with the front end," Jink admits. "Can't seem to keep her aligned, but the powertrain's solid." He taps the steering wheel affectionately. "Good thing, too. Need her to get to work."

Reef tries not to show his surprise. "You got a job now?"

Jink nods, making the snake tattoo surrounding his neck writhe momentarily. "Bigger, too. With Scotia Paving. We been with them, what, eight months now?" he asks Bigger.

"Almost nine," Bigger replies. "Pay's good. It's a bitch in this heat, though, so we were glad our boss gave us the afternoon off for the funeral."

"You were there?" Reef asks. "I didn't see you."

Bigger shrugs. "Funerals aren't—"

"—your thing," Reef finishes. "I know. Mine neither."

"We waited outside in Beauty," says Jink.

"Beauty?"

Bigger rolls his eyes at him over the seat. "*This* piece 'a shit." He winks at Reef slyly. "Guy who gives his car a name like that probably has a special tag for his gonads, right?" He exaggerates the word *special* in a three-syllable lisp.

Reef reaches ahead and claps Jink on the shoulder. "He's just yankin' your chain, buddy. You only ever have one first car, right? Hell, I remember my first *bike*. I named *her*, too." Of course, technically, she wasn't *his* bike. He'd stolen her from outside a community centre where some Boy Scouts were meeting. He'd kept her a couple of days before ditching her, but not before giving her a name: *Free*. Lame, yeah, but he hadn't called her that because she'd cost him nothing. It was the feeling that coursed through him each time he crested a hill and let her go, the wind tearing at his face and clothes as he flew flat out. He'd been living with his third foster family at the time, and it helped him forget for a few minutes what he no longer had.

It's gotten easy forgetting things over the years. If not forgetting them, at least filing them away. There are some memories, though, that he hopes will never fade. "Look," he says, "I don't know if you guys got any place special to go . . ."

"Anywhere you want," Jink says. "We're at your . . ." He seems to grope for a word, then shrugs. "Anywhere you want."

"Thanks, buddy. There's a couple things I wanna do before I go back tomorrow."

"You're not stayin'?" Bigger's voice is incredulous.

Reef shrugs. "My boss is a great guy. Gave me time off to come for the funeral, but this is his busiest season. I don't wanna let him down."

"You're workin' construction, right?"

"Yeah. Mostly commercial buildings, but we started a condominium complex just before I left."

Bigger nods. "I figured you was either into construction or weight-trainin'. You packed on some more muscle since we seen you. You look great, man."

"Where d'ya wanna go?" asks Jink. He has been driving aimlessly, and Reef sees they're now approaching the harbour.

"Waverley okay?" Reef asks.

Jink and Bigger look at each other and nod knowingly. "Sure, man," says Jink, turning onto Barrington. From there they can see the MacKay Bridge, which will take them to the 118 and then on to North Hills.

In moments, Beauty is climbing the span, and Reef digs in his pockets for the change they'll need at the toll booth on the other side. He is barely aware of the quarters he counts out, seeing instead memories unfold in his head, all those times he rode shotgun in Frank's pickup after a day of volunteering. Heading back toward the only real home he's known since his grandmother died.

* * *

"Still look the same?" asks Bigger, nodding toward the sprawling Victorian structure.

In front of it is the sign Reef had ridiculed the day Greg Matheson first brought him here. Above a painted backdrop of rolling hills, a star throws jagged rays down on the silhouette of a figure carrying a heavy load. One of North Hills's first residents had made the sign as a parting gift to Frank, and on his first day there Reef thought it was the corniest thing he'd ever seen. Now he swallows hard against the lump in his throat. He gets out of the car. "Yeah," he replies, his voice gruffer than he intends. "Still looks the same."

Jink and Bigger get out, too, following him up the short driveway. But instead of climbing the steps leading to the wraparound veranda, Reef continues past them.

"You not goin' in?" Jink asks.

Reef shakes his head. He no longer trusts himself to speak. He cuts across a narrow strip of lawn and walks around the side of the building, his friends at his heels. And then he sees it.

"That's some greenhouse," says Bigger as they follow him into the backyard.

It *is* some greenhouse. Not huge, but fully functional. Through the glass, Reef can see it's filled with vegetable plants— tomatoes, cucumbers, even some squash, all of them ready to be picked. Reef wonders whose job that will be now.

"I remember you sayin' he made you fix it your first month here."

Reef nods. He complained to no end that summer about the job Frank assigned him when he'd arrived there. His first day at North Hills, Reef could see it had been unattended for many years—much of the wooden structure had rotted and several of the glass panels had either fallen clean through or been smashed—and Frank told him it was his job to repair everything.

He'd cursed continually the first few days, fuming at Frank in his head for what he assumed was just the man's way to get free labour. He knows better now, understands the real reason Frank assigned him that task. Lashing out in anger after Nan's death, he had destroyed so many things in the years since then. The greenhouse was the first he'd repaired.

It was more than that, though. Working on the greenhouse helped Reef see what he was capable of. He had no idea what he was doing and he refused to ask Frank for help or advice, so he spent much of the first few days fixing the many mistakes he made. But the more he worked at it, the better he got, and he began to think hard about the repairs that were needed, began to see where he was going wrong and what he could do about it. And the day he replaced the last panel and stood back to look at the finished project, he didn't feel the relief he'd expected. He was sorry the job was over.

And he felt something else, too, something he didn't recognize at first. How many times had his grandfather told him he was worthless, a waste of blood, the reason for every bad thing that had ever happened to them? How many times had court-appointed foster parents told him the same thing? It didn't matter. He'd believed it every time, even did his best to prove them right. But standing there in North Hills's backyard the day he finished those repairs, he saw something that made him think that maybe, just maybe, he wasn't worthless after all. The emotion he didn't recognize was pride. It was Frank's first gift to him.

Suddenly, Frank is beside him again now, his hand on Reef's shoulder like the last time they stood together—the morning Reef left for Calgary and the construction job Frank had gotten him with a contractor he knew. *I e-mailed Wayne a picture of the greenhouse*, he'd told Reef, *so he could see how good you are.*

There were so many things Reef had wanted to say to him at that moment, but he couldn't get the words out. All he'd managed was *Thanks, Frank.* He was afraid if he tried to say more he'd break down.

There is no stopping him now, though. His shoulders quake as he sobs, and he doesn't even try to wipe the tears away. There are too many.

This time, the hand on his shoulder is real. Bigger's hand, squeezing. "It's okay, man." He and Jink look away, give Reef some semblance of privacy in that backyard.

"Hey! Something I can do for you guys?"

Reef turns. Through his tears, he sees a man standing on the back deck, probably one of the caseworkers Matheson said was staying there temporarily.

Jink and Bigger turn, too. "Yeah, asswipe," Jink snarls, "you can take a flyin' f—"

"It's okay," Reef says, his voice little more than a croak as he struggles to regain control. He coughs, then coughs again, dragging his shirt sleeve over his face. "We were just leavin'." He takes one last look at the greenhouse, then turns and heads back to the driveway.

"Sorry about that, guys," he mutters as they walk toward Beauty.

"Forget it, man," says Bigger.

"Yeah," says Jink. As they reach the car, he continues, "You said there's a *couple* things you wanna do before you go back. You still up for the other one?"

Reef forces a grin. "Probably not," he replies, his voice still thick, "but I can't go back without doin' it."

CHAPTER 8

"DISCUSS THE THEME OF BETRAYAL IN GEORGE LAMMING'S NOVEL *In the Castle of My Skin.*" Even reading the essay topic aloud, Leeza feels disconnected from the words. She might just as easily be reading the nutritional content on the back of a cereal box, the niacin, riboflavin, and God-knows-what-else in *Special K.* She scans the other topics that Dr. Drake, her British Colonial Studies professor, has listed for their next assignment, sees nothing that holds greater appeal, and returns once more to the first.

It's not that she has no interest in the topic. She enjoyed Lamming's novel but, staring at the title, she realizes that for the past two years she has lived in a castle of her *own* skin. No. More *fortress* than castle, a thick membrane of scars both real and emotional that keep others at a distance. Like the guy who used to sit beside her in class and twice asked her out for coffee. Both times she told him no, that she had things to do, and last week he began sitting by a redhead named Jessica, who wears mostly tight T-shirts with beer logos printed across them and often dozes off in class. The guy hasn't spoken to Leeza since, just nods at her as he passes. Not that she blames him. He was trying to be friendly and she shut him down. Twice.

She tries to force herself to be friendlier sometimes but even casual relationships seem unnatural to her now, like she's learning the steps to a complicated dance and she's always one beat behind. In conversation, she finds herself always asking people questions and, during their replies, thinking up something else to ask, afraid of a lull that might focus attention on her. She dislikes telling people what she really thinks, how she really feels. Brett is her only friend who sees through her, won't let her get away with saying nothing, but even with her it isn't easy. Like today.

When she allows herself to think about it, Leeza knows there have been only three people in her life—besides her mother, of course—whom she has opened up to completely: her father, her sister, and Reef Kennedy. *And how many of those people are still in my life?* she thinks. *Oh, right. None of them.*

Her eyes return to the list of essay topics. *Discuss the theme of betrayal . . .* Christ, her life is a case study.

To be fair, she knows that Ellen would still be here if the cancer hadn't taken her. But even earlier in Leeza's life, people had a way of disappearing. Like her father. Not her stepfather, Jack, who is as constant as breathing; her biological father: Scott Hemming. Leeza has always preferred the term *biological* to *real father*, which, in his case, is a complete misnomer since he renounced that role years ago.

As a youngster, Leeza used to tell him everything. One of her earliest memories is of curling up on his lap in his study and sharing everything she'd done at preschool that day: the games she played, the people she played them with, the songs she sang. She'd show him the pictures she drew, telling him what moment she'd drawn and who the people were. Sometimes he would guess but he was usually wrong, except when he picked out himself because he was always the tallest one with the blond hair, the same colour as hers. His hair *felt* like hers, too, so much softer than her mother's coarser locks. She loved how it smelled, and she loved how *he* smelled, too, how whatever cologne he used would linger on her for hours afterwards, especially if he wasn't too busy that day to give her a whisker rub, his sandpapery face tickling her soft skin. Most of the time, though, he was usually doing something else while she chattered, checking his e-mail or updating his calendar.

Leeza was nine when her mother told her and Ellen about the divorce. Although devastating, the news hadn't come as a surprise since their father was rarely home in his last years with them, the result of the travelling he did in his work as an insurance investigator. What *was* a surprise was the news he was getting married again, this time to a flight attendant he'd apparently been having an affair with for some time, and he had already moved to Toronto where she lived with her twin sons from a previous marriage. Two years later, she gave birth to a third.

None of this information came from their father—their mother learned it second-hand from a friend who'd bumped into Scott and his new family in Toronto. And Diane had taken her time telling Leeza and Ellen the news. Had, in fact, waited until she and Jack were engaged, as if a stepfather were a kind of consolation prize.

The goodbye their father said to Leeza and Ellen was almost formal, like change-of-address information you'd submit to Canada Post. His work still brought him to Halifax in the year following the divorce, and he seemed to make an effort to see them in the beginning. But then weeks between visits became months, and then the visits stopped altogether.

"'Discuss the theme of betrayal in George Lamming's novel *In the Castle of My Skin*,'" she reads aloud again, waiting for inspiration that will fill her blank notepad, but her thoughts once more return to Scott Hemming. He hadn't even come to Ellen's funeral. It shouldn't have surprised her, of course. He'd long since stopped sending birthday and Christmas cards with cheques for the same amount each time, and the only evidence that he continues to exist are the monthly deposits he makes to the education account her mother set up, the sole support Diane demanded from him in the divorce. Those deposits were reduced by half when Ellen died, proof that he knew of her passing, and Leeza knows that these, too, will end when she finishes her degree at Dalhousie. She briefly wonders how he'll know this—will he scan lists of graduates from Atlantic universities?—then wonders how she'll react when the deposits finally stop. Will this, too, seem like a betrayal?

"Did you say something, dear?" her mother calls from her office off the kitchen.

Leeza grimaces. She knows she should be working at her desk in her room upstairs, but she likes being able to spread out her materials on the large granite-surfaced island, likes being able to see everything at once instead of sorting through careful piles. She has always been a big-picture person, probably the reason why she now finds relationships so difficult, why she sabotages something as simple as an invitation to go for coffee. Rather than focusing on the here and now, her mind leaps toward inevitable outcomes, all of which involve an intimacy she is unwilling even to consider.

"Leeza, honey? Were you talking to me?"

Leeza sighs. "Just reading the assignment the prof gave us."

"Anything I can help with?"

She looks at the paper in her hands, puts it down. "I think I'll go for that run after all."

"Don't forget sunscreen, dear."

Leeza sees her fingernails making red half-moons in the heels of both hands. She straightens her fingers, then pushes back from the island and stands up. "I'll put some on now," she says, sighing.

"I got a new bottle of SPF 70," her mother continues from her office. "It's on the shelf in the hall closet."

Might as well wear latex paint, thinks Leeza. "Thanks," she says.

"You'll watch out for traffic when you cross the street, right?"

Leeza draws a deep breath, holds it until she's confident she can release it without shrieking. "Yes," she says finally. "I'll watch out for traffic."

CHAPTER 9

"WE'RE JUST GONNA SIT HERE?" ASKS JINK.

"Yeah," says Reef, "if that's okay with you."

"Fine by me," Jink says. He reaches for the key and switches off the ignition. The engine continues to knock for a few seconds until finally shaking itself into silence.

"Beauty," murmurs Bigger beside him.

Jink hasn't missed the sarcasm. "She's good enough for you to park your worthless ass in every morning when I pick you up, ain't she?" he snarls. "Look, you wanna find your own goddamn way to work tomorrow, you go right ahead."

Reef grins at the backs of their heads. A casual listener overhearing their conversation might think the two sitting in the front seat can barely stand to share the same space, but that couldn't be further from the truth. Despite their continual ragging on each other, neither would tolerate for a second someone else doing the same.

Bigger turns to look at Reef over the seat. "You sure this is the right house?"

Reef shakes his head. "She said it was on Connaught, and that two-storey looks like how she described it, but I'm just guessin'. We won't stay long. Even if it *is* her house, she probably don't live there now. Probably off at university somewhere."

"Why don't you just call her?"

Reef turns to look at the cars that pass them as they sit parked on the side of the street. With the vehicle's windows open, the shade cast by the maples overhead makes the heat inside Beauty almost bearable. "I'm not allowed to contact her, remember?"

"So what're we doin' here?" asks Jink.

Reef shrugs. "I guess I just wanna make sure she's okay."

"Is that her?" asks Bigger. He points toward the house and they watch as a blonde girl comes out the side door.

Reef's heart staggers in his chest. Dressed in baggy sweats and a tank top, she is even more beautiful than he remembers. Her honey-coloured hair, much longer now, is pulled back in a smooth ponytail that swings from side to side as she walks down the steps. Her skin seems to glisten, and he imagines her applying sunscreen only moments before. Then imagines his own hands touching that skin, rubbing in the sunscreen with smooth circular motions. It is all he can do not to call her name through the open window.

All three watch as she moves to the small patch of lawn beside the driveway, where she stands motionless for a moment. Then she reaches over her head, bending smoothly from side to side, holding each pose for a long moment before sitting down on the freshly mown grass. She slowly stretches out one leg, then the other, and Reef thinks he sees her favour her left. This is probably his imagination—after all, it's been two years since the accident—but he is convinced he sees this, feels regret clutch at him for the millionth time.

Now she stands and slides on an armband pulled from her pocket, puts in earbuds, then adjusts the iPod that Reef can't see but knows is there. Sliding her hands over her hair and tightening her ponytail, she walks down the short driveway and stands for a moment, waiting for the traffic to pass on the divided boulevard.

Suddenly, Reef realizes she is going to cross the street without going to the intersection behind them. Her path will take her directly in front of Beauty. He can barely breathe. "Let's go," he tells Jink, his voice little more than a whisper.

"Now? But we just—"

"Now!" he hisses.

But it's too late. She is already moving toward them, and in three heartbeats she is beside the car and heading toward the sidewalk on Reef's right. In that single moment, she is less than an arm's reach from him, and he can almost hear her breathing as she passes. *Does* hear her breathing because his own has stopped.

And then she begins to run, her long legs taking her away from him.

By now, Beauty has ground to life, and Jink signals as he waits for traffic to pass. "You shoulda called out to her, man," he says as he swings the car into the street. "Woulda been so easy."

Staring unseeingly at the houses they now pass, Reef says nothing.

"What're we doin' here?" asks Reef as the car pulls into the driveway of a three-storey apartment building that looks like it survived the 1917 Halifax Explosion. Barely.

Jink glances in the rear-view mirror. "Thought maybe you could use a little fun after . . . you know . . ."

"Zeus lives here," interrupts Bigger, shooting Jink a sidelong glance.

"Zeus?" asks Reef. "What part 'a the guy's in traction now?" It's been a long time since he's seen Zeus Williams, but it's a sure bet he's got at least one broken bone. In all the years Reef has known him, he can't remember more than a couple of times Zeus wasn't stoned, and physical activity on his part often ended with him in an emergency room.

Bigger and Jink grin at each other. "You can see for yourself."

"Kennedy, you sonuvabitch!" bellows Zeus when Reef enters the apartment. "How the hell are you?"

"By the looks 'a things, a lot better 'n you," Reef replies, nodding at the casts on the guy's left arm and leg.

Lying on the moth-eaten sofa in his living room, Zeus waves off the remark with his one good arm. "Ah, this ain't nothin'. You should see my motorcycle. Had to sell what was left for scrap."

"You weren't ridin' high again, were you?"

"Any other way?"

Reef shakes his head. One of these days Zeus Williams's luck will run out. Unfortunately, he'll probably use up someone else's at the same time.

The friends come in and make themselves as comfortable as they can on the remaining furniture in the room—three chairs that look to have come from either a thrift-store or a Dumpster, and the smell wafting off the one Reef sits in makes him pretty sure it's the latter. In marked contrast to the furniture, though, is what looks to be a nearly new flat-screen mounted on the wall, some Nickelodeon cartoon flickering across its enormous surface.

"So whaddya been up to, Reef?" asks Zeus. Even from across the room, Reef can see his eyes are glassy, and the pungent haze floating in the air explains why.

Reef is in the middle of telling him about Calgary when Jink picks up a steel rod from the floor beside the sofa. "What's this?" he asks.

"My scratcher," says Zeus. "The casts itch like a bugger, 'specially as warm as it's been. Give it here."

Of course, that's the last thing Jink has in mind, not when he can milk entertainment out of a situation, and he dangles it mercilessly out of Zeus's reach for the next five minutes, all the while taunting him with a running commentary on burning rashes and flaky skin. By this time, Bigger is hooting and even Reef can't help laughing at Zeus's reaction, a rant that might have stunted the growth of nearby houseplants if the guy had any. However, the only vegetation in Zeus's apartment is a remarkably healthy crop of potted marijuana plants growing in what should have been a bedroom, something Reef sees when he gets up to use the bathroom. When he comes back, Jink has finally relinquished the metal rod, which Zeus pistons in and out of his leg cast at warp speed, his face a sudden rendering of bliss.

Once he settles down again, Zeus offers to share a joint from his homegrown stash. "Primo stuff," he tells them.

Both Bigger and Jink are game but Reef declines. He hasn't toked in two years, which is Frank's doing. *Respect yourself*—one of Frank's five rules that have guided his choices ever since—included respecting your body, too, and that meant no alcohol or drugs. "Thanks anyway, man," he tells Zeus, whose face telegraphs his immediate astonishment. After all, the nickname Reef's been called for years came from the dope he used to smoke.

Despite his choice, Reef finds it hard watching his friends smoke up, hard breathing in that pungent sweetness and not wanting more of the same. It's been a long, emotionally draining day, and he'd give anything for a hit to take the edge off what he's feeling. But he knows one will only lead to more, so instead he opens a window and leans out to clear his head. Zeus, of course, has a field day with that and begins taunting him for "bein' such a pussy," but Bigger and Jink tell Zeus—in graphic terms—to back off.

When they finally leave Zeus's place, Jink and Bigger try to convince Reef to go with them to The Keg for steaks and then to a party in Rockingham, but he asks them to drop him at Matheson's instead. He doesn't want to keep the social worker and his family waiting any longer. As it is, it's nearly 7:30 by the time they reach his modest North End bungalow.

"I was hopin' this was the right place," says Reef as the door opens.

"Glad you found us," Greg Matheson replies, all smiles. He glances over Reef's shoulder at the Buick in the driveway. "Jink and Bigger want to come in, too? There's plenty of food."

The first thing that Reef had liked about this man was how different he was from other social workers he'd known. Unlike the others, Matheson had never been intimidated by Bigger and Jink and, despite their frequent brushes with the law, he seemed to understand immediately how important they were in Reef's life. And his buddies obviously liked the social worker, too. On the way over here, they'd told him how Matheson still calls them once in a while to see how they're doing. And they'd never even been on his caseload.

Reef shakes his head. "Thanks, but they've got plans." He turns and nods at his buddies, who give him a thumbs-up. Because he's leaving tomorrow morning, they said their good-byes in the driveway. Jink had gotten something in his eye, Bigger had kept punching Reef in the shoulder, and both had complained several times about him not staying longer. But he'd invited them to Calgary any time they wanted to visit, and this seemed to placate them enough to get them back in the car.

Reef watches as the Buick now backs toward the street. In the middle of a three-point turn, Beauty stalls, and Reef hears the starter grind as Jink tries the ignition twice, then a third time. Finally, the engine roars to life and the car lurches off slowly, picking up speed before backfiring twice around the corner and out of sight.

"After riding around in that thing," Matheson offers dryly, "you can't say another word about my Escort, okay?"

Reef grins. "Deal," he says.

The man claps him on the shoulder. "C'mon in. I want you to meet my girls."

Six-year-old Abby looks a lot like her father, minus the thinning hair, and she begins chattering nonstop about puppies and unicorns even before Matheson finishes introducing their guest. Having never been around little kids, Reef isn't sure how to react, but it doesn't take him long to realize that Abby's quite happy doing the talking for both of them—all he has to do is nod from time to time.

Eight-year-old Taylor, on the other hand, is much shyer, hanging back and letting her sister monopolize the moment. Reef can see immediately that she's the image of her mother, Jenny, an attractive, dark-haired woman who is barely a head taller than her daughter.

"I'm glad to finally meet you, Reef," Jenny says warmly, ignoring his outstretched hand and giving him a hug instead. "You have no idea how many times Greg has spoken about you."

Reef flushes. "I hope some of it was good," he says when she steps back.

"All of it," she assures him. "Now, are you hungry?"

Reef is, in fact, ravenous as he hasn't eaten anything since the flight from Calgary that morning. "I could eat a bite," he says. "I hope you didn't go to any trouble, though."

"No trouble," she says. "Greg loves any excuse to fire up his new barbecue, and we've got some pork chops in the fridge with your name on them." She turns to her daughters. "Now that you've met Reef, it's time for your bath, okay?"

Taylor turns and heads down the hall but Abby stands her ground, her face suddenly dark. "Will Reef still be here after?"

"Yes, honey," says Matheson. "You can say good-night to him before I come read your story."

Her face brightens and she turns to follow her sister, her mother behind them both. Reef watches as Jenny scoops Abby up in her arms, nuzzling her neck as she carries her daughter down the hall, and he can't help wonder what his life might have been like if he'd grown up with parents like the Mathesons. He looks away.

"So, how many chops do you think you can eat?" Matheson asks.

"How many ya got?" Reef returns.

The man laughs. "More than enough." He leads Reef into the kitchen and opens the refrigerator to reveal a platter piled high with thumb-thick pork chops. Beside it are large bowls of garden and macaroni salads, and behind them are plates and bowls with even more food. Matheson was right. There looks to be enough here to feed even Bigger.

Reef whistles. "You got an army comin' by later?"

Matheson grins. "Jenny wasn't kidding about me and bar-becuing. Come see my new Grillmaster." He opens the patio door off the kitchen and Reef follows him outside onto a large deck. Beyond it is a small back lawn, in its centre a swing set, slide, sand-box, wading pool, and myriad children's toys scattered around all of them. But it's the huge propane barbecue on the deck that grabs Reef's attention: tri-level porcelain grills, dual side burners, electronic temperature controls, even a rotisserie, all in a sleek, stainless-steel housing that rolls effortlessly on large rubber tires. Reef half-expects to see outlets for Internet and cable TV.

"Now I know why you haven't bought a new car," he jokes.

Matheson nods. "Cost me an arm and a leg, but I like buying stuff the whole family can enjoy. And hey, I'm no seasonal griller. I barbecue all year round, so we'll get plenty of use out of this baby." He turns to go back into the kitchen.

"Can I help?" asks Reef. A sudden yawn embarrasses him, and he covers his widening mouth with his hand.

Matheson shakes his head. "You can take a load off. You look beat. Time difference must be killing you."

Reef glances at his watch and realizes he's been up since two o'clock Atlantic Time. Because he flew standby, he'd gotten to the Calgary airport long before any of the morning flights to Halifax were leaving, and he feels it catching up with him now. He yawns again. "You sure there's nothin' I can do?"

"You can open us some drinks, then have a seat on the deck and prepare to be dazzled by my grilling expertise."

"Deal." He follows Matheson inside and waits as the man forks several chops onto a plate.

"I'll have a beer," says Matheson as he steps back from the fridge. "You're welcome to as many as you want."

"A Coke'll be fine," he says, reaching for a can after grabbing a Coors Light for his friend.

"You don't drink?"

Reef shakes his head.

"Rule number one?"

Reef nods. And then he reddens. "Not that *you* shouldn't," he mumbles as he sees Matheson staring at him, the man's face a strange mixture of emotions.

"It's okay," says Matheson. "I was just thinking again how I wish Frank could see you now."

Reef puts his hand up. "Don't," he says, his eyes growing misty. "I already embarrassed myself plenty today."

Matheson sets the plate on the counter and reaches out, puts his hand on Reef's shoulder. "Don't you ever be ashamed of showing people how you feel, okay? Keeping everything nailed down was part of your problem, remember?"

Reef nods, swallowing hard.

"Okay, then," says Matheson, clapping him on the back before stepping away. "Let's fire up that beast."

"Can Reef read me my story?" asks Abby. She stands in the patio doorway holding a battered stuffed animal that, at one time, might have been a rabbit. Now it resembles the shapeless clouds that cover her pyjamas.

Surprised at the child's request, Reef squirms in his chair. What does he know about reading bedtime stories?

"Won't I do?" her father asks.

Abby crosses her arms. "I want Reef."

"Look, honey, Reef's tired—"

"It's okay," says Reef, pushing back from the table on the patio where they ate their meal. "You wouldn't let me help with supper." He turns to the child. "I've never read someone a story before. You'll have to show me how."

She takes his big hand in her tiny one, tugging him. "It's easy. You gotta pay 'tention to the pictures."

Reef turns to Matheson. "Okay with you?"

"Be my guest. But you don't know what you're in for," he adds.

He was right. Reef assumed he'd be reading a book while the child beside him simply listened, but storytime turned out to be a lot more interactive than that: Abby jumping in to read her favourite parts, Abby offering her own analysis of why certain characters did what they did ("He's an ol' smarty-pants" and "They *never* listen"), Abby asking "what if" questions. On and on, but Reef didn't care. She reminded him a lot of Leeza the first time he tried to teach her how to play poker, how she'd interrupted the game with question after question to make sure she understood the rules.

"Okay, sweetheart," says Jenny, standing now in the doorway of Abby's pink bedroom. "That's enough stories for one night."

The child burrows deeper against Reef's long frame. Even with his back propped against the pillows and headboard, his feet hang over the end of the princess bed, something Abby has commented on several times. "Just one more?" she pleads.

"It's okay with me," Reef tells her mother.

"Thanks," says Jenny, "but she'll keep you going for hours. And then she'll be a bear in the morning. *Won't* you, sweetie?"

"I'm not tired," Abby asserts, but her face stretches in a huge yawn.

Reef grins, then yawns, too. Pushing up off the bed, he tells her, "I wanna help your dad with the dishes anyway."

"Will you read me one tomorrow?" she asks, yawning again.

"I'm goin' home tomorrow," he tells her, but her eyes are already closing. He steps aside to give Jenny room to tuck in her daughter.

Back in the kitchen, he sees that Matheson has already done the dishes and cleaned up. Reef finds him sitting on the deck nursing a final beer and admiring the ruby-coloured sky.

"Red sky at night, sailor's delight," he says as Reef takes a seat beside him.

"What about us landlubbers?" asks Reef.

"Business as usual, I'm afraid."

"I figured."

They share an easy silence, and then Matheson turns to him. "Do you *have* to go back tomorrow? You can't stay longer?"

"Wayne, my boss, was great about givin' me the time off, but it's crazy out there now, and the crew's short-handed as it is. Two of 'em quit last week, Maritimers who wanted to come home."

"Ever think you might want to come home, too?"

Reef sighs. "Doesn't matter what I want."

"Why's that?"

Reef looks across the backyard at the lengthening summer shadows. Voices float to them from the sidewalk, people out for a stroll, and their words are swallowed up in the wash of a car passing on the street. A distant ship's horn signals activity on the harbour, probably one of the cruise ships he saw from the MacKay Bridge earlier that day. So much sound and movement around them all the time, people with plans heading toward destinations they've chosen. Unlike him. "What I want ain't somethin' I can have," he says quietly.

"What's that?"

Reef doesn't say anything for a moment. Then, "You remember me talkin' at the funeral about that girl? Leeza?"

"I remember."

Reef takes a deep breath. "I think about her every day."

"Look, Reef, you've paid for that mistake—"

"A person can't ever really *pay* for somethin' like that," he murmurs. "But that's not what I meant. I don't just think about how I *hurt* her. I think about *her.*"

Matheson raises his eyebrows. "You have feelings for her." It isn't a question.

Reef looks away, his eyes returning to the shadows that look like dark lace against the green grass.

"Do you love her?" asks Matheson.

His eyes still averted, Reef replies, "I know it's crazy. I only knew her for a few weeks. And that was two years ago."

"When you really love someone," says Matheson, "it doesn't matter how long—"

"We were just kids."

"You're not a kid now, Reef."

"Yeah, but I'll always be the guy who nearly killed her." He gets up and walks to the edge of the deck, his face shrouded with sadness. "I kidded myself for a while, though. That last week I was with her at the rehab? I began to think—" He stops, stares at his feet.

"Think what?"

Reef looks away again and a long moment passes before he speaks. "I thought we could be together. The two of us." He turns to Matheson. "Not right away, I know. She had so much pain still ahead of her, so much healin' to do. But I wanted to help, to make it easier. I thought maybe we could work through it together, even build a life together." He shrugs. "Like I said. Crazy."

Matheson sets his beer on the table, leans forward with his hands on his knees. "Did you ever tell her how you felt?"

"I tried to that last day, but . . ." His voice trails off as he remembers Leeza's mother entering her room at rehab screaming at him, calling him a monster.

"Did she have feelings for you?"

Reef remembers Leeza sobbing, telling him to go away, telling Brett, *He did this to me!* "Oh, yeah," he replies, giving a short, humourless laugh, "she had feelin's for me, all right."

"I don't mean when she found out who you were. What about before?"

Reef lets his mind drift back to the afternoons he and Leeza spent together, the things they shared with each other. "I thought maybe there might be somethin'. I dunno."

"What about your life in Calgary? Met anyone else since you moved out there?"

"I dated some. Most of 'em were girls that buddies at work set me up with. But no one for long."

"Why not?"

"None of 'em . . ."

"None of them what?"

Reef runs a hand through his hair. "None of 'em were Leeza." He looks away, embarrassment reddening his face. "Pathetic, huh?"

Matheson smiles. "It's not pathetic at all. You met someone who touched you in a way no one else has. Probably in a way you didn't think was possible."

Reef turns to him. "How'd you know?"

Matheson nods toward the house behind them. "That's how I felt with Jenny. And I don't mean that love-at-first-sight nonsense. Jenny and I were friends long before we were lovers.

In fact, the first night we spent together, we talked until dawn. How's *that* for pathetic?"

Reef laughs softly, then sobers. "So now you know why I can't move back here. I'd wanna see her."

"You're worried about the restraining order," says Matheson. Reef nods.

"Those things only last twelve months. It expired almost a year ago."

Reef shakes his head. "Her mother renewed it. The court sent me the papers."

Matheson looks down at the now-empty bottle in his hands. "The restraining order isn't the whole story, is it?"

Reef shouldn't be surprised by the man's perceptiveness, but he is. "Wouldn't be fair to her," he says. "I put her through hell. Twice."

"That's not the reason, Reef, and you know it."

Reef stares at the social worker for a moment, mystified. "So what *is* the reason?"

"You're scared."

Reef snorts. "No, I'm not."

"Yes," says Matheson, "you are."

The annoyance Reef feels threatens to flare into something more, and he struggles to shrug it off. "I ain't scared, okay?"

"It's nothing to be ashamed of, Reef. Women terrify all of us."

"Look, I'm *not*—" Reef begins, but Matheson cuts him off.

"Of *course* you are. Who *wouldn't* be? Here's a girl you can't stop thinking about, a girl you *love*, for heaven's sake, and the last time you saw her she was reeling from the news that you'd nearly killed her. If I were you and I had to choose between seeing that girl again and staring down a grizzly, I'd go with the bear. *Any* guy would."

Reef blinks at him. Suddenly, everything Matheson is telling him makes sense. Like how he felt this afternoon when Leeza was walking toward Jink's car, walking toward *him*. How he couldn't breathe. He'd felt the same way the night his grandmother died, the night he realized he was all alone, that he'd be alone forever. He had been afraid then, too. "You're right," he says, his voice little more than a whisper. "I'm scared."

Matheson nods. "You know what you have to do."

Reef looks at him. "I can't." The words surprise him, make him think of all the times a cocky Reef Kennedy roared *I can do anything!* when a foster parent or principal or police officer tried to tell him otherwise. What a fool he'd been.

"Yes, you can. I'll help you. Tomorrow I'll call the judge who issued the restraining order. Maybe if the court knows about the situation, they'll allow a meeting. Probably with conditions, but that's to be expected." Matheson paces across the deck and back. "And if that doesn't work, we'll contact Judge Thomas. She knows all the good you've been doing since she sent you to North Hills. Frank kept her informed of everything, including all those extra visits to schools, over and above what she assigned. And he told her about the outreach work you've been doing in Calgary, too, with those street kids."

"You know about that?"

"Do I *know*? How could I *not*? Every chance he got, it was 'Reef this, Reef that.'" Matheson's voice softens. "Reef, he couldn't have been more proud of you if you'd been his own son."

Reef looks away, struggles against the feeling of loss that threatens to overwhelm him again.

"Anyway, the point is, Reef, you've got a lot in your favour. Judge Thomas knows about your work out there, too. She knows how much you've changed since you stood in her courtroom two years ago. I think you've got a good chance of seeing Leeza again. That is, if you really want to."

"But she may not want to see *him*," says a voice behind them.

Both Matheson and Reef turn to see Jenny standing in the patio doorway. "Why's that?" Matheson asks her.

"Come see," she says.

They follow her inside to the living room, where she picks up a remote control and points it at the video recorder. "I was watching the news and they said there was a story coming up about Frank's funeral. I went to get you but you were in the middle of some heavy stuff." She pauses and smiles at her husband. "What you said about us being friends first? Totally makes up for forgetting our anniversary last month." She turns again to Reef. "Anyway, I didn't want to interrupt you so I recorded the segment. Did you know that someone videoed the funeral service?"

Reef shakes his head.

She clicks the remote and an advertisement for an anti-aging cream is immediately replaced by a shot of a news studio. The short reporter Reef had seen outside the church is sitting at a desk facing the camera. His name—John Peterson—floats on the bottom of the screen, and a photograph of Frank appears on a monitor behind him. Jenny presses another button on the remote and the volume increases.

"Today," says Peterson, "mourners paid their respects to Frank Silas Colville, the driving force behind North Hills Group Home and several youth programs, who died tragically in an automobile accident earlier this week." Frank's photo is replaced by an image of his pickup, nearly unrecognizable to Reef in its now T-boned condition. "A sixteen-year-old male now in hospital has confessed to stealing a car from a parking garage in downtown Halifax.

While trying to evade police in a high-speed chase, he lost control of the vehicle and hit Colville's truck broadside, killing the man instantly. The young offender's injuries aren't life-threatening and he is expected to recover fully."

The camera pulls back to reveal one of the TV personalities Reef saw at the funeral, the network's anchorman, Richard Langstroth. "John," he says, "any life lost to a senseless act like this is sad indeed, but Frank Colville's death is even more tragic, isn't it?"

"Yes," replies Peterson, "Colville devoted much of his adult life to helping young offenders become productive members of the community, yet it was a young offender who brought an end to that work."

"It's my understanding," says Langstroth, "that one of the teenagers he worked with was responsible for another motor vehicle accident."

"Yes, Richard. That case caught the attention of the media two years ago when Judge Hilary Thomas chose not to incarcerate that teenager, who had thrown a rock from a Halifax overpass and nearly killed a female driver. Instead, Judge Thomas assigned him to live at North Hills for a year and to perform volunteer work in the community."

"And many people were outraged by that decision," comments Langstroth.

"Many people continue to be," Peterson affirms. "Seventeen at the time, that young offender is now an adult, and he spoke at Colville's funeral this afternoon."

"And you have video of his comments?" asks Langstroth.

"I do." Both Peterson and Langstroth turn toward the monitor, which now shows Reef frozen in place behind a podium. "His name," continues Peterson, "is Chad Kennedy, also known as Reef Kennedy, and he chose today to discard the anonymity provided him by the Youth Criminal Justice Act when he committed the offence. Moments after revealing his role in the accident he caused, he had this to say about the young man whose actions took Colville's life on Monday."

The onscreen Reef unfreezes and says, "The moment I heard about the accident, about the car that rammed into Frank's pickup, I wanted to kill the kid who'd stolen it and tried to outrun those police. I wanted to kill him." The image freezes again, and the camera pulls back to show Langstroth shaking his head. "Doesn't sound like his community service had much impact on him," he says.

Reef gapes at the television, then turns to Matheson, his voice a growl. "That's not all I said!"

Matheson shushes him, and Reef looks at the screen again. Peterson is nodding.

"You're not the only one," says Peterson, "to think that Kennedy didn't learn anything from Judge Thomas's sentence. Following the funeral, I spoke to Roland Decker, who, as you know, is running in the upcoming federal election on a platform that promises a tougher stance on youth crime."

The onscreen Reef is replaced by Decker in the church-yard. "This," says Decker, his voice passionate, "is exactly the kind of result we can expect from judicial application of the current legislation. If I'm elected, the legislation I propose will put young offenders where they belong—in prison away from the good citizens of this country. If these kids are old enough to commit violent crimes like the one Kennedy admitted to, they're old enough to face the consequences and do the time."

The image of Decker freezes and the camera pulls back once more to show Peterson and the anchorman. Langstroth asks, "Did Kennedy speak about his own victim?"

"Interesting you should ask, Richard," replies Peterson. "After the service, I asked Kennedy to comment on the young woman he nearly killed, and this was his response." They turn again to the monitor, which now shows Reef in the churchyard, microphones thrust toward him. "I got nothin' to say about her," the onscreen Reef says.

The scene immediately switches again to Roland Decker, who comments, "It's clear that Kennedy has given little thought to his unfortunate victim and the devastating impact his action had on her. Sadly, he's typical of many young offenders who don't accept responsibility for their actions. And why should he? He got a free ride, didn't he?"

The camera returns to Peterson, who begins to say something else, but Jenny presses a button on the remote and the television darkens.

Reef groans. "None 'a that—" he begins, then gropes for words. "Yeah, I said those things, but—"

"You don't have to explain, Reef," says Jenny. "Greg told me about your eulogy, how you asked for understanding the way Frank would have. Greg also told me what happened afterwards. He sat with the boys in the car and saw what those reporters did, how they tried to goad you into talking about Leeza. He even got out to help set the record straight but then you put an end to it." She sighs. "Not all journalists are like that. Peterson's just trying to make a name for himself on Decker's coattails."

"Jenny's right," says Matheson. "There'll be other reports that won't be so slanted. I'm sure of it."

But Reef barely hears their words of assurance. In his mind he's picturing another news conference, the one after his hearing in which Leeza's mother sobbed in front of a video camera, *That ruling was a slap in the face! My daughter is lying in a hospital bed with injuries to more than half her body, and that animal was sentenced to be a* volunteer! *For Christ's sake, can* anyone *call that fair?*

He wonders what Diane Morrison would think if she saw the segment he and the Mathesons just watched, but he's pretty sure he knows. What bothers him more is what Leeza would think.

CHAPTER 10

SITTING AT THE KITCHEN ISLAND, THE FIRST DRAFT OF HER *In the Castle of My Skin* essay nearly finished, Leeza hears the volume of the living room TV suddenly increase. Voices suggest two men having a conversation, and she shakes her head. Her mother is addicted to reality TV, despite being told by Leeza that there's very little about it that's genuine. One of her professors last year described how skilled editors cut and splice video segments to create tension and drama where there is none—*frankenbiting*, he called it—but her mother refuses to even consider the possibility that everything she sees isn't real. Hearing those men's voices now, Leeza assumes she's immersed in yet another program where people with no lives—or, at least, no self-respect—welcome cameras into their homes.

"Leeza! Jack!" her mother calls. "Come see this!"

Leeza groans. She's been forced to watch segments in the past when her mother has tried to prove how authentic those shows are, and she ignores the command. But she hears her stepfather walk from his study down the hall into the living room and, a moment later, he calls her name.

"Leeza, I think you might be interested in this."

She sighs. Apparently, George Lamming will have to wait. She gets up from the island and makes her way to the living room. "You're watching the *news?*" she asks when she enters and sees the Channel Nine news logo frozen on the flat-screen. When was the last time her mother chose news over nonsense?

"I recorded this while I was watching *World's Wackiest Weddings,*" says Diane when Leeza enters. "You remember me talking about Roland Decker?"

Leeza nods. "That guy who's running for office."

"He's not just *any* guy running for office," says her mother. "He's the one who's promising to get tough on young offenders. They interviewed him about it earlier today."

Leeza looks at her. "And you thought I'd be interested because . . ."

Diane frowns. "Here's a man who knows how the judicial system needs to respond to young people who do bad things. Like what happened to you, sweetheart."

It's Leeza's turn to frown. "You know I don't like talking about that," she says softly.

"I'm not asking you to, sweetheart. Just listen to what the man has to say on the matter. This is the first election you'll be voting in, so you should be aware of the issues. Especially this one."

"Look," says Leeza, trying to keep her voice light, "you and I didn't agree on this two years ago. What makes you think I'll change my mind now?"

Diane's eyes flicker to Jack, who shakes his head at her, but she ignores his warning. "We didn't agree because you weren't yourself. That Kennedy boy played on your emotions, made you think what he did to you wasn't his fault."

"No, he didn't," says Leeza, more to her feet than to her mother. "He didn't even know who I was."

"That's what he *claimed*," Diane says.

Leeza feels her irritation begin to grow into something more. Something like the scream she's been holding back for so long now. "Don't you think I would've known otherwise? We spent *weeks* together."

"You were vulnerable, dear. You were confined to a wheel-chair and a hospital bed. You were broken, both physically and emotionally, and he *used* that."

"No, he didn't," says Leeza, determination in her jawline. "He *helped* me."

Diane's eyes widen. "Why are you defending him? How *can* you after how he hurt you?"

"The person you're describing isn't the person I knew that summer. He might have been like that before, but not afterwards. He changed."

"You knew this guy for a few weeks but you're an expert on him," Diane says, scorn tingeing her voice.

Although Leeza knows it's useless to try to make her mother understand, she says, "It felt longer, like I knew him better than friends I'd grown up with. We'd shared so many of the same experiences."

"Really?" her mother asks, scorn now evident on her face, too. "You mugged people? Committed break-and-enters? Pushed drugs like he did?"

"Not that," replies Leeza, trying to keep the frustration from her voice. "He knew what it was like to lose someone close to him. Like I lost Ellen."

Diane's face flushes. "And *I* didn't lose Ellen, too? This *criminal* knew more about loss than a mother whose first-born died in her arms?"

Leeza shakes her head. "That's not what I meant."

"Well, why don't you *enlighten* me, Leeza?"

"Diane," says Jack, his voice cautious, "this talk isn't accomplishing anything."

"No!" she says, whirling to face him. "I want to *hear* this. I want to hear how a criminal—" She pauses, turns again to Leeza. "No, how a *monster* could have been more supportive than I was."

"I could be *myself*!" The words are out of Leeza's mouth before she realizes she's said them.

Diane recoils as if slapped. "And *I* didn't let you be yourself?"

Leeza takes a breath, then another, the scream clawing at her, pulsing at the base of her throat. She struggles to speak evenly. "When Ellen died, I had to be strong for you. I'd lost a sister, but you'd lost a child. Your *first-born*, like you said. There were times I felt guilty just being alive. Do you think I could have shared *that* with you? Do you think you would have understood *that*?" She lowers her eyes. "Reef did."

There. She has said his name aloud after all this time, and a sudden thrumming in her chest reminds her of the hummingbird in the backyard.

"Really," says her mother, the word less a statement than a manifestation of utter disbelief.

"Yes, really. Reef showed me how to start living again."

"After nearly *killing* you!"

The shriek startles everyone, including Leeza, who has finally released it. "He wasn't trying to kill me or anyone!" she cries, thinking of the things Brett told her after calling North Hills. "He was just lashing out!"

"See?" Diane says to Jack, her voice indignant. "*This* is why I had to get that restraining order. To keep her away from that manipulative son of a—"

"Don't," says Leeza, her voice suddenly like scissors.

"Don't what?"

"Don't talk to me about manipulation." She pauses, takes another deep breath. "You've been controlling everything I've done since the accident."

"That's not true!"

"It *is* true." Leeza sees the wounded look on her mother's face, but she presses on. "I know you do it because you love me, but you treat me like a child. You watch my every move, tell me constantly what I should do, what I should wear. Today you even told me to watch out for cars when I cross the street!"

"Is it so wrong that I *care* what happens to you?"

"Look," says Jack, "enough is enough, okay? There's no need to—"

"Caring is one thing," says Leeza, ignoring her stepfather. "*Controlling* is another." She hears her voice rising, wants to bite back the words, but too much has been bottled up for too long. She can't stop it. "Like that restraining order."

"That restraining order was *necessary*! Why do you think I renewed it?"

Leeza blinks at her. "You *renewed* it? *When*?"

"They expire after twelve months, and I wasn't about to give that monster an opportunity to see you again."

Leeza's mind reels at this information. "*I* should have decided whether or not I would talk to Reef again, not *you*."

"You weren't thinking straight! I couldn't let—"

"That's just it!" Leeza points at the TV screen on which the news logo still hangs frozen. "You want to control what I *think*, too, even tell me who to *vote* for!"

"I want what's best for you!"

"No, you don't. You want what's *safe* for me."

"Aren't they the same thing?"

"No. They aren't." She walks toward the door, then pauses. "I've been tiptoeing around my own life for the past two years. It's time I started living it." She leaves the room, walks down the hall toward the kitchen, stares at the papers spread out on the island, then heads for the back door instead. She's going for a run. At night. In the dark. She might even close her eyes.

When she returns, she's exhausted and dripping with sweat but feeling better than she's felt in a long time. Because of the heat this afternoon, her earlier run had been far less satisfying, like forcing her body through liquid wool. The cooler evening air made the miles almost effortless.

The light is on in the upstairs hallway, which means that her mother and Jack have already gone to bed. She's relieved. She didn't want to face a continuation of their earlier battle. Her mother is famous in their family for always having the last word.

Then she sees the disc on top of her Lamming paper with a note in her mother's handwriting: *I'm not forcing you to do anything, but I'd appreciate it if you watched this recording. I think you'll be interested to see just how much your "friend" has changed.*

CHAPTER 11

REEF OPENS HIS EYES IN THE DARKNESS, WONDERING FOR A MOMENT where he is. Then it comes to him—the Mathesons' basement guest room, although Greg had grinned sheepishly when he'd called it that a few hours ago. "I don't think home designers have invented a word yet for playroom-with-sofa-bed," he'd said when he showed Reef where he'd be sleeping.

Reef feels a vibration beside him and realizes it's his cell-phone that has woken him. Reaching for it, he looks blearily at the display, sees it's an Alberta area code and, although he doesn't recognize the number, figures it's Jacob Paul or Wayne McLaren or maybe one of the guys he works with calling on a friend's phone. "Hello," he says, his voice still thick with sleep.

"I have spoken with all of my men, Mr. Kennedy," Alexi Sukorov says in his perfect English. No hello, no pretense at politeness. "And I have shared with each of them the video footage of your visit. None of them recalls ever seeing you before." The Russian pauses for a moment, and Reef imagines him nearly a continent away, steepling his fingers together.

"Which leads me to question, if you will, the veracity of the tale you spun for me."

Reef's mind is spinning now as he struggles to respond, grasping for something to say. "If you will," he begins, layering his words with sarcasm, "those men 'a yours ain't the brightest bulbs in the store. You willin' to bet they just didn't notice me?"

"I pay my men to be observant."

"Yeah, and I pay for shoes that fit but that don't stop me from gettin' blisters."

There is a brief silence. "You assured me, Mr. Kennedy, that you do not play games. Neither do I. There are things far worse than couriering sealed packages that boys do to survive on the street."

The line goes dead.

"You look terrible," Matheson says when Reef enters the kitchen the next morning. "Sorry about that sofa bed. I'm hoping one of these years to build an addition that'll include a real guest room."

"It was fine," says Reef. "Really." In fact, he far preferred it to a sterile hotel suite. Everywhere around him last night was evidence of the life that unfolded daily in that North End bungalow, including the toys and books and puzzles and games that littered the floor of the playroom. The closest thing to a toy or game in the tenements where he'd lived with his grandparents was the collection of rocks he kept in his closet, rocks he'd found on roadsides and in parking lots and only brought out when his grandfather wasn't around.

Before falling asleep last night in that playroom, Reef had wondered yet again what his life might have been like if his mother had lived. Would she have loved him the way the Mathesons clearly love their daughters? Could she have kept him from making the mistakes that marred the second half of his life? He'd still been pondering those questions when sleep dragged him under, weariness shutting off the world. Until the phone call from Sukorov. Sleep hadn't come again after that.

"Coffee?" asks Matheson.

"Thanks." Reef pulls up a chair and sits down.

The social worker reaches over and pours him a cup from the carafe on the table. Reef takes a long swallow of the steaming black liquid, enjoying the heat as it finds his belly.

"Where are the girls?" he asks after a second swallow.

"On their way to school. We carpool with neighbours and it's Jenny's turn today. I hope the TV didn't wake you. They like to watch cartoons while we get their breakfast."

"It didn't wake me," says Reef. In fact, he'd enjoyed listening to the girls' soft laughter as he lay waiting downstairs, reluctant to disrupt the family's morning routine. Those happy sounds had made it easier for him to push aside—at least for a while—the threat in Sukorov's final words. And as the sounds of the children's program filtered below, he thought again about the news program he'd watched last night, thought again about Leeza and hoped she hadn't seen it. But that hope, he knows, is pointless. Someone's probably posted the segment on YouTube already.

"We've got bacon and eggs for breakfast," says Matheson. "Or cereal, fruit, toast, whatever you want."

"Thanks, but coffee's all I need." He has no appetite.

Matheson studies him for a moment. "So, what'd you decide? Are you going to see her or what?"

Reef looks out the window at the swing set, slide, and sandbox in the backyard, more evidence of the family in that North

End home, and the image grips him suddenly like it's a photo advertising everything he'll never have. He turns to Matheson. "Before last night," he says, "I mighta considered it. But that reporter and Decker aren't the only people who feel like that about me. And, really, who can blame 'em? For some people, I'll always be that guy."

"For Leeza, you mean."

Reef nods.

"You don't know that—" Matheson begins.

"Yeah, I think I do," he says quietly. He's remembering the picture that appeared in the newspaper the previous spring. During his year at North Hills, Judge Thomas had required him to take part in extracurriculars, and he'd surprised everyone—including himself—when he turned out to be a strong volleyball player. In fact, he'd scored the tie-breaking and match points that earned his team the provincial title, and he'd gotten his photo in *The Chronicle Herald* with his medal. Months had gone by since he'd seen Leeza, and Reef had hoped she might see that picture and call to congratulate him, or at least send him a note. But there'd been nothing. "I think I do," he says again.

"So that's it? You're not even going to try?"

Reef takes a final swallow of his coffee and sets the cup down. "What I'm *gonna* do is catch the first flight possible."

"You don't have a return ticket?" When Reef shakes his head, Matheson continues, "You thought there was a chance you might stay longer, didn't you. You were hoping she'd be at the funeral."

Reef flushes. "Dumb and dumber, right?" He glances at his watch. "I'll probably have to lay over in Toronto or Montreal, but I'd like to get to Calgary by early this evening if I can." He gets up from the table. "Okay if I grab a shower first?"

"Of course. Jenny put fresh towels in the bathroom for you. I'll drive you to the airport when you're ready."

"Thanks, Greg, but I can take a cab."

"You're just afraid to be seen in the Escort."

Reef grins. "It's not that. You'll be late for work if you take me way out there."

"Slow morning anyway. A home visit. Completely doable."

"You're sure?"

"Absolutely."

"Okay, then," says Reef. "I appreciate it."

CHAPTER 12

BREAKFAST THAT MORNING HAD BEEN QUIETER THAN USUAL. JACK had tried to make conversation several times, but neither Leeza nor her mother had responded with more than single syllables. From the look on her mother's face, Leeza knew she was still hurt, still waiting for an apology, but Leeza hadn't offered one. In fact, she welcomed the silence. Her class had been moved up to 9:00 that morning instead of the usual 10:30, and she'd wanted to finish breakfast as quickly as possible so she could review her class notes before she left.

Sitting in the lecture hall now waiting for the other students to arrive, she admits to herself that her earlier class time isn't the only reason she wanted to get out of the house. She knew that once her mother thawed out, she would no doubt bring up the news segment, after which she would gloat about her excellent understanding of human nature—or, more specifically, *inhuman* nature. Leeza wasn't prepared to go down that road. She still isn't.

"You choose your essay topic yet?"

Leeza glances up to see red-haired Jessica taking the seat next to her, today's T-shirt proclaiming the great taste of Moosehead Lager. "Yes," she replies.

"Which one?"

"The first. The one about betrayal."

The redhead raises her eyebrows, which have been plucked to pencil-line perfection. "I haven't even read that book yet," she says. "Besides, the whole betrayal thing seems like such a downer."

You have no idea, thinks Leeza, the news segment surfacing in her thoughts, but she forces herself to make conversation. Maybe talking will keep her from thinking about last night. "Have you chosen one?"

"I'm thinking of doing the comparative analysis since he's letting us choose which books to write about. I can't keep up with all the reading. I've only gotten through three of the assigned texts. How about you?"

Leeza isn't surprised the girl has read so few—Jessica is clearly more interested in slamming shots than doing course-work—but she doesn't want to tell her she's already read all the books on the syllabus. "A little more than that," Leeza offers, wanting to change the subject. "You busy with other things?" *Like wet T-shirt contests?*

"I work part time as a bartender downtown, but two of the girls on staff are away and I've been pretty much full time the past couple weeks. *More* than full time, actually."

Bartender, thinks Leeza. Which explains the T-shirts and the dozing off in class. "Can't your boss get someone else to cover for them?" she asks.

"I need the hours."

"But if it's interfering with your classwork . . ." Leeza doesn't want to complete the thought, doesn't want to state the obvious.

Jessica shrugs. "My dad lost his job a few months ago and his pogey ran out. And I have three younger brothers." Now she's the one who doesn't state the obvious.

Just then, the young man who offered to take Leeza for coffee arrives, and he nods at her as he sits down, then begins chatting animatedly with the redhead. Suddenly on the outside of their conversation, Leeza is actually grateful for not having to interact with them. She is embarrassed by the girl's honesty and suddenly ashamed for judging her so harshly. There is always so much she doesn't know about people. So much she *thinks* she understands but really doesn't.

As the class waits for the professor to arrive, her mind drifts back to the news segment her mother recorded for her. When she'd seen her note last night and knew Reef was on the disc, she'd nearly run to the living room, where she'd slid it into the player. And when she'd seen the image of Reef frozen on the screen behind those news people, she'd felt exactly as she had each day Reef entered her room at rehab. Every time, it was like someone had switched on a light—everything was suddenly different, illuminated, thrown into vivid relief. It was like that again last night.

She'd paused the recording then and stared at that high-definition image for a long moment. He was even better looking than she remembered. Two years had given him maturity, of course, but something else as well. An air of assurance? He seemed broader, too, more solid, somehow even stronger than the teenager who had taken a broken girl and put her back together, made her feel human again. She felt her heart lift in a way it hadn't in two years. Then she'd pressed Play. And experienced the betrayal.

He hadn't changed. *I wanted to kill him*, he'd said at that funeral. Said it while standing in the pulpit of a church! Her mother was right after all. He was still the violent person who'd stood on that overpass, would always be that person despite what she thought she felt, thought she knew. Why is there always so much she doesn't know about people?

Amazingly, she'd managed to hold back her tears while she watched most of the recording, listened to Roland Decker say words much like her mother's, wishes now that she'd listened to them, *believed* them two years ago. But it was the statement Reef made in the churchyard that opened the floodgates, racked her with sobs: *I got nothin' to say about her.* As if she wasn't worth a single comment, not one word. He couldn't even be bothered to say he was sorry. Because he wasn't.

"Good morning, people," says Professor Drake as he enters the room. "I hope the earlier time this morning hasn't been too inconvenient for you. It's only for today. My wife and I received some good news yesterday—"

Wiping at sudden tears, Leeza gathers up her books and stands, crossing in front of Jessica and the coffee guy to get to the door. "I'm sorry," she mumbles to the professor as she hurries past him.

Someone else's good news is the last thing she can bear to hear right now.

CHAPTER 13

MATHESON EASES THE ESCORT TO A STOP IN FRONT OF THE TERMINAL
entrance. "See? I told you she'd make it," he says.

Reef grins. "Don't jinx it. You still have to get back."

Matheson smiles broadly, but then his face grows serious.
"You're sure I can't talk you into staying a while longer?"

"I wish I could . . ." Reef lets the words go unsaid.

"Abby's going to pitch a fit when she gets home from school
and finds you gone. But, hey," he jokes, "at least it gets you out of
never-ending story time." ·

Reef thinks of the child curled against him last night as they
read and chatted to each other. "I liked it," he says, which he
realizes sounds lame. He wishes he could put into words what it
meant to him; it was the most intimate interaction he had had
with another human being since Leeza. For a moment, he is
overwhelmed by this thought, and he has to force out his next
words. "Say goodbye for me, okay? To Jenny and Taylor, too. You
got a great family there."

"You're welcome back any time. You know that, right?"

"Thanks." He is reluctant to say more, afraid of the feelings welling up in him. *It'll be good to get back to Calgary*, he thinks. Halifax has been an emotional roller coaster for him.

He reaches out to shake Matheson's hand, but the social worker has turned and opened his door. They both get out of the car, and Matheson comes around to the curb and hugs him.

"You take care of yourself, okay?" he says as he steps back. "And call us sometime. *Any* time. I don't want someone else to have to die before we hear from you again."

"I will. And if you call *me* again," says Reef, "use the cell number I gave you. I'm not in my apartment much to answer my land line." He opens the Escort's rear door and grabs his back-pack off the seat. "Thanks for everything. I mean it." He wants to say more, but a speaker somewhere overhead announces flights departing to Toronto and Edmonton, and he wonders if one of those might be a leg to Calgary.

Matheson seems to understand. "You'd better go," he says. He walks around to the driver's door but, instead of getting in, he stands looking at Reef across the Escort's roof. "Remember what I told you last night, Reef. It's okay to be afraid. Fear is a part of life. It gives us pause, forces us to think about what we're doing. Fear is *useful.* But one feeling that *isn't* useful is regret. Anything we learn from regret is always too late. Bear that in mind, okay?"

Reef nods.

Matheson climbs into the car, taps the horn, and pulls away.

Standing in the terminal a few minutes later scanning the monitors for information about westbound flights, Reef thinks about Matheson's comment. *Anything we learn from regret is always too late.* He sees there are two flights before lunch that will get him to Calgary, one of them an Air Canada Airbus leaving in forty minutes. There are several people lined up in front of the airline's service desk, but at least he has no luggage to check. He makes his way toward the end of the line and stands behind a mother with two small children, both of them much younger than Abby and Taylor.

It's okay to be afraid. Fear is a part of life.

He glances at his watch, then pulls out his cellphone, staring at it for several seconds before calling directory assistance. After an operator gives him the number he's asked for, he keys it into his phone, but his thumb hesitates over the Talk button. He looks at the number on the display, wonders whether this is the right thing to do, then slides his thumb over the End button.

He hesitates for nearly a minute—*Anything we learn from regret is always too late*—then presses Talk.

CHAPTER 14

WHEN LEEZA REACHES THE HOUSE, SHE'S GLAD TO SEE BOTH HER mother's and Jack's cars are gone. Her mother, she remembers now, had a meeting this morning with a man who recently bought a restaurant in Bedford and wants to redecorate it. Ironically, Diane had redecorated this same restaurant a couple of years ago, fuming when the previous owner insisted on a fifties theme. She said the retro look might actually have worked if he hadn't been so cheap and, more to the point, adamant about using as much red vinyl as possible. *The whole place,* she'd moaned to Jack and Leeza, *looks like the back seat of a prostitute's old Pontiac.*

Leeza unlocks the door, trudges in, and climbs the stairs to her room. She sets her book bag on her desk, then pulls out her cellphone and turns the ringer back on—Professor Drake has a strict no-cells-in-class policy—and sees she has five missed calls from Brett. Leeza shrugs—no way does she want to go another round with *her* right now—and turns the phone off again, then sprawls on the bed, her face buried in one of the oversized pillows her mother picked up at Bed and Bath during their spring sale. It occurs to Leeza at that moment that almost everything in her room, from the bedding and curtains to the dresser, nightstand, desk, scatter rug, and even the closet organizer, was selected by her mother. And why not? Her mother is always right, isn't she? Look at what she knew about Reef.

Just then the land line on her nightstand rings and Leeza picks it up, expecting to see Brett's number on the call display. She frowns when she sees the out-of-province area code. Probably a telemarketer. How much crappier can her day get? She intends to ignore it, just let the damn thing ring, but *that* scenario also involves her moping around in her room for the next hour—or four—which holds zero appeal for her. Maybe the telemarketer will be calling from one of those research companies asking endless survey questions she'll have to respond to by choosing a number from one to ten. Good for at least half an hour. That's how pathetic her life is at this moment.

She clicks the phone on. "Hello?"

"Hello," says a male voice. "Do you know who this is?"

CHAPTER 15

"GOSH, REEF, IT'S GOOD TO SEE YOU!" TRILLS CARLY REYNOLDS WHEN she opens the door. "I couldn't believe it was you when you called. I'm just glad I'm working afternoons this week or I would've missed you." She hugs Reef on the doorstep, despite the obvious interest of the elderly man across the street who stands at his picture window, peering at them through a lace curtain. "Ignore Mr. Frost," she mutters. "He's a one-man Neighbourhood Watch. He'll be telling my husband this evening all about the handsome young guy I'm having an affair with." She gives the elderly man an exaggerated two-arm wave like those airport personnel who guide airplanes to terminal gates, then leads Reef inside.

"Sorry if I'm interrupting anything," he says.

"Yeah, like I'm dying to get back to folding my laundry. The excitement never stops here."

Reef grins. Although he'd felt awkward as hell his first day volunteering at the Halifax Rehabilitation Centre two years ago, it hadn't taken him long to recognize how much everyone on the sixth floor liked Carly Reynolds. Intuitive, sincere, and good-humoured, she was dedicated to her patients and worked tirelessly to ensure their recovery and transition to life beyond the rehab's walls. With the help of a patient named Brett, Carly was the one who arranged to have Reef spend time with another patient whose recovery had been derailed by a deepening depression. Leeza.

Carly takes his jacket and backpack from him, laying them on a chair while he settles himself on the living room sofa, plush leather furniture that he's pretty sure doesn't unfold into a bed. "Can I get you something to eat?" she asks.

"No thanks." Although he had only coffee at Matheson's that morning, eating is about the last thing he wants to do right now. Twice during the cab ride here, he almost told the driver to turn around and take him back to the airport, and even now he wonders whether he's doing the right thing. Despite Carly's warmth on the phone when he called, he'd worried how she might respond to him in person. This is, after all, the first he's seen her since she learned he was the guy who'd put Leeza in the rehab in the first place. But he needn't have been concerned.

"I'm really glad you called," she says. "I'm sorry, though, about what brought you back to Halifax. I heard about Frank Colville."

"Thanks," he says.

"You're living out west now?"

He tells Carly about his construction job in Calgary, then asks if she's still working at the rehab.

She nods. "Still on the sixth floor, too. An administrative position opened up last fall that my husband hoped I'd be interested in. Better hours, more money, things like that."

"But you didn't apply, right?"

She shakes her head. "The business end of health care never appealed to me. I'd rather work with patients than papers."

"I'm glad," he tells her. "Hey, is Stephen still there?" Stephen Hayes had received severe brain trauma in an accident while four-wheeling, and Reef had read to him during his first days volunteering on the sixth floor.

"They moved him to a unit in New Glasgow shortly after . . ." Carly hesitates, and Reef can see her cheeks turn pink.

"After they asked me to leave," he finishes for her, and he feels heat in his own cheeks now. "Look, I never got a chance to thank you for everything you did for me while I was there." He shakes his head. "I can only imagine what you thought when you, uh, found out about me."

"I couldn't get over the chances of you and Leeza ending up at the same place. Whoever arranged *that* should've bought a lottery ticket on the same day, huh?"

Reef appreciates her attempt at humour, but it doesn't stop the shame from welling up inside him. "What I did—" he begins, groping for words. "It was terrible."

"Yes," Carly agrees, "it *was* terrible. But there's been good that's come of it."

"I think you probably had better volunteers," he mutters, looking down at his feet.

"That's not what I meant. Do you remember doing a presentation for students at John C. Miles High School? It would have been the winter after you left the rehab."

Reef looks up at her. "I did quite a few. The schools started to blur after a while."

"My sister's son, Reid, goes to John C. Miles. Janet called me that evening, told me how Reid came home talking a blue streak about you and the things you told his class. You really made an impact."

Reef shrugs.

"You have no idea how remarkable that was," she insists, and Reef sees her eyes grow moist. "Reid went through some tough times. He'd been heavy into drugs for a couple years, got involved with a bad crowd, even stole a car the summer before. The thing is, Janet and my brother-in-law were at their wits' end with him. They'd done everything they could to help bring him around, even tried tough love, but nothing worked. Reid lived in the same house with them, but he hadn't spoken to them in months, not a real conversation anyway. And then that afternoon he comes home from school talking nonstop about you. Janet cried that night on the phone when she told me." Carly gets up and walks into another room, returns carrying a tissue that she dabs at the corners of her eyes. "Sorry, I'm getting more emotional in my old age."

Reef nods and looks away.

"I'm not saying everything was perfect after that," Carly continues. "He still has problems at school, and those so-called friends of his aren't completely out of the picture. But he and his parents are working through stuff and he's been coming around bit by bit. He may even graduate this year, which no one *ever* thought would happen." She dabs at her eyes again. "You were the beginning of that, Reef. I talked to Reid about it once. Even though it was weeks after you spoke at his school, you could see he was still really affected by what you shared."

Reef shrugs again, embarrassed. "Sounds like he was ready for a change."

Carly shakes her head. "That's just it. He wasn't. He'd even planned to skip the assembly where you were speaking, but the vice-principal caught him sneaking out and forced him to stay. When Reid talked to me about your presentation, he said part of what made it so real for him was your name. It was so close to his that you could have been talking about *him*, could have been describing where his *own* life was taking him if he didn't wise up."

Reef nods again, not sure what to say.

"The other part was the pain you were carrying around. Reid said he wouldn't want to have to live with something like that every day."

Reef looks at the polished oak flooring at his feet, thinks about this Reid guy, wonders if maybe something good could have come after all from the terrible thing he did.

"And just so you know," adds Carly, grinning through her tears, "I got elevated to 'cool aunt' status because I happened to *know* this amazing Reef Kennedy."

"Amazin'," he scoffs, embarrassment colouring his words. "Give me a break."

Carly frowns. "Don't brush it off like that, Reef. You did a really good thing. Just like you did a good thing with Leeza that summer. She might never have worked through her recovery if you hadn't been there."

He shakes his head sadly. "She wouldn't've been there in the first place if I hadn't thrown that rock."

"You know," says Carly, "I'm a firm believer in things happening for a reason. If you hadn't thrown that rock, where would my nephew be today? Where would *you* be?"

It's small comfort, but he allows her comment to go unchallenged.

"So," Carly says, "I know you didn't come all this way just to hang out with a cool aunt. What can I do for you?"

CHAPTER 16

"WHO ARE YOU?" ASKS LEEZA. SHE'S ALWAYS HATED IT WHEN CALLERS ask, "Do you know who this is?" Hasn't her morning been miserable enough without her having to cope with somebody who doesn't have a clue about phone etiquette?

"Are you alone?" the voice asks.

Christ! Leeza clicks off the phone and tosses it on the bed beside her. Getting a call from a pervert pretty much clinches it. This has been one shitty day, and it's not even 10:00. It wouldn't surprise her if, by noon, a tsunami roared up Halifax Harbour or some geological catastrophe levelled Citadel Hill.

She lies there for a moment looking at the ceiling, trying to resist the inertia that has suddenly set in, seeped into every part of her. It would be so easy just to crawl under the covers and sleep the day away, but she knows she should do something constructive. She probably has only an hour's work left on her Lamming paper—writing the conclusion, citing her sources, formatting the essay, printing it off—but summing up her thoughts on betrayal really isn't something she feels inspired to do right now.

And then, of course, she's thinking of the other betrayal in her life, the one she watched in high definition last night. What she *does* feel suddenly inspired to do is retrieve that disc from the player in the living room and Frisbee it into Connaught Avenue traffic. Of course, the easier action would be to erase it, but that wouldn't offer nearly the same cathartic release as seeing that disc mashed by passing cars into a thousand silver slivers. She's nearly convinced herself to go get it when the phone rings again, the call display revealing the same number as before.

She realizes the best thing to do is ignore it, but the day has sucked so hard that she thinks it might be helpful, even therapeutic, to share some of her misery, take it out on the sick bastard who apparently can't get off without talking filth on a phone to a faceless female. She presses the Talk button.

"Listen, you creep, I've got your number. Do you hear me? You call one more time and I'll be handing it over to the police. Now why don't you *grow* a pair and get a life!" She holds the phone out in front of her and is just about to click it off when she hears a voice say, "Leeza?"

Astonished, she stares at the phone for a moment, then brings it to her ear again. "Who *is* this?"

"I'm sorry. I just wanted to make sure your mother isn't there. She's not, is she?"

"I'm hanging up now," Leeza says, annoyance replacing astonishment.

"No, please, don't hang up. Look, I'd really like to see you."

"And I'd like to know who I'm talking to. You've got two seconds."

Leeza listens to the silence on the line. Then, just as her finger moves to the End button, she hears the voice again: "It's me, Leeza. It's your father."

CHAPTER 17

"SO YOU STILL HAVE FEELINGS FOR HER," SAYS CARLY. "EVEN AFTER all this time."

Reef nods.

"Well," she says, grinning broadly, "I guess Brett was right after all."

"About what?" he asks.

"About this. She said she'd never seen two people more connected than you and Leeza. I don't know how many times that summer Brett described the transformation that came over Leeza each time you arrived. Even when the three of you were playing poker together, it was like Brett wasn't even in the room."

"She said that?" Reef has often wondered if Leeza felt the same way about him. *Hoped* she did and sometimes, in his imagination, even convinced himself of this, but he couldn't be sure. They'd never even kissed.

"She said you two were soulmates," continues Carly. "Believe me, I kidded her about *that* one, told her she'd been watching that soap opera of hers way too long. Remember how every afternoon she'd drop everything, no matter what was going on, and go get a Pepsi from the pop machine and head for the big-screen TV on the third floor?"

Reef smiles. "I remember."

Carly is smiling, too. "She was really pissed at me for suggesting that. She told me she knew the difference between real life and acting, thank you very much, and she was darn sure you two weren't acting." Carly's eyes soften. "Guess she was right about *you*, anyway."

Reef stands and walks to the window, sees Mr. Frost still standing in his, surveying Carly's house. Is that a clipboard in his hand? Is he taking *notes*? Reef resists the urge to wave at him and turns to Carly. "Do you ever see her? Leeza? Ever talk to her?"

"I ran into her at the mall last Christmas, but you know what that's like. She had shopping to do and so did I. We only chatted for a minute."

"She doesn't come back to the rehab? Even to visit?"

Carly shakes her head. "Some people do. To see patients who were there the same time they were. Some drop by to visit the nurses on their unit. When patients are in rehab for several months with the same people caring for them all that time, strong bonds can form. Some patients even return to volunteer. But there are lots who *never* come back. Who can blame them? Rehab isn't exactly a place of happy memories."

"Do you ever hear from Brett?"

"Quite a bit. She and Sam live two hours from the city, so she's only been back to the rehab a couple times, but she calls every few weeks. Sometimes more often, depending on how things are going at work and if she needs to vent." Carly grins. "She told me once that a person has to be crazy to work at Brookdale's Home Hardware, and I told her if that's the case, she never has to worry about getting fired."

Reef smiles absently, his mind on everything she's told him. "Does she—?" he falters, trying to find a way to ask his question without making it seem like an invasion of privacy. "Do you know if she stayed in contact with Leeza?"

Carly nods. "And *yes* to your next question, too." She gets up and walks down the hallway, returning in a minute with a piece of paper. "Brett's phone number," she says as she hands it to him.

Reef stands. "Thanks, Carly. I owe you."

She shakes her head. "After what you did for my nephew, you don't owe me a thing. If there's anything else I can do, you just call, okay?"

"Where to?" asks the cab driver.

Reef wishes he knew the right answer to that question. If he had any sense, he'd return to the airport to see if he can make that second flight to Calgary. According to his watch, it leaves in just over an hour, and midday flights sometimes offer a good chance of getting a standby seat, provided you arrive early enough to get your name near the top of the list.

But doesn't he now have what he wanted from Carly? Confirmation that Leeza had feelings for him? And now that he has that, what does he *do* about it?

"Connaught Avenue," he says, and he gives the driver the address.

The driver radioes his status to his dispatcher, turns on the meter, then eases the taxi into the street.

The moment they're moving, though, Reef feels his guts clench. He tries to distract himself, looks at the photo and information mounted on the back of the seat in front of him, identifying the driver as Barry Outhouse.

Looking in the rear-view mirror, the driver notices Reef eyeing his information. "Yeah. No matter how bad your day is, count yourself lucky you don't gotta carry around a last name like mine."

Any other day, Reef might have laughed at the comment. After last night's newscast, though, the name Kennedy is baggage enough. He smiles politely.

"You from around here?" asks the driver after a moment.

"Used to be," Reef replies.

"Visitin' friends?"

Reef looks out the window. "Somethin' like that."

"I'm from Charlottetown originally," says the driver. "Followed a girl here."

Reef doesn't know how to respond to this information, so he doesn't.

"Didn't last, though," the driver adds. "You got someone?"

Reef shakes his head.

"Ah, you're probably better off single. Women. Who understands 'em? One day everything's great, then you make one mistake and they can't get beyond it. Whole thing falls apart."

He continues to talk, explaining what went wrong, but Reef isn't listening, hearing instead five words loop over and over in his head—*they can't get beyond it.* Even if Brett was right, even if Leeza did have feelings for him, that was two years ago and, more important, *before* she learned he'd thrown the rock that nearly killed her. Any feelings she might have had for him probably vanished. Wasn't that obvious when he tried to see her again the following morning? Even with Brett in the room supporting him, telling Leeza, *You need to hear him out . . . He really didn't know who you were,* Leeza had sobbed, *Does that even matter? He did this to me!*

Reef interrupts the driver. "Sorry," he says. "Change 'a plans. Take me to the airport instead."

"You're sure?" the driver asks.

"Yeah," says Reef. "Hope that's not a problem."

"No problem." He radios his dispatcher the change and turns right at the next intersection, pointing the car toward the airport.

Anything we learn from regret is always too late.

Reef ignores Matheson's voice in his head, watches the city slide by.

It's okay to be afraid. Fear is a part of life.

Easy for *him* to say. He's got it all: a wife who loves him, two great kids, a comfortable home where he knows all three will be waiting every evening he turns in the driveway. Even a goddamn Grillmaster.

But the voice is persistent. *You know what you have to do.*

Reef sighs. He pulls out the paper Carly gave him, stares at it for at least a block, then takes out his cellphone and keys in the number.

Someone picks up after the first ring. "Hello?"

For a moment, Reef can't find words.

"Okay," says the voice, "I hear you breathing. We got a couple options here. The two of us can go on inhaling and exhaling, or I can just put the phone down and you can listen to me vacuum, which is what I was doing when you called. On my day off. Trust me, though, I'll do just about anything to get out of vacuuming."

The girl has not changed one bit.

"Hey, Brett," Reef manages to say.

"Hey, yourself."

"I don't know if you remember me, but—"

"Reef? Is that you?" The voice on the other end of the line has gone up two octaves.

Reef's eyes widen. "Yeah, it's me. How'd you know?"

"I saw you on YouTube this morning. My mom tweeted me the link." Reef hears a chuckle. "I don't know if you remember my mom, but the woman *lives* on-line now. If she's not chatting, tweeting, or Facebooking, she's looking for things to chat, tweet, or Facebook *about*. She saw you a couple times at the rehab and recognized you this morning in a video someone had just uploaded."

Reef nearly groans. Apparently, that news clip will haunt him forever. "About that—" he begins.

"What you said about your friend Frank was awesome. I wish I'd met him. He sounded like an incredible guy."

"You saw that?" he asks.

"And how you handled those reporters afterwards? I was impressed. A couple of 'em really tried to get a rise out of you, but you kept your cool. And I'm so glad you didn't let them hound you into talking about Leeza. She's paranoid about her privacy, even more now than before."

Reef suddenly realizes that the video Brett saw isn't the heavily edited version that aired last night, and he wonders if Leeza has seen this longer one. Before he can ask, though, Brett plunges on.

"So what are you doing now? Are you still in Halifax?"

"No, I moved to Calgary a year ago."

"Calgary?"

"I work for a construction company out there. Look, do you—?"

"But you're back in Halifax now."

"I just came for Frank's funeral."

"I'm really sorry about what happened, Reef. I know he was important to you."

"Thanks," he says.

"When do you go home?"

"Today."

There is, at last, a moment of silence on the other end, and Reef is about to ask Brett his question when she fires up on all cylinders again. "When's your flight?"

"I'm hopin' to get one around noon, but first—"

"Are you gonna see Leeza before you leave?"

He hesitates. That, of course, is the question. "I was thinkin' of it, but I don't know how she'd feel about findin' me on her doorstep. You remember what happened the last time I saw her."

"Yeah," she says. "My ears are still ringing."

Reef doesn't know if she's referring to Leeza's crying or her mother's screaming. It doesn't matter. Remembering that moment, he knows he was crazy even to think of contacting her.

Apparently, Brett doesn't agree. Her voice suddenly serious, she insists, "You need to see her, Reef. It would do her good. Maybe even do you *both* good."

"Why do you say that?"

Brett doesn't answer right away. "That thing you said to those reporters, how there isn't a day that you don't think about her. Did you mean it?"

Reef's voice is subdued when he replies, "Yeah. I did."

"Sounds to me like you and Leeza both need closure, but it's never gonna happen until one of you takes the first step."

"Big step," he says quietly.

"You're a big guy," she says. "Can you hold on a second? I've got a beep."

Reef looks out the window, his eyes seeing everything and nothing, vehicles and trees and houses a blur as the cab sweeps past them, heading toward the airport.

Anything we learn from regret is always too late.

He suddenly leans forward. "Look," he says to the driver, "I changed my mind. I'd like to go to the Connaught Avenue address after all. Is that okay?"

The driver shrugs. "Doesn't matter to me," he says, nodding toward the meter. "It's your money. I'll drive around all day if you want."

"Reef?" Brett's voice again. "I gotta run. Someone left work sick and they want me to fill in."

"No worries. You take it easy, okay?"

"Will you call me before you go back to Calgary? I'd like to hear how this thing with Leeza goes."

"You'll probably see the mushroom cloud from where you are," he says, trying to keep his voice light.

"You've got my phone number," she says. "Let's stay in touch." She gives him her e-mail address and Facebook identity with her married name, then adds, "No excuses, okay?"

He gives her his information, too, and promises he'll contact her. And then she's gone.

In much less time than he would have liked, the cab pulls to a stop on Connaught. "Here," he says, handing the driver the amount on the meter along with a tip.

"Thanks, buddy."

Reef makes no move to get out.

"Anything wrong?" the driver asks.

Reef shrugs and reaches across the seat for his backpack.

Just as he grips the door handle, he sees the side door of the Connaught Avenue colonial open and Leeza appear wearing a tank top, jeans, and running shoes. He jerks back into the seat, watching her hurry toward the detached garage.

"Look," the driver says, "if you're gonna stay in the car, I gotta start the meter again."

"Start it," Reef replies, his eyes lasering the now-open garage door. "I don't think I'll be stayin.'"

Leeza reappears wearing a helmet and pushing a bicycle— a sleek, silver multi-speed—that, even seen from the street, appears almost brand new. She closes the garage door, lifts her leg over the seat, and coasts the bike down the driveway, barely giving the parked taxi a glance as she looks for an opening in traffic. She pedals it across the two lanes, carries it over the grass divider, then gets back on and rides north, heading in the opposite direction.

His head whirling with indecision, Reef asks, "Can you follow that bicycle?"

The driver turns and looks at him. "Dude, are you for real?"

Reef reaches for the door handle. "If you can't—"

"I didn't say that." The driver puts on his signal light, shifts, and punches the car into traffic. "Keep an eye on her until I can get us turned around."

Reef peers out the back window, watching Leeza pedal away from him. As if he's willed it, the light at the next intersection turns yellow and then red, and she brings the bike to a stop among the vehicles waiting for the green.

The taxi driver takes the next left and loops around to the northbound lane. By the time they've completed the turn, there's no sign of Leeza, but the driver is undaunted. "We'll catch her," he says.

Sure enough, as they crest the hill where London crosses Connaught, Reef can see Leeza in the distance moving swiftly toward the Bayers Road intersection, and she signals a left turn with her arm. Before she reaches it, though, the green arrow turns amber, and then left-turning traffic gets the red.

The taxi reaches the end of the line of traffic and idles as they wait for the green arrow to return. "Just so we're clear," says the driver, "we're not stalking her, are we?"

"Uh-uh," says Reef, shaking his head.

"Is she the one you were talkin' about on the phone? The one you weren't sure about seein' again, didn't know how she would react?" When Reef nods, he continues, "None 'a my business, but it sounds like the last time you were together didn't go so good."

Reef doesn't respond.

"Women, huh?" the driver says again, grinning.

They watch as Leeza stays in the left lane leading to the Halifax Shopping Centre. In a few seconds, she turns left, then right into the upper parking lot. Reef continues to watch her as the taxi stops at the three-way intersection and waits for a van to pull out.

By the time the taxi enters the parking lot, Leeza has pedalled to the glass entrance, dismounted, and put her bike in the rack by the door, pausing only to thread a chain through the frame and her helmet and lock it. Then she disappears inside.

As the taxi brakes in front of the entrance, Reef thrusts more money over the seat. "Thanks," he says, grabbing his backpack and getting out.

"Good luck," the driver calls through the open window.

I'll need it, thinks Reef as he heads toward the entrance.

CHAPTER 18

NOW OUT OF THE DAZZLING SUNSHINE, LEEZA'S EYES TAKE A
moment to adjust. She's grateful for the shopping centre's air-
conditioning, which eases the stickiness of her moist skin. She
enjoyed the exercise, though, likes the sudden heaviness of her
legs now after pedalling to keep pace with the traffic, and she
wishes she'd used the bike more often. She hasn't ridden it in
more than two years, not since before the accident, but she
vows to make good use of it from now on.

Thinking about the bike, of course, keeps her from thinking about the phone call from her father. On the ride over here,
she'd remembered the last time she saw him, remembered how
uncomfortable he'd seemed. It had been more than a month
since his previous visit, yet he'd stayed only a few minutes. Barely
ten years old at the time, she'd found the hugs he gave her and
Ellen at the end stiff, something offered out of duty rather than
love. Some part of her knew even then that she'd never see him
again. Yet now he's returned.

She walks briskly, afraid that if she slows her stride she'll be
tempted to stop, to rethink what she's doing. She feels like she's

just leaped from a plane and is now plunging in free fall, rushing headlong toward uncertainty. The comparison, of course, makes her think of Brett, whose first and only skydive ended in disaster.

And suddenly, out of nowhere, Leeza feels an overwhelming sense of her *own* disaster—Reef Kennedy. For a brief moment, she actually imagines his presence and the sensation is so intense that she slows, nearly turning to scan the shoppers behind her. But she realizes, of course, how ridiculous this is, realizes that what she's feeling is simply nerves, and she resumes her pace. Even if Reef *were* here—and she knows he is not—she has nothing to say to him. Ever again.

Thoughts of Reef remind her of her conversation with Brett yesterday, and she remembers turning off her phone after seeing all those missed calls. She reaches into her jeans and pulls out her cell, powering it on again, and immediately the phone burbles, alerting her to a text from Brett: *Call me!* Right. Like *that'll* happen. After Brett ragged on her about Reef, Leeza can only imagine what her friend would have to say if she knew what Leeza is about to do now.

She allows her thoughts to return to her father. She has in her mind an image of what he looks like, but that was nine years ago. She knows he's probably changed, no doubt gained weight and lost hair like so many of her friends' fathers have in that time. All the same, though, she is looking for an attractive, trim man with sandy-coloured hair. It was, after all, his genes that gave her the blonde mane she now runs her hands through as she walks toward the food court.

She was hoping to be able to slip into the washroom to freshen up, but she now sees there isn't time—he is already waiting for her at one of the tables. And, astonishingly, it's as though the years never passed for him. He still has all his hair and none of it appears grey, and she wonders if it's dyed or if the sandy colour hides it. Even though he's sitting down, his attention focused on the cup of Perks coffee in front of him, she can tell he's still trim, and his white polo shirt contrasts vividly with a deep tan that makes him look much younger than his age. He could pass for someone under thirty, a man waiting to meet his date rather than his daughter.

Leeza freezes amid a whirl of uncertainty, suddenly questioning why she's here, why she's agreed to meet a man who hasn't seen her or contacted her in nine years, a man whose presence in her life is marked only by direct deposits in an education account. A man who not only failed to attend his older daughter's funeral but couldn't even be bothered to phone his younger daughter following the accident that nearly killed her. *Why am I here?*

Part of the answer, she knows, is curiosity. What could have brought him to Halifax? What can he possibly want from her after all this time? Although they spoke only briefly on the phone, she thought she detected a note of desperation in his voice as he pleaded with her to meet him.

Another reason she's here, of course, has to do with her mother. On the phone, her father specifically asked her not to tell Diane about their meeting, which was easy enough to do since her mother wasn't home. In the note she left on the kitchen island, Leeza simply said she'd be at the Halifax Shopping Centre, not with whom, and this omission appeals to the part of her that has suffocated under her mother's constant surveillance. The fact that she automatically left that note in the first place accounting for her whereabouts now underscores that feeling—wouldn't Diane have assumed she was in class anyway? Leeza grimaces at how compliance to her mother has become an unthinking reflex for her.

Mostly, though, she's here because she has nothing to lose. After watching the recording of last night's newscast, after witnessing that public betrayal, she feels empty, unassailable. What more can her father do to her that Reef hasn't already done?

Still, she hesitates, standing motionless near the top of the escalators, looking across the food court at the man waiting for her. She tries to summon the anger and resentment she felt for so long after he abandoned them, but there is only that emptiness. Then he looks up from his coffee and sees her. For a handful of heartbeats, he studies her as if trying to subtract years from her face. Then he smiles, gets up and hurries toward her, his arms extended.

Leeza is horrified when she realizes he intends to embrace her. He is, after all, a total stranger to her now, and she has no idea how to react. She would like to step back, ward him off in some way, but before she can do anything, he's upon her, wrapping his arms around her, pulling her into him. This is nothing like the last hug he gave her, and she can only wait as he holds her, can only wait as the moment stretches itself out. Standing there helplessly enfolded, she smells the polo shirt against her face, breathes in the very same cologne he wore all those years ago. Is that possible, she wonders, or has memory simply inserted itself into this moment?

Finally, he steps back, holds her at arm's length and looks at her. "You're beautiful," he says.

Leeza flushes but, before she can say anything, he is leading her to his table. "Can I get you something?" he asks as she sits down.

She shakes her head.

"Maybe an ice cream?" He nods at the Dairy Queen counter that Leeza is surprised to see is open even at this hour.

"No." She's suddenly aware of how abrupt that sounds and adds, "Thanks, but it's early for ice cream." This despite the four people already lined up for DQ.

He sits back in his chair and stares at her, shaking his head. "I know it's been a long time," he says, "but I wasn't prepared for a young woman. You're all grown up." He reaches across the table and takes her hands in his. "I remember the day you were born, how tiny your fingers were." He shakes his head again.

Leeza looks at her slim hands in his, feels the warmth of his palms against her skin. Something inside her simply wants to enjoy this moment, one she dreamt about for months after he'd left them for the last time, but the realist in her can't. She pulls away. "Why are you here?" she asks.

"To see you," he replies. "To see my daughter."

That was the line she always imagined him saying: *To see my daughter.* In her fantasy, it wouldn't matter that he'd been gone for weeks, then months, then years. That line would magically undo all the hurt she'd carried around for so long.

But she isn't ten years old anymore. She frowns, leans back in the hard metal chair that's screwed to the floor. It isn't going anywhere—unlike, she suspects, her father.

He looks at her for a long moment and she sees something like a shadow cross his face. Has she hurt his feelings? What did he expect? And what does he want from her now?

"I'm sorry I stopped being your father," he tells her. "You must hate me."

She returns his gaze. "I did for a long time," she says, annoyed at the sudden emotion in her voice. Yet another betrayal.

He nods, looking down at his hands that now hold nothing. "I'm not surprised."

"Why didn't you—?" she begins but then looks away. She doesn't want the answer to this question, doesn't want to know what could keep a father from a dying daughter and, later, from a second daughter nearly dead.

It's as if he's read her mind. "I didn't feel I had the right to come," he explains. "I'd been away for so long, I wasn't sure how you'd react." He shrugs. "I knew how your *mother* would react, though. She would've crucified me. I could practically hear her screaming in my head—" He stops abruptly. "I'm sorry. That isn't fair."

No, it isn't. She doesn't want to listen to him talk about her mother. He gave up that right, too, a long time ago. In fact, he gave up every right. She suddenly regrets coming, doesn't want to be sitting here in the food court on a beautiful day across from a man who is but is not her father.

"I'd like to get to know you," he says. "I want to make up for not being there all those years."

That was the other line she'd imagined him saying when she fantasized about this moment. *I want to make up for not being there.* As if that were possible. Hadn't he missed every milestone in the last nine years? Birthdays? Christmases? A graduation? A funeral? "How can you expect to make up for that?" she asks, disbelief etching her words.

"You're right to be skeptical," he says. "But all I'm asking for is a chance."

For a moment, Leeza expects him to reach across and clasp her hands again, and she places them in her lap. Then she sees the expression on his face. It's like she's looking at something raw. An open wound.

"Do you think you could find it in your heart to give me that chance?" he asks softly and, even amid the hollow clatter of the food court, Leeza hears the pleading in his voice again. "I'm so sorry. You have to believe me."

Leeza recalls someone else saying words very much like these. Reef, the last time she saw him: *I'm so sorry. You gotta believe me.* But her mother had thrown him out seconds later, then turned and sneered, *How could he think saying he was sorry would make up for what he did?* Leeza is pretty sure her mother would say the same thing now. And hadn't the woman been right about Reef all along? Didn't that newscast prove it?

But a part of her, the part that manufactured fantasies about her father returning to her someday, chooses to ignore the misgivings her heart whispers to her now. Her heart has been wrong before, as she discovered last night.

She looks down at her hands in her lap, hands that have unconsciously twisted the hem of her tank top, wrinkling the material. She smoothes out the fabric, then looks up at the man who sits across from her, waiting.

She smiles.

CHAPTER 19

WATCHING LEEZA STRIDE AHEAD OF HIM THROUGH THE MALL A FEW
moments ago, her shoulders back, her stride determined, Reef
could tell she hadn't come here to shop. She had another purpose,
a destination in mind as she moved deliberately through the knots
of early-morning bargain hunters whose vehicles were already
filling the parking lot behind them.

His heart and mind racing as he followed, Reef had practised
in his head a dozen things to say to her, discarding each of them.
Too abrupt. Too ridiculous. Too everything. What should he say
to a person he hasn't seen in two years? What *could* he say?

There was a moment when she seemed to hesitate, to falter,
and he was afraid she might turn and see him following, but then
she'd resumed her pace, reaching into her pocket and checking
her cellphone as she walked. He hadn't wanted to approach her
while she was on the way to wherever she was going, wanted
instead to wait until she'd reached her objective. After all this
time, talking to her was going to be difficult enough without her
assuming he was stalking her. Which, technically, he was. But

he loved watching her move. The whole time he'd known her that summer, she'd been confined to a wheelchair and her bed, and it lifted his heart to see her walk so gracefully through the mall. Yes, he would wait for her to get to where she was going.

And then she did.

Reef stands near the escalator now, watching the scene unfold across the food court from him, wishing he had asked Brett one final question: *Is Leeza seeing anyone now?* Because she is. A man who, from here, looks to be in his late twenties. She had seemed to stiffen as he approached her, hugged her, but watching them sit together now at the table across from New York Fries, Reef can clearly see they have feelings for each other. The man had held both her hands in his, his eyes never leaving her face, and she now offers him a smile that Reef remembers only too well. That smile had shone light into places that had been dark for too long, had moved something inside him he thought was incapable of ever being moved again.

He turns away. There is nothing here for him now. All this time he has been fooling himself into believing there might be, but at last he knows better.

Heading back toward the mall entrance, Reef pulls out his cell and brings up the menu, retrieving the number of the cab company he called before. He hopes they don't send the same driver, who will only ask questions Reef doesn't want to answer.

He has, of course, missed the second flight, but there's another—this one WestJet—leaving for Edmonton in twenty minutes, and it shouldn't be a problem for him to get a connector flight from there to Calgary. Glancing at his watch, he sees he may just be able to make it if he hurries—and, of course, if there's a seat still available. Even if he catches this flight, it will be late before he gets home, but the time difference will work in his favour—he will get back the three hours he lost on the way to Nova Scotia. That three hours, he now knows, is the only thing he lost here that he'll ever see again.

As he approaches the lone agent at the WestJet counter, he notices a man with a boy who looks about Taylor's age wearing what are obviously new high-tops, cargo pants, a denim shirt, and a backpack with an Iron Man decal on it. They stand near the terminal windows to the right of the now-empty queue corrals, and the man is bent over the boy, muttering. Seeing tears in the boy's eyes, Reef slows his pace, hears the anger in the man's voice.

"—good for nothin' little shit! I told you when I gave you that ten bucks to put it in a safe place, but *did* you, dummy? No! And now it's lost. You're about as useful as tits on a bull!" he sneers as he straightens. "Well, don't expect me to cough up cash for your lunch, numbskull. Maybe when you get hungry enough, you'll finally start usin' that brain 'a yours."

Reef suddenly sees in his head a hundred moments just like this one. Except the boy in his head doesn't have new clothes and an Iron Man backpack. The boy in his head wears too-short jeans and a second-hand T-shirt washed so many times it's nearly transparent. The words being muttered, though, are much the same: *dummy*, *numbskull*, and a string of others the man snarls every time he's reminded that his illegitimate grandson breathes the same air he does. And there are tears in this boy's eyes, too.

Despite his efforts to ignore the scene, Reef feels the familiar heat ignite in his belly, the beginnings of the same fire he'd fanned for years before he met Frank. The beginnings of the same fire that had held him in its grip the afternoon he'd stood on an overpass with a rock in his hand. Shrugging, he takes out his wallet, pulls out a ten-dollar bill, palms it, and returns the wallet to his back pocket in one fluid motion.

"Sir?" he says, stopping beside the two.

The man glances at him, his face a dark scowl. "Yeah?"

Reef holds out the money. "I think your boy dropped this."

The man stares at the bill, his eyes filled with suspicion.

"Found it on the floor back there," Reef adds, nodding over his shoulder.

Three different expressions slide across the man's face. Then he grins. "Thanks," he says, taking the money and handing it to the boy. "Looks like this is your lucky day," he says, his voice noticeably warmer.

The boy looks at the money, then at Reef, then at the money again.

"Take it," the man says.

The boy reaches out, takes the bill.

"What do you say now?"

"It isn't my—"

"Just *thank* the guy, okay?" says the man, an edge to each word.

The boy looks up at Reef shyly. "Thanks, mister."

"No problem," says Reef, turning and walking away.

He is steps from the WestJet counter when he feels a tug on his sleeve. Looking down, he sees the boy holding out the ten-dollar bill. "What's up?" he asks. The boy's father remains by the queue corrals, his face red.

The boy looks embarrassed. "Here, mister. It isn't mine."

"Sure it is."

The boy shakes his head solemnly.

"How do you know?" asks Reef.

"I lost two five-dollar bills."

Reef drops his backpack and squats beside the boy so they're at eye level with each other. "Keep it, kid," he tells him. "I got a feelin' you've earned it." He pats the boy's shoulder and then stands. "And just so you know? *Everybody* loses things, okay? I bet even your dad does, too."

The boy nods, then returns to his father, who says something to him that Reef can't hear. The boy just shrugs and the two walk off down the concourse. Reef watches them go, sees the boy look back at him and give a small, shy wave. Reef lifts his hand in return, and then father and son turn a corner and are gone.

Reef turns toward the WestJet counter and sees the agent is now gone, too. He glances at his watch and knows it's too late to make that flight. He sighs, begins to scan the monitor for other options.

Just then his cell vibrates in his pocket and he reaches for it. "Hello?"

"Reef? Jeez, I'm glad you picked up," says Matheson.

"Somethin' wrong?" Reef asks.

"Everything!"

CHAPTER 20

DIANE IS SITTING ON THE DECK—UNDER THE SHADE OF THE PATIO umbrella, of course—sipping an iced tea when Leeza returns, coasting her bike to a stop in front of the garage. "You didn't buy anything," she observes after Leeza puts the bike and helmet away and climbs the steps.

Leeza shakes her head.

"I could've taken you shopping myself later this afternoon," says her mother, who, surprisingly, hasn't asked about Leeza's class.

This exchange is the first since their argument last night, and it would appear that her mother has moved beyond it. Leeza knows there's more to it than forgiveness, though. "That's okay," she says, pouring herself a tall glass of iced tea from the pitcher on the patio table. She brings it to her lips and drains half in even swallows, waiting for the inevitable inquisition.

"Seems a shame to bike all that way in this heat."

"I needed the exercise," says Leeza before finishing the rest of the iced tea.

"What couldn't wait until this afternoon?"

Leeza's fingers tighten around the empty glass. She sets it on the table, drawing from a well of patience she didn't know she had. "How'd your meeting go with the guy in Bedford?"

Diane looks at her for a moment, her eyebrows arched, then begins telling Leeza about the client's ideas for a French restaurant.

"Is he prepared to spend some serious decorating dollars?" Leeza asks, determined to keep the conversation away from her trip to the shopping centre.

"That's the best part," replies Diane, clearly warming to her subject. "He wants me to forget about cost for now and work up two or three concepts to run by him. For the time being, his focus is on doing everything as well as he can to attract high-end clientele."

"And he doesn't think the red vinyl will cut it?" Leeza teases, pouring herself more iced tea.

Diane laughs. "He's already got a crew tearing that out, thank God."

"Does he know—?"

"Of *course* not," interrupts Diane, grinning. "If he knew I was responsible for that hooker's nightmare, I don't think he'd give me the time of day." She sighs. "I've got my work cut out for me."

"You enjoy a challenge," says Leeza, finishing her drink and getting up. There are things she has to do.

"Sweetheart?"

Leeza turns, suppressing a sigh. "Yes?" She knows what's coming, of course, knows her mother has waited until now to bring up the newscast. But she's wrong.

"Everything okay?"

Leeza nods. "Sure. Why wouldn't it be?"

Her mother tilts her head to one side. "I don't know. You just have this look on your face."

"A look?"

"Like when you were younger and I'd catch you doing something you shouldn't, like getting into Ellen's things when she wasn't home. You'd get this innocent expression on your face that always made you look twice as guilty."

Leeza shakes her head. "Everything's fine."

"You'd tell me, wouldn't you?" her mother asks.

"Tell you what?"

"If something were wrong."

Leeza forces a chuckle, bends down to brush her lips over her mother's forehead. "Nothing's wrong, okay?" She straightens and heads for the door, but she's conscious of her mother's eyes on her back, following her inside.

In her room, Leeza prints off her completed essay, which she has revised a final time and formatted according to her professor's requirements. It feels good to have that job behind her, something she can cross off her to-do list.

Funny, her father had said this morning how that was one of the things he remembered most clearly about her. How, even as a six-year-old, she was forever making lists—misspelled, of course—and crossing things off one at a time. "Like a little CEO," he'd joked. That memory pleases her, her penchant for lists an obvious reflection of a Type A personality that used to drive her sister crazy. But her father's recollection pleases Leeza for another reason, too. She likes that there's someone else besides her mother who seems to know her so well.

She does, of course, feel guilty about lying. Well, not lying, really, since she was telling the truth when she said nothing was wrong. She just didn't tell her mother the *whole* truth.

Her mind wanders back to her morning at the food court and she thinks of how her father began by asking questions about her first year at university: which courses she liked best, had she chosen a major, did any particular careers appeal to her yet, on and on. Leeza gave guarded answers at first, distrustful of this sudden interest in her and unwilling to disclose personal information to someone who was a stranger to her, despite what it might say on her birth certificate. But the questions kept coming and he seemed genuinely engrossed in everything she had to say, nodding, smiling, never critical or judgmental like her mother. And despite her initial misgivings, Leeza found herself slowly opening up to him, moving beyond single-word replies to more detailed responses.

He had opened up to her, too, talking about moments he remembered when they'd been a family of four, and the memory of her list-making wasn't the only one he'd shared that struck a chord with her. Most of them she recalled only vaguely or not at all. Like the time she was five and had an allergic reaction to something she'd eaten and they'd rushed her to emergency, her face swollen like a balloon. The time she was three and she wandered off in a Superstore, falling asleep on a chair in the pharmacy's waiting area while they searched frantically up and down every aisle. The time she was a week old and had croup so bad he and her mother took turns holding her upright in their arms for two days to keep her congested lungs from collapsing. As she listened to him share those memories, she felt like she was watching her life unfold backwards, like one of those movies where the scenes appear in reverse order and it's only when you see the beginning that you understand the end.

He'd eventually bought both of them ice cream after all, which they'd eaten outside on a bench in the sunshine. The heat had melted it faster than they could eat it, of course, and before long her fingers were webbed with chocolate. Her father's, too.

She thinks of those two words and lets them slide off her tongue like ice cream: "My father." Hearing herself say them aloud in her bedroom, she replays in her mind how he wiped off both their hands with a wad of Dairy Queen napkins. She'd nearly pulled away again, uncomfortable at this sudden physical intimacy, but then something about his action tugged at her memory. As he dabbed at the sticky chocolate, she'd recalled him doing the same thing when she was little, wiping off Popsicle drippings or the bright orange residue of Cheezies, and she could see from his expression that he was suddenly remembering the same thing. Sitting there on that bench in the sunshine as shoppers breezed past them, he'd looked up from her hands, his face suddenly serious. "I've been such a fool, Leeza," he'd said softly, his voice a husky whisper. "I wish there was a way I could get back all those years."

For nearly half her life, she has harboured a steely bitterness toward him. Has, in fact, even nursed that feeling as she struggled with the loss and rejection she experienced when it slowly became clear he'd abandoned both her and Ellen for good. That bitterness made her stronger, made it easier somehow when she saw other fathers arrive to watch their daughters play on sports teams, perform in theatrical productions, even graduate from high school. Not that her stepfather hadn't done all those things—Jack came to as many events as his work schedule allowed—but it wasn't the same, not when you knew your real father had chosen a second family over his first. Yes, that bitterness gave her strength. But it also set her apart, helped her build walls, made it difficult for her to trust the young men who tried to get close to her.

I wish there was a way I could get back all those years. It is those words she realizes she has most wanted to hear, those words that resonated with her on the bench outside the shopping centre, thawing the bitterness she has embraced for so long, undermining her resolve to remain detached from a father who'd discarded his family like trash. A father who has suddenly reappeared in her life just when she needs him most.

"My father," she murmurs again as she stands staring out her bedroom window, seeing nothing but memory.

CHAPTER 21

EVEN AMID THE NOISE OF THE BUSY AIRPORT TERMINAL, REEF HAD heard the urgency in Matheson's voice on the phone, and he'd told the social worker to hang on while he ran to the arrivals area and hailed a cab. "The provincial courthouse on Spring Garden Road," he'd told the driver, then waited for the roar of an approaching 737 to diminish before speaking into his cell.

"Sorry, Greg," says Reef now as the cab merges with other outbound traffic, "I missed that last part."

Matheson repeats it. "Decker held a news conference this morning. I just heard the end of it on the radio. He was speaking in front of the courthouse just before heading inside for the hearing."

"I don't get it. What's the hearin' about?"

"He's trying to get a judge to shut down North Hills."

"That's crazy!" growls Reef. "How could he get a hearin' so fast?" Thinking of his own experience before a judge after throwing that rock from the overpass, he knows that courtroom calendars are booked up weeks, even months, in advance.

"From what Decker said to reporters, I guess he made the application weeks ago, when he first decided to run for office. Apparently, he's been gunning for North Hills from the beginning. Frank's death just threw a spotlight on it."

"And Frank never said anything to you about it?"

"Not a word."

Which, Reef realizes, was so like Frank. In the two years he knew the man, Reef had never heard him complain. About anything. Frank only had time for *other* people's problems.

"But how can Decker go through with it now?" Reef asks. "Won't he look like a fool?" After all, hadn't the guy just yesterday attended the funeral that honoured Frank Colville and the work he had done with young offenders? Hadn't he spoken to the media immediately after that funeral? Surely any effort to sabotage Frank's work would just send a mixed message to voters—and Reef points that out to his friend now.

"The voting public has a notoriously short memory, Reef. The best way for a would-be politician like Decker to capitalize on an issue is to keep it front and centre in the news. Yes, Decker honoured the work Frank did, but now he can present himself as someone who's able to rise above the emotion associated with his death and take a cold, hard look at how he operated North Hills."

"Then we got nothin' to worry about," says Reef. "Nobody was better at what he did than Frank."

"Decker apparently has something up his sleeve. He told reporters he has—how'd he put it?—compelling evidence of North Hills's ineffectiveness that he feels the court should see."

"He's got nothin'. He's more about the cameras than the court," mutters Reef.

"You're right, but he also claims he's out to save the province money, and that's getting him a lot of attention. In today's eroding economy where every misspent government dollar alienates voters further, Decker knows he can whip up considerable support if he convinces the public he can save tax dollars by closing North Hills. You should've heard him," continues Matheson, his words layered with disgust. "He claimed North Hills was little more than a country club for some of the province's worst young offenders. You have to hand it to the guy—he knows how to play it. What hard-working citizen who's having trouble feeding and clothing his own kids wouldn't want to see someone shut down a place that coddles teenage criminals?"

The image of Frank Colville coddling anyone makes Reef snort into the phone. "That's bullshit!" he mutters as the cab cruises toward the city. "Besides, Greg, government fundin' only pays for *part* 'a North Hills's operating costs. The rest is covered by the fundraisin' Frank did." And then he sees the problem.

"Right," says Matheson. "And now that Frank is gone, fundraising will be tough. Decker's smart. All he has to do is present North Hills as a fiscal liability."

"But what about all the people Frank helped at that place? What about all the good he did?"

"That's why you need to be at that hearing, Reef. Decker's voice shouldn't be the only one the judge hears."

"I'm really sorry you had to miss your flight," says Matheson as Reef climbs out of the cab.

Reef waves off the apology. "This is more important. I called Wayne and told him I'd be at least another day gettin' back. He was cool with it when he heard what was goin' on."

"He was a good friend of Frank's, right?" Matheson asks as they hurry along the walkway leading to the provincial courthouse.

Reef nods. "He's as pissed as I am. Do you think Decker really stands a chance of gettin' North Hills shut down?"

Matheson shrugs. "From what I hear, Oliver West is a reasonable judge, but he'll obviously be aware of the public pressure that's being brought to bear here."

Reef casts a glance behind them at the news vehicles parked at the corner of Grafton and Spring Garden Road, and he scowls. "Decker don't go anywhere without his posse, does he?"

Entering the building, they stop at the security checkpoint to remove their cellphones and other metal objects, which they place in baskets, and Reef passes his backpack to a guard, who looks at him with bored eyes. Matheson walks through the metal detector first, immediately setting off the alarm, and a second guard waves an electronic wand over him and finds another set of keys in his jacket pocket before letting him through.

When Reef passes through the metal detector, he triggers no alarm, and he collects his backpack and cell from the guard and follows Matheson up the central staircase, its thick wooden railings and balusters stained a brown so dark they're almost black. Carpeting muffles their footsteps on the wooden treads as they head to courtroom three on the second floor, where the hearing is being held.

At the top of the staircase, they see a heavy oak door bearing three signs, the first warning that the door may open suddenly. The others instruct visitors to turn off cellphones and to refrain from entering while a witness is on the stand, so both Reef and Matheson pull out their phones and power them off, then peer through the door's narrow window. Seeing the witness stand empty, they slip inside and look for a seat in one of the pew-like wooden benches, finding two spaces at the back. The rest are full.

A man wearing a robe—presumably Judge West—sits at the front of the room listening as a clerk calls forward the first person to take the stand: Roland Decker. Around them, Reef is conscious of people scribbling on notepads, and he remembers many of their faces from yesterday. One of them is John Peterson, the pint-sized reporter from the churchyard and the newscast, and when he sees Reef, his face reflects what appears to be smug satisfaction. He turns toward the witness stand and grins at Decker, who has also seen the two new arrivals, and a similar grin creases Decker's face as he turns his attention to the clerk.

"Please state your name for the court," instructs the clerk after swearing in the witness.

"Roland Bernard Decker."

A lawyer approaches the stand and asks Decker to state his occupation.

"I'm a financial analyst for the investment firm Stoffler, Weinberg, and Grant."

"Mr. Decker, please tell us why you're petitioning the court."

Decker glances around the large room, obviously pleased to see so many members of the media present. Nearly preening, he says, "As both a private citizen and a financial expert, I have a keen interest in how taxpayers' money is spent, and I have grave concerns about government money being used to support an institution that is ineffective at best and, at worst, detrimental to the public good."

"And to which institution are you referring?" asks the lawyer.

"North Hills Group Home in Waverley."

A rustling passes through the courtroom like a wave, and then there is silence again as everyone waits for the lawyer's next question. They don't have to wait long.

"Mr. Decker," says the lawyer, "can you tell us what makes you think North Hills is failing to meet its mandate of successfully transitioning male offenders back into mainstream society?"

"I'm not here to tell you what I *think*," says Decker. "I have tangible, irrefutable evidence that proves North Hills is merely a rest stop for low-lifes on the way to becoming hardened criminals."

CHAPTER 22

"LEEZA, HONEY?"

"In here." Having showered again after her bike ride, Leeza's almost finished dressing. She's chosen yet another tank top because the day promises to be uncomfortably warm. Once again, she longed to put on shorts, but she's settled on another pair of jeans, which she pulls up as her mother opens her bedroom door.

"Can you tell me who this call was from?" Diane enters the room holding out one of the house phones, its display showing the last caller's number. "It's not our area code."

Leeza recognizes her father's cell number and nearly groans. *Why didn't I delete the caller history?* "Telemarketer?" she asks, running a brush through her damp hair.

"Shouldn't be. We're on that no-call list."

"I don't think that stops all of them," Leeza murmurs. She sits down at her desk, takes the pages of her essay from the printer and staples them together.

"I called the operator and she told me it was a cellphone. Telemarketers don't usually use cells."

"Did you check the voice-mail?" asks Leeza. Reluctant to face her mother, she makes a production of opening the leather book-bag she carries to class and sliding the completed assignment inside. She's annoyed that she feels guilty. *All I did was answer the damn phone.*

"Whoever it was didn't leave a message."

Leeza feels her face grow warm. She's more than annoyed now, exasperated at being made to feel like she's twelve and just caught skipping school. But she struggles to keep her voice from betraying her. "If it's important, I'm sure they'll call back."

"They already did. Within moments of the first call. The second one lasted over nine minutes." Her mother holds out the phone again to show her the elapsed time on the display.

Leeza makes an effort to unclench her jaw as she turns to her. "What are you asking me?"

Her mother stares at her for a long moment, then sighs. "Was it that Kennedy boy? Has he been calling here? Have you been talking to him?"

Leeza pushes back from her desk and gets up, the twinge in her left leg fuelling her anger. "It wasn't him!" she snaps. "I *saw* the newscast you recorded for me, okay? Even if he *were* to call here, I have nothing to say to him."

"Then who was it?" demands her mother. "Why won't you tell me?"

Leeza struggles against the same shriek she couldn't suppress last night. "Why must you know every detail about every second of my life? It was a *phone* call, for God's sake."

"You're hiding something from me, Leeza. I *know* it! And so help me, if this is about that monster who almost killed you—"

"It was my *father*!" Leeza hisses, her clenched fists trembling.

"That's not Jack's cellphone, Leeza."

"I don't mean Jack."

Her mother stares at her blankly for a moment, and then comprehension suddenly surfaces in her eyes, along with something else that Leeza thinks could be horror. "Your *father?*"

"Yes. My father." She says the words with quiet vehemence, enjoying the way they feel in her mouth, the way they sound in the room.

Her mother's mouth twists into something like a scar. "Why would *he* be calling here? What in *hell* could he possibly want?"

Her fingernails pressing into her palms, Leeza is barely able to keep from shouting her next words. "To *see* me!"

"To see you?" Astonishment like sharp stones in her mother's voice.

"Yes," says Leeza, still struggling to control her anger. "He wants to make up for all the time he's wasted."

Her mother stares at her, an expression of incredulity rippling across her face, then shakes her head sadly. "If you believe he's here just to see you, Leeza, you're even more gullible than I thought. Honey, that man couldn't even be bothered to *call* when you were in intensive care two years ago." She shakes her head again, and her next words are laced with sarcasm. "Wants to make up for all the time he's wasted. *Christ!*"

Leeza grinds her teeth together, forces herself to breathe before speaking again. "Is it so hard to believe that someone *else* might care about me? Someone besides *you?* Are you so threatened that you'd—?"

"*Threatened?*" Diane draws back as though Leeza has physically struck her. "What a thing to say about your own moth—" But the ringing of the telephone in her hand interrupts her. Glancing at the display, her face changes from shock to anger. She clicks the Talk button and brings the phone to her ear.

"Hello, Scott," she says. "You've got some nerve to—"

Leeza reaches for the phone, but her mother steps back, turning away from her, a move that doesn't stop Leeza from hearing her father's voice through the receiver. Although she can't make out the words, she can guess what he's asking, and she reaches for her bedside extension.

"No," says Diane, "you may *not* talk to her. I don't know what it is you think you're doing, but—"

"Dad? It's me."

"Leeza!" her mother snaps. "Put that phone down!"

Leeza ignores her. "I'm here, Dad. What's up?"

"Leeza," says Scott, "could you meet me again?"

Diane stares open-mouthed at her. "*Again?* You've already *seen* him?"

Leeza turns away from equal parts disgust and disappointment in her mother's eyes. "I thought we agreed to get together tomorrow," she tells him.

"You're doing no such th—" Diane begins.

"I know," her father says, "but I need to see you now. It's important."

Leeza watches her mother's face work oddly as she tries to process what she's hearing. "Now?" Leeza asks. She thinks she can hear something in her father's voice. Something that wasn't there when she saw him earlier. An urgency. "Is something wrong?"

"Something's wrong, all right," Diane scoffs. "It's thinking that this *man*," and her voice gives the word the emotional weight of *maggot*, "might actually *care* for you." She savagely clicks off the phone in her hand. "Leeza, I absolutely forbid you to see him again."

Leeza gapes at her mother. "You *didn't* just say that. You *forbid* me? I'm nineteen years old!"

"Then *act* like it! Scott Hemming couldn't care *less* about you. He's—"

"—my father!" Leeza finishes. "And if he needs to see me, you aren't going to stop me."

"We'll see about that." Diane clicks the phone on again. "Leeza's having nothing to do with you, Scott. Do you hear me?"

Apparently, he doesn't. "Leeza, I'll come pick you up."

Looking at the fury on her mother's face, Leeza says, "No, Dad, I'll come to you. The same place we met this morning?"

"I'll be there. And Leeza?"

"Yes?"

"Please hurry."

"Give me five minutes." Leeza hangs up the phone and turns toward the door.

"Leeza!" her mother pleads. "Don't do this!"

Leeza doesn't even pause. She takes the stairs two at a time.

CHAPTER 23

THE REACTION IN THE COURTROOM IS IMMEDIATE. MURMURS RESONATE as the spectators respond to Decker's allegations.

Shocked at this attack on Frank's work, Reef watches Decker and his lawyer exchange a smile, clearly pleased with the observers' reactions. Reef's body shifts as he physically tries to harness his anger, and he feels Matheson's hand on his shoulder, steadying him.

"So, Mr. Decker," says the lawyer when the murmurs fade, "what evidence do you have to support your claim that North Hills Group Home is ineffective in its capacity to rehabilitate young offenders?"

Decker raises his arms and brings both hands together as though, Reef thinks, he's a pope posing for a portrait. "First, I would like to say that criticizing the work of someone like Frank Colville is something I do today with extreme reluctance. Mr. Colville was obviously a fine man who rose above adversity to become an admired member of our community, and in no way do I want to diminish the intent of his work. Just its results."

Reef clenches his jaw. Hearing Decker speak Frank's name makes his skin crawl. It's obvious from the man's easy posture and smile exactly how reluctant he is to be sitting on that witness stand shitting all over Frank's reputation.

Matheson leans toward Reef. "He looks like a cat with feathers in his mouth," the social worker whispers. "You have any idea what this is about?"

Reef shakes his head.

The judge addresses Decker's lawyer. "Mr. Sheppard, I have a full docket today, so I'd appreciate it if we could move these proceedings along. The court notes your client's reluctance but requests expediency."

"Certainly, Your Honour," Sheppard replies. "By all means." Turning to Decker, he resumes his line of questioning. "Can you explain for the court, Mr. Decker, the nature of your evidence?"

Decker nods. "Since beginning my inquiry into North Hills, I've been investigating a young man who spent a year at the facility after having caused a multi-vehicle collision that nearly killed a seventeen-year-old girl."

Reef snaps to attention. "What the—?"

Decker holds up a folder. "I have here a number of articles written by many of our province's fine reporters that describe how he viciously threw a rock off an overpass into that girl's windshield." Passing the folder to Sheppard, Decker leans forward, whispering something to the lawyer. Sheppard turns, surprise evident on his face when he sees Reef, and he looks at Decker and nods.

Philippa Maltby, the attorney representing the province and, therefore, the institutions it supports, stands and addresses the judge. "Your Honour, I think we're all familiar with the incident, which was reported in the media ad nauseam. However, news articles don't qualify as hard evidence, nor do I see their relevance. If Mr. Decker is going to give us a history of every offender who passed through North Hills's doors, we're going to be here a very long time."

"I can assure you," Sheppard tells the judge, "that Mr. Decker plans to speak only about this one individual."

Reef looks at Decker, the man's cat-with-feathers smirk increasingly evident. Even from across the room, Reef can see the gleam in Decker's eyes.

"I have my own concerns about relevance," says the judge. He nods at the witness. "You may continue, Mr. Decker, but please get to the point."

"My point, Your Honour, is that this young man was, you might say, a *graduate* of North Hills's rehabilitation program and yet, a year later at age nineteen, he remains a danger to society."

"You lousy—" mutters Reef under his breath, struggling to stay seated. Again he feels Matheson's hand on his shoulder.

Maltby stands again. "Your Honour, the details of this case aren't open to discussion since the person at its focus was a young offender at the time of the incident—age seventeen, if memory serves me. I'm sure I don't need to remind Mr. Sheppard that information about a minor's criminal record is safeguarded by the Youth Criminal Justice Act."

"Your Honour," says Sheppard, turning to the judge, "the person in question already spoke to the media about this event yesterday, so this particular criminal activity is already a matter of public record. I refer, of course, to Section 110 subsection (3) of the Criminal Code. And Mr. Decker has just informed me that the individual, Chad Kennedy, is in the courtroom right now. He's the tall young man back there on the left."

As everyone in the courtroom turns to look at him, Reef's hands tighten into fists.

"Your Honour, my client is more than willing to continue presenting his evidence, but he's just suggested that my questioning this young man now could speed things along. When Mr. Decker filed his petition, neither he nor I was aware Mr. Kennedy would be present today, so I understand that the request I'm about to make is highly irregular. However, my giving this young man the opportunity to respond directly to Mr. Decker's evidence could save the court considerable time. With your permission, I would like to call Mr. Kennedy to the stand."

Judge West pauses. "Ms. Maltby, do you have any objections?"

"Not if it will save time, Your Honour," the Crown attorney replies.

The judge turns toward Reef. "Mr. Kennedy?"

Reef stands. "Yes, sir?"

"Mr. Sheppard is right. His request is highly irregular, but this is a hearing, not a trial, and I'm inclined to do anything that will expedite this matter. However, you are under no obligation to comply. The decision is yours."

"Sir," says Reef, "this guy, Mr. Decker, has had lots to say about Frank Colville and North Hills, and I wouldn't mind the chance to set the record straight."

"Very well," says the judge. He turns to the witness. "Mr. Decker, you may step down."

Decker nods. Getting up, he glances at Sheppard, his smirk now a full-blown smile. The lawyer grins in return.

Matheson puts his hand on Reef's arm. "You sure about this?"

Reef nods as the clerk rises and calls Chad Kennedy to the stand, and Reef moves toward the front of the room.

Once he has stated his full name and sworn to tell the truth, he sits down and responds to questions about his age, occupation, and place of residence, questions that once more remind Reef of his own hearing more than two years ago. Then comes the question he has dreaded.

"Are you," asks Sheppard, folding his hands behind his back in a pose that reminds Reef of a penguin, "the same Chad Kennedy who threw a rock off the Park Street overpass two years ago in—" The attorney opens a folder and reads the date, then continues, "—an act that caused a multi-vehicle collision and nearly killed a seventeen-year-old girl?"

Looking out at the dozens of faces waiting for him to answer, Reef has to remind himself that he's not on trial here. "Yes," he replies, "I'm the guy who nearly killed that girl." The reaction of the people before him now echoes the one he received at Frank's funeral, the people in the courtroom shaking their heads, murmuring to each other. "That's something I regret more than anyth—"

"Just answer the question, please," interrupts the lawyer.

Reef glares at him, then nods curtly. "Yes, I'm the guy."

The lawyer turns and moves toward the table behind him, opening a briefcase and removing two documents, one of them wrist-thick. He carries both to the judge, handing him the heavier of the two. "Your Honour, this is the transcript of Mr. Kennedy's hearing. And this," he says, passing him the second document, "is Judge Hilary Thomas's subsequent ruling that confined him to North Hills Group Home for a period of one year."

The judge barely glances at either. "Mr. Sheppard, I'm well aware of Judge Thomas's ruling, as well as the hearing that preceded it."

The lawyer is undeterred. "Your Honour, please note the date of that ruling on the page I've tabbed."

The judge flips to that page, quickly locating the information. "Noted," he says.

Sheppard returns to his briefcase and retrieves another paper, which he also hands to the judge. "This document," says the lawyer, "is a copy of a Section 810 recognizance ordering Mr. Kennedy to refrain from contacting or approaching his victim." He emphasizes the last word, giving it an audible capital letter.

The judge nods.

"If you'll look at the top right corner of this document, you'll see it's dated three months after Mr. Kennedy moved to North Hills. Even after living at the group home for a quarter of the time he was required to spend there, Mr. Kennedy was conducting himself in a manner that required a court order to prevent him from contacting his victim." Again, he capitalizes the *V* with his voice.

"May I say something?" asks Reef.

"Your Honour," says Sheppard, giving Reef a baleful look, "would you please instruct Mr. Kennedy to adhere to answering the questions I ask him?"

"Mr. Sheppard," the judge replies, "Mr. Kennedy has agreed to your request to be examined without having an opportunity to prepare. I believe we can dispense with the formalities to allow him to comment, don't you?"

The lawyer glances behind him at Roland Decker, who frowns. "By all means," he replies, but his tone is anything but generous.

Judge West turns to Reef. "What would you like to say, Mr. Kennedy?"

"Sir, totally by accident or fluke or whatever you wanna call it, I ended up volunteerin' at the same rehabilitation centre where—" He hesitates, unwilling to use Leeza's name in front of these reporters. "—where the girl I hurt was bein' treated. We became friends."

"Friends?" the judge asks, clearly surprised.

Reef nods. "Neither of us knew who the other one was. We didn't find out until much later."

"Go on," says the judge.

Reef takes a deep breath, looks toward the back of the courtroom and sees Greg Matheson nod encouragingly. "Both of us had lost someone to cancer," he continues, "someone very close to us, and she was the first person I ever talked to about that. She was the first person I ever told a *lot* 'a things. I volunteered at that rehab for weeks, and I spent every day with her. I liked her a lot." Thinking about his conversation that morning with Carly, he adds, "And I think she felt the same way about me." He pauses, afraid to give those reporters details they could distort.

"Your point, Mr. Kennedy?"

"It was a shock to both of us when she found out I was the one—" He looks down at his hands gripping the arms of the chair he sits on, then turns again to the judge. "It was a real shock. I tried to see her to tell her how sorry I was, but her mother—"

"Your Honour," interrupts Sheppard, "this is all very interesting, I'm sure," his tone suggesting the exact opposite, "but I have more questions for Mr. Kennedy."

"Let's give him another minute, Mr. Sheppard."

The lawyer shrugs, his gesture—not unlike that of a petulant child—followed by a grudging nod.

"It was her mother who got the restraining order," Reef explains, "not the girl."

"Which was her right," says the judge, "since her daughter was a minor at the time."

"Yes, it was her right." Reef pauses again, considering how to phrase his next remark. "I just want you to know that I never harassed the girl. The last time I saw her, I was only tryin' to apologize for what I did to her. And I never saw her again after the restraining order was issued."

"Your Honour," interjects Sheppard, his face suddenly brightening, "may I continue with my questioning now?"

"Go ahead, Mr. Sheppard."

The lawyer turns to Reef again, and Reef senses that something is different now. Something has changed. "Mr. Kennedy, you just said that you never saw the young woman again. Is that correct?"

Reef thinks about seeing Leeza yesterday and again today, but those times don't count. He never tried to speak to her, and she didn't even see him. "That's right."

"And are you aware that the Section 810 recognizance is still in effect, that the victim's mother applied for a second restraining order when the first one expired?"

"Yes."

The attorney does the penguin thing with his hands again. "The recognizance stipulates a specific distance beyond which you are not permitted to approach the young woman, does it not?"

Reef nods. "I think it's two hundred metres."

"Yes," says the lawyer, "that's correct. Two hundred metres." He brings his hands forward and clasps them, and Reef can almost imagine him struggling not to rub his palms together.

And all at once, Reef realizes the mistake he's made.

"Yet," says Sheppard, "since the restraining order was issued, you've been far closer to her than that, have you not?"

Reef thinks of Leeza walking past Beauty. And then he sees across the courtroom another broad grin on Roland Decker's face.

"In fact," continues the lawyer, "you've been far closer than two hundred metres on more than one occasion. Isn't that right, Mr. Kennedy?"

Reef sees Matheson looking at him questioningly. Other faces reflect more hostile expressions.

"Mr. Kennedy," says Judge West, "please answer Mr. Sheppard's question."

"Don't bother," the lawyer says, pivoting like a dancer and walking toward his briefcase again, returning with a large envelope in his hands. He takes out two eight-by-ten colour photographs and holds them up. "Is this you in these pictures, Mr. Kennedy?"

Reef looks at them, astonished by their detail, both obviously having been taken by a telephoto lens. "Yeah," he says, his voice barely a whisper.

"Mr. Kennedy," says the judge, "you'll have to speak up."

"I said yes. That's me in those pictures."

"And the young woman near you," says Sheppard. "Isn't she the girl identified in the recognizance? The girl you were required by law not to approach within two hundred metres?"

Reef looks across the room at Decker, longs to feel his fist obliterate that smile. "Yeah. That's her."

The lawyer passes both photos to the judge. "These were taken within the past twenty-four hours, Your Honour, as the time-stamp in the bottom right corner of each clearly indicates. The first shows Mr. Kennedy sitting in a car outside the young woman's home as she walks unsuspectingly past the vehicle, and the second shows him walking a few metres behind her in the Halifax Shopping Centre. In fact, that second photo was taken a little more than two hours ago." He turns to Reef. "You've been back in Halifax for two days, and on both those days you *stalked* this young woman. Isn't that right, Mr. Kennedy?"

"I wasn't stalkin' her," Reef replies, struggling to keep the anger from his voice. He slides his right hand into his pocket and grips the smooth round stone from Crystal Crescent Beach.

"Well, then, how would *you* describe what you were doing in that car yesterday and then in the mall this morning? Clearly the young woman didn't know you were there. And clearly you were watching her, following her. That certainly sounds like stalking to me."

Reef seethes, and his silence evokes a wave of murmuring that sweeps across the courtroom.

Judge West raps his gavel. "This is a courtroom, not a coffee house. If anyone here feels the need to chat, I'll ask the sheriff to escort you out." The murmurs cease and the judge turns again to Reef. "Mr. Kennedy," he says, "you haven't answered Mr. Sheppard's question."

Obviously pleased with himself, the lawyer gives a magnanimous shrug. "Your Honour, I'll be happy to withdraw the question in an effort to move these proceedings along. I have something else I'd like to ask Mr. Kennedy."

"It's your call, Mr. Sheppard."

The lawyer looks up as if inspecting the plastered ceiling, drawing out the moment before he speaks again. "Mr. Kennedy, when you lived in Halifax, you were known to associate with some fairly—" He pauses, as if groping for a word. Or, as it turns out, heightening the drama. "—*unsavoury* characters," he finishes. "Isn't that so?"

Reef can see from the expressions around the courtroom that Sheppard's emphasis on the word "unsavoury" has probably conjured images of murderers and rapists rather than guys like Bigger, Jink, and Zeus. Yeah, all his buddies had run-ins with the cops, but more often from boozing and brawling than anything else. However, Reef had also known Rowdy Brewster, the badass gangbanger who nearly killed Jink, and although he had steered clear of Rowdy as much as he could, he's afraid to deny that relationship now in case Sheppard knows about it and plans to use it against him.

"Yes," Reef replies, his eyes hard, "but that was before I ended up at North Hills."

The lawyer turns his back on him, facing the spectators so that his next question addresses the rear courtroom wall. "So since your time at North Hills, have you associated with any known criminal?"

"No. Absolutely not."

Even though he's looking at the lawyer's back, Reef can hear the smile shaping the man's next words. "Then how do you explain your meeting with Alexi Sukorov?" When Reef does not answer immediately, the lawyer turns to face him. "Sukorov is well known to both the RCMP and the Calgary Police Service, is he not?"

Clutching the stone in his pocket, Reef knows his sudden silence condemns him, but he is afraid to speak, afraid his anger will boil over. "Yes," he manages to say at last.

"My sources," continues Sheppard, "tell me that Alexi Sukorov is suspected of trafficking in narcotics and living off the avails of women. Pimping, in other words," he adds, as if offering a vocabulary lesson. "Is that your understanding?" But he doesn't wait for an answer. "Although you claim to have had no association whatsoever with the criminal element since your time at North Hills, you met with Sukorov two days ago. Isn't that correct?"

Reef tastes something coppery and is only dimly aware that he has ground the inside of his cheek between his teeth, the blood now pooling around his tongue. His left temple pulses and his face feels stove-hot, but it's cool compared to the furnace now blazing in his chest as he stares at Decker's ever-broadening grin. "You sonuvabitch," he breathes.

"Reef! Wait up!" calls Matheson, but Reef ignores him, pushing his way through the throng of reporters outside the courtroom who clamour for his attention. He needs to get outside, to get beyond the voices that shout his name, the hands that brush against his arms as he moves down the stairs. But it's like walking through chest-high water, the waves around him made of flesh and bone.

Finally, he makes it to the bottom of the staircase, but standing in front of the security checkpoint are two men: John Peterson with a microphone in his hand and another man carrying on his shoulder a videocamera and portable light-source, a miniature sun throwing a rectangular slash of brilliance before it. Reef will have to pass both men to get out.

"Mr. Kennedy!" calls Peterson as Reef approaches, his voice penetrating the melee, rising above it so that the reporters behind him actually pause in their clamouring. "Would you like to make a statement?"

Reef feels the bodies around him draw back, and for a moment he actually believes he'll make it out of the courthouse without doing more damage than he already has. He increases his pace toward the exit, focusing on the sunshine beyond those double doors.

But it's clear that Peterson has other plans. He plants himself directly in front of Reef, shoving the microphone toward him.

As Reef attempts to sidestep him, he is suddenly dazzled by the cameraman's light. "Outta my way," he says through clenched teeth, but Peterson only grins.

"Mr. Kennedy," says the reporter, "you lied under oath in Judge Oliver West's courtroom. And on more than one occasion in the past twenty-four hours, you violated the conditions of a court-issued restraining order. Not only that, you've consorted with a suspected felon in Calgary. And only moments ago, Judge West was prepared to cite you for contempt for your verbal abuse of attorney Martin Sheppard. As a former resident of North Hills Group Home for young offenders, do you have anything to say for yourself?"

From among the bodies behind him, Reef can hear Matheson shout, "He's baiting you, Reef! Ignore him!"

Reef knows he was ambushed by Decker, who until two days ago probably planned to talk only about the restraining order Leeza's mother had taken out against him. But Reef had given him so much more in the past forty-eight hours, information Decker must have paid top dollar to a private investigator to get. Decker had no doubt planned to offer up all that evidence himself until he saw Reef appear in the courtroom. And to Sheppard's credit, the attorney had altered their game plan seamlessly, providing enough drama to rival any carefully edited reality show.

Reef also knows he didn't consciously lie when he said he hadn't seen Leeza since the restraining order was issued. He knows his outburst in the courtroom—directed, in fact, at Decker, not Sheppard—was an accident, a verbal slip. And he knows that no matter how hard he has tried these past two days, everything up to this point has somehow been beyond his control. But he is suddenly tired of being the powerless patsy, the whipping boy everyone gets to drag through the dirt.

"Do you have anything to say?" repeats Peterson, his eyes nearly as intense as the cameraman's light.

More than anything, Reef wants to wrench that microphone away and pulverize it beneath his foot, wants to ram his fist into Peterson's face and watch the little weasel crash to the floor in a bloody, crumpled heap. Wants to curse the media intent on vilifying him, wants to lash out with every profanity he has ever heard, most of them learned from his grandfather. He wants to rip the air with oaths and expletives that might somehow douse the fire that blazes more fiercely in his chest every second.

But suddenly he hears Frank's voice in his head: *Do the right thing.*

"No comment," he mutters as he brushes past the reporter and cameraman and pushes out through the double doors.

CHAPTER 24

LEEZA DOESN'T MAKE IT TO THE FOOD COURT. HER FATHER IS WAITING for her outside the shopping centre's entrance, his eyes scanning the people streaming toward the doors, obviously looking for his daughter.

She expected to have to wait for him. Rather than bother with her bike, she'd taken her mother's car, something else she'll be chastised for when she returns home. But she was certain about the panic she'd heard in her father's voice so she came as fast as she could, hurriedly parking the car and running toward the entrance.

He must have called from the shopping centre, having stayed behind after she left. And as she gets closer now, she sees she is right. Hanging from both his hands are bags bearing names that surprise her: Gap Kids and The Children's Place. But those names *shouldn't* surprise her, of course, since her father has a young son—the son he and his second wife were making together while she and Ellen were learning what it was like not to have a father anymore.

As this flashes through Leeza's mind, she finds herself slowing, as though her feet know something her brain has yet to understand. *But should any of it make a difference?* she wonders. Hasn't he told her he wants to get to know her, wants to make up for not being there all those years? Buying gifts for a brother she's never met doesn't make any of that less real. Does it?

Before she can answer that question, he sees her. "Leeza!" he calls, hurrying to meet her. No longer does he look like the young man from this morning. Lines in his face make him appear far older than his forty-two years.

"What's wrong?" Leeza asks, thoughts of his other family disappearing in the face of his obvious distress.

But he doesn't reply, merely leads her across the parking lot, weaving through rows of vehicles until he arrives at a new sedan with a rental agency's decal on the back bumper.

He transfers all the bags to one hand, then pulls out a remote entry device and presses it. The trunk lid swings up, and after tossing the bags inside, he bangs it shut. Then he goes around to the passenger door and holds it open. "Get in," he tells her, and she hears that same urgency in his voice.

She slides into the car and he closes the door behind her, then goes to the driver's side and gets in. He sits with his hands on the steering wheel, staring ahead.

"Are you going to tell me what's wrong?" she asks, her own anxiety increasing by the second.

He turns to her, staring into her eyes for a moment, his own eyes like those of someone in pain, and Leeza feels fear tug at her.

"In a minute," he says, sliding the key into the ignition and starting the car. He backs it out of the parking space, then heads for the exit, turning toward the Bayers Road inbound lane.

And despite a minute passing, and then a second and a third, he doesn't speak, intent only on manoeuvring the car through traffic as they travel east across the city. Soon she sees the harbour, and Leeza expects her father to head toward Seaview Memorial Park, one of the places along the water where he can park so they can talk. Instead, he turns south, taking them under the Halifax span of the MacDonald Bridge and continuing down Barrington. Traffic is heavy in the downtown core, but soon they're beyond it and heading toward Point Pleasant.

Nearly fifteen minutes have passed since they left the shopping centre, and it's only now as her father swings the rental car into the parking area beside Black Rock Beach that Leeza remembers. Her father used to bring her and Ellen to Point Pleasant when they were little and their mother needed them out of the house, but that was before Hurricane Juan ripped through the park one September, snapping off and uprooting seventy percent of Point Pleasant's trees. It's a much more open space now, although efforts have been made to replant and restore. As they get out of the car and silently follow the path called Soldiers Memorial Way, she can tell her father is surprised by what he sees here. So much loss.

Finally, he stops beside a bench overlooking the Atlantic Ocean. "Let's sit here," he says. They do.

Even after so much silence, he still doesn't offer an explanation. Instead, his eyes scan the waves as though looking for the words he needs.

"Please," Leeza begs him. "Just say it."

"This isn't how I wanted to do it," her father tells her.

"Do what?"

He turns to her, and he appears to have aged even more on the drive here. In the harsh sunlight, the lines on his face seem even deeper, and now she can see grey threaded throughout his sandy hair. "I wanted you to get to know me better first. I wanted you to understand why. But there isn't time."

She knows that something is terribly wrong. She can hear it in his voice. "What did you want me to understand?"

"Why I have to ask you what I came for."

What I came for. She's confused. She *knows* what he came for. To get to know her better, right? To make up for all that time, all those lost years. "What do you have to ask me?" She barely recognizes her voice as she says this.

He looks once more at the water. And then at her.

Leeza's tank top is drenched with sweat and her breath comes in ragged gasps, but still she forces herself forward, her feet thudding the sidewalk in an unconscious rhythm. If she can just keep running, just keep moving her body along the concrete, perhaps she can keep her mind from straying to those minutes in the park. She reaches yet another corner and some part of her hopes that traffic will honour the crosswalk as she darts across the intersection. She cannot bear to stop.

A horn blares and tires shriek against pavement, a bumper halting within inches of her legs. "Idiot!" she hears someone yell, but she doesn't respond, simply pistons her legs faster, increasing the distance between her and her father.

She was crying at first, her gasps initially sobs, and she'd had to wipe at tears repeatedly so she could see where she was going. But her tears have stopped now. She has none left.

Two men ahead of her struggle to lift a sofa from the back of a red half-ton truck parked at the curb, no doubt intent on carrying it into the house on Leeza's right. A mountain range of boxes covers the mat-sized patch of lawn in front, and plants of every imaginable variety sway in pots on a freshly painted veranda. Moving day. A new beginning.

Which only makes her think of the new beginning with her father she had imagined until minutes ago. Another sob suddenly racks her body, and the men with the sofa turn to stare at her as she sprints past.

That sob only releases others and the tears begin to flow again. What had her mother said? *If you believe he's here just to see you, Leeza, you're even more gullible than I thought.* Why does her mother always have to be right?

Struggling to stop crying, she approaches another intersection, and this time she knows she'll have to stop and wait for the walk sign. She hasn't survived a car accident and months of agonizing rehabilitation to throw her life away crossing streets. She's stronger than that. She tells herself this now, under her breath. *You're stronger than that.* But there's a part of her that doesn't believe this mantra. *You're kidding yourself,* that part says now. *Just look at you.*

And as she comes to a stop at the corner of Spring Garden Road, she sees herself reflected in the window of a blue Hyundai, its signal light flashing while the driver waits to turn. Her hair, no longer in a neat ponytail, flares wildly in all directions. Her cheeks are streaked with mascara, and a string of snot dangles from one nostril. She tries to wipe it away with the back of her bare arm, but she only succeeds in smearing it across her cheek. She tugs at her tank top, stretching the material so it serves as a makeshift tissue that she wipes across her face. And still she sobs.

"Are you all right, dear?"

She turns and sees beside her a white-haired woman holding the hand of a small child who looks up at her with wide, dark eyes. Leeza nods, tries to say, "I'm fine," but the words come out in gulps that sound like "I'm frying." And she may as well be. Her face burns with humiliation, not just because she looks like something escaped from a nightmare but because she has been fooled once again. *I wish there was a way I could get back all those years.* She nearly chokes at that memory. Because it isn't years her father wishes he could have. He wants something far more tangible.

"Are you sure, dear?" the woman asks.

But the red hand changes to a green man and Leeza leaps into the crosswalk, grateful to be running again.

She has no idea where she is going until she gets there. After all this time, she has finally come full circle.

CHAPTER 25

"LOOK, GIVE ME A BREAK, OKAY? I'M NOT AS YOUNG AS I USED TO BE."

Reef turns to see a red-faced Matheson jogging several metres behind him, and he finally slows his pace. There are, he notes with relief, no reporters following him. Not that this should come as a surprise. They already have the information they need about Chad Kennedy because attorney Martin Sheppard has seen to that. Besides, they're probably far more interested in getting Roland Decker's response to that information. They won't have to worry about a *No comment* there, can count on Decker to give them the juicy sound bite they need for the newscasts they'll be filming for their respective TV stations.

Matheson reaches him a few moments later. "I'm sorry, Reef," he gasps, bending over with his hands on his knees.

"What do *you* have to be sorry for?" he snarls, rage still flaring in his chest.

"If I hadn't encouraged you to see Leeza—"

"No, I *should've* listened to you. That way, they'd have pictures of me *speakin'* to her instead of *stalkin'* her."

Matheson straightens up, wipes an arm across his glistening forehead. "I am *so* out of shape," he says. "Gotta cut back on the pork chops."

Reef knows the social worker is trying to lighten the mood, is at least grateful for the effort if not the effect. But there is little chance he can forget, even for a moment, the damage he has done. "I never should've come back," he mutters now. "I only made things worse."

Matheson reaches out, lays his hand on Reef's arm. "There's no way you could've known what Decker was up to."

Reef pulls away, the anger still churning inside him. "Like that *matters?*" He nods toward the courthouse far behind them. "I'm surprised the judge didn't charge me with *contempt*, or for lyin' under oath. *That* would've driven a few more nails in North Hills's coffin."

"Look," says Matheson, "if people knew how you've turned your life around, how you're helping others like those street kids in Calgary—"

"No!" interrupts Reef.

"What?"

"I'm *not* draggin' them into this. The last thing those guys need is to have reporters shovin' cameras in their faces all for the sake of a story." He thinks of how hard it's been trying to reach those kids, how hard it's been just getting some of them to show up in that basement of the Unitarian church. How many will come if there are reporters on the steps? And if the kids don't go there, where *will* they go? To Sukorov? *There are things far worse than couriering sealed packages that boys do to survive on the street.* Reef's stomach twists at the thought of what the Russian will force them to do. "Greg," he says firmly now, "we gotta keep those kids out of it."

"Even if it might save North Hills?"

Reef stares at him for a moment, then nods. "I can't take the chance."

"But it looks bad, Reef. Those lies Sheppard told about you getting involved with that felon—"

"They weren't lies. I went to see him."

Matheson blinks at him, his expression a blend of bewilderment and shock. "Reef . . ."

"It's not what you think. I was tryin' to keep him away from those kids."

"Then you have to *tell* people that," says Matheson.

Experience has taught me that winning is a completely arbitrary concept. The only thing that truly matters is the last man standing.

"Please, Greg, you gotta trust me on this. Those kids . . ." He shakes his head. "You gotta trust me."

Reef looks away, his eyes drawn to the figure of a young woman in a tank top and jeans standing at an intersection west of them, an older woman and a child beside her. Seen from this distance, the younger woman could be anyone, but her long blonde hair makes him think of Leeza and he wonders where she is now. He'd give anything to be able to see her one more time, to speak to her, to tell her again how sorry he is for everything that happened. Even though she's found someone else now, even though there is no chance she could ever return what he has felt for her all this time, he longs to make that single thing right.

But every action he takes only backfires, blows up in his face.

"I gotta get outta here," he says as the girl jogs across the street and disappears from view. "The sooner I get on a plane, the better for everybody."

"I never saw you as a quitter," says Matheson.

Reef turns to him again. "What'd you say?"

"You heard me."

The fire in his chest flares again. "Look, Greg, you don't wanna go there. Not now."

"Why *not* now? In a minute you'll be in a cab heading for the airport, right? Seems like this is as good a time as any."

"You've been a good friend," says Reef, struggling to contain the edges of his anger. "Let's keep it that way, okay?"

But Matheson is not dissuaded. "What do you think Frank would say if he were here?"

"Leave Frank out of it." Even amid the noise of downtown traffic, there is no mistaking the heat in Reef's words.

Matheson shakes his head. "I can't. How do you think he'd feel about your giving up like this? Running off when things get tough?"

Reef can barely see through the red haze that clouds his vision, can hardly hear Matheson's words above the blood-rush in his ears, and he forces his fingers not to curl into fists as he struggles to keep from lashing out. "I know what you're tryin' to do, Greg. It's not gonna work."

Matheson stares at him for a moment before continuing. "Remember that home visit I told you I had to do this morning?"

Reef gives a grudging nod.

"A university professor and his wife. They tried for years to have kids but nothing happened. Nothing physically wrong with either of them, but they just couldn't seem to make a baby. They applied for foster care last month, and we just got an eleven-month-old that we hope to place with them this week."

"Good for them," says Reef, sarcasm underlining each word.

"No. Good for the baby." Matheson watches as a bus rumbles noisily by them, a piece of paper in the gutter swirling in its back-wash. When it passes and the rumbling subsides, he continues,

"Cigarette burns on his hands and feet, and X-rays show evidence of at least three fractures, although he's never been to a hospital to have them treated. The only reason he ended up there this time was the broken arm. Looks like the mother's boyfriend threw him against a wall."

Reef looks at his feet, immediately regretting his comment.

"I know the foster homes you lived in weren't great, Reef. But they're not all like that. There are lots of good ones, and this will be one of them. I can tell. And not just because these people have a nice home and money in the bank. You should've seen that couple when I visited them this morning. The guy was so excited he could barely talk, kept stumbling over the answers to my questions. Here's a *professor*, for God's sake, a man with a doctorate teaching university English courses, and he couldn't put two sentences together the first five minutes I was there. It was his wife who finally got him settled down." He grins as if remembering the moment. "They have a lot of love to give a baby. And that's good because he's going to need it."

Reef looks up again. "Why're you tellin' me all this?"

"They're going to make a difference in that kid's life. I know it. Just like Frank made a difference in yours. I keep thinking of all the kids who go off the rails. And lots of those have parents who love them, who'd never hurt them in a million years, but things happen and suddenly they're in the system. The ones who ended up at North Hills were the lucky ones."

Suddenly, Reef remembers a moment following his own hearing when Judge Thomas sentenced him to a year at the group home. Before leaving the courtroom, his lawyer had told him, "You don't know how lucky you are." And, of course, at the time he *hadn't* known. Had, in fact, thought the judge's ruling was a joke. He'd actually been looking forward to a couple months at Riverview Correctional Institute, which he'd handled easily enough before.

Where would I be now, he wonders, if Thomas had given me what I'd expected? *You don't know how lucky you are.*

Matheson puts his hand on Reef's arm again. "Frank had faith in you, and so do I. Don't let Decker win. If you do, you're going to regret it. North Hills can still be a place that puts lives back together. Like it did yours."

Before Reef can respond, a taxi pulls over to the curb. Its rear door opens and he hears a woman tell the driver "This won't take long" before getting out, the taxi continuing to idle beside them. Reef recognizes her immediately—Frank Colville's sister, Catherine Powell. He is too drained for conversation right now, but he can't just ignore her.

"Mrs. Powell," he says, reaching out to shake her hand.

She looks at his open palm hanging in the air and makes no move to take it. Instead, she raises her eyes to his, and he can see in them a look he recognizes well, having seen it in his grandfather's eyes many times. Disgust.

"How *could* you?" she asks him.

"Excuse me?" he says, his hand dropping to his side.

"I was in that courtroom," she says, and Reef feels his heart plummet. "I was planning to return to Fredericton this morning, but I heard about the hearing so I stayed." She gives him a hard stare.

"What that lawyer said—" he begins, but she cuts him off.

"To think that my brother *trusted* you," she tells him, her voiced layered with contempt. "You should be *ashamed* of yourself!"

Reef gapes at her, unable to respond, and it's Matheson who speaks next. "Mrs. Powell," he begins, introducing himself. "I knew your brother. He couldn't have been *prouder* of Reef—"

"Really?" she asks, turning her fury on him now. "You're saying he'd have been proud of someone who commits *perjury?* Someone who spends his time now with *criminals?* He'd have *sanctioned* the repeated stalking of a defenceless girl? If you think Frank would have supported any of *that*, you most certainly did *not* know my brother!" She whirls toward Reef again. "Frank was no saint. He made lots of mistakes that he regretted, that he spent the last half of his life trying to pay for. I'm just glad he isn't here today to see his *biggest* mistake, having faith in the likes of *you!* You've tarnished his name and everything he worked so hard for. You're—" She pauses, groping for words. "You're *reprehensible!*" And before Reef can reply, she turns her back on him and climbs into the taxi, slamming the door behind her.

Reef can only watch as the car drives off, fury replacing his astonishment. He ignores Matheson as the man tries to apologize for the woman's behaviour ("She only has half the story, Reef"), takes no notice of his soothing tone, comforting gestures. There is only one thing on his mind now as he strides away, oblivious to Matheson's cries to come back.

Roland Decker will pay for this.

CHAPTER 26

"LEEZA! WHAT ARE *YOU* DOING HERE?"

Leeza turns and sees Carly Reynolds just coming through the building's entrance. She hadn't expected to find the nurse so easily. In fact, she'd expected to roam the Halifax Rehabilitation Centre looking for her since she wasn't even sure Carly still worked on the sixth floor—or, for that matter, if she still worked in the rehab at all. But no sooner had she entered the lobby and approached the woman at the information desk than she heard her name called.

"Hi, Carly," Leeza says as the nurse reaches her, arms outstretched, embracing her warmly.

"Well, this is certainly a day for coincidences," says Carly. "I was just talking about you this morning. What brings you here?" she asks, stepping back to look at her.

Leeza promised herself that she wouldn't cry again. Promised herself that she's stronger than that. But she isn't. Tears brim her eyelids and she cannot trust herself to speak.

"Look, honey," Carly says softly, "you come with me. I'm plenty early for my shift so I have time to sit and chat for a while. That okay with you?"

Carly, it seems, has not changed. Two years ago, Leeza hadn't been in rehab more than a week before she realized that Carly always arrived at least an hour early for work and never left immediately after. The nurse told people it was because she liked having the extra time to get up to speed at the beginning of a shift and then, at the end, to make sure all her charts were completed, but Leeza soon learned it was more than that. God knows she spent a lot of that extra time in Leeza's room during her first few weeks there, trying to cheer her up.

"I'd like that," Leeza manages to whisper, and the nurse squeezes her arm, leading her toward the elevator.

"So we're not talking about your *step*father," says Carly, pouring herself a cup of coffee in the staff lounge. "You sure you don't want one?" she asks, holding up the pot.

Leeza shakes her head. The tissues in her hand are a soggy mass, and although she thinks she's gotten herself under control at last, she reaches for more from the box on the table. Just in case. "No, I don't mean Jack. My *biological* father." She can't bear to use the words *real father* again. Not after what he said to her. What he asked her for.

"I didn't know he was still in the picture," says Carly. "I don't remember ever seeing him here when you were a patient."

"You didn't." Taking a deep breath, Leeza tells Carly about her father's affair, her parents' divorce, his move to Ontario where he married the woman he'd been sleeping with, his eventual decision to sever all ties with his Halifax family. "She already had two sons, and they had another one together," she adds quietly. "He's eight."

"So he chose them over you and your sister," Carly says gently.

Leeza nods, struggling not to give in to the tears that threaten again.

"And you just found out about their youngest boy today?"

"No, I knew."

"Oh," says Carly, clearly confused. "I just assumed that's why you were so upset."

Leeza shakes her head, wiping away more tears with the tissue. "He said he wanted to get to know me," she sobs, "wanted to make up for all the years he'd lost."

"And you didn't believe him?"

It takes Leeza several seconds before she can reply. "I *did* believe him," she gulps. "At first." She brushes the tissue over her eyes once more. "But he lied."

"How do you know?"

Leeza takes another deep breath, letting her mind return to that bench in Point Pleasant Park. As much as it hurts her to relive that moment, she needs to talk about it, needs to hear someone else tell her that she's right to feel betrayed.

Her father looks once more at the water. And then at her. "I have a son," he says.

Leeza nods. "I know. Mom told us a long time ago." He seems to be waiting for her to say something more, but what? Something inane like "That's wonderful" or "I'm happy for you"? What can he possibly *expect* her to say?

But his expectation, she will soon discover, has more to do with action than words.

"We named him Liam. After his grandfather."

Leeza has an odd moment trying to reconcile that information with the name of her father's father, Aubrey Hemming, who died along with her grandmother before she was born. And then she realizes it's not her *father's* father whose name Liam bears. "Your wife's father," she says. It's easier for her to say "your wife" than to use the woman's name. The woman who slept with her father and destroyed their family.

Leeza knows she is being unfair, of course. It takes two people to commit adultery, to break a trust. Her father is not blameless. But still she prefers "your wife" to the name she has never spoken aloud. Not once.

He nods. "Her father's name is William, actually, but we liked Liam better."

She notices that he hasn't spoken his wife's name, either, and she wonders if this is intentional. Following this thought gives her something else to roll around her mind, something besides the words "I have a son."

"He's eight now," her father continues. "Quite the soccer player already," he adds, as if forgetting that both she and Ellen played for years.

Or maybe he's told her this so she'll know they have something in common. *Liam likes soccer, too.* Kinship.

And it's only now that her mind hears the cruel similarity in the sounds of their names. *Liam. Leeza.*

"But he hasn't been able to play this year," her father says, and she sees his face cloud. He turns away from her, looking at the Atlantic waves rolling toward them, one after the other, breaking on the rocks. Every once in a while, a bigger one shatters, sending spray in the air that Leeza feels on her face.

She knows he expects her to ask why, but she doesn't, preferring instead to watch the waves roll and shatter, roll and shatter. She will not break their silence with another question. And she's not being childish here. Whatever he has to say, whatever he has come to ask her for, she will not make it easier for him. She has earned that right. She has the scars on her body to prove it, not to mention the headstone in St. Anthony's Cemetery that bears her sister's name.

"He's been sick for a while," says her father, and she hears him swallow twice before continuing. "At first, we thought it was just the flu. All his friends had this bug. I came down with it, too." He doesn't mention Liam's mother, and Leeza assumes she's as impervious to flu as she was to fidelity and other people's families.

"It didn't go away, though. We finally took him to Sick Kids." It takes Leeza a moment to realize he's talking about the children's hospital in Toronto. "It's leukemia," he says.

For a brief, ridiculous moment, Leeza nearly laughs at the brutal coincidence.

Leukemia.

Cancer.

She recalls, of course, the day Ellen returned from the doctor's office with the diagnosis of her own cancer, recalls her disbelief, recalls accusing Ellen of being a drama queen and manufacturing that news just to scare her. She recalls the anger she felt toward Ellen—first, for making up such a thing, and then, later, because it was true. Sisters don't get cancer. And they certainly don't die from it.

But they do.

And she did.

"Cancer," Leeza says now, that impulse to laugh now gone.

"He's had almost every treatment, but nothing's worked." And then her father is crying, the waves still rolling and shattering in front of them.

She doesn't know what to do, what to say. Is he asking to be comforted? She's hardly the person to offer that. During the long, dark period that was Ellen's cancer, the hardest part was acceptance—accepting that the diagnosis was correct, accepting that she was helpless to do more than support her sister as the disease ate away at her, accepting the cancer's inevitable conclusion and then the loss afterwards. Acceptance isn't comfort. Only one person had been able to give her that.

Reef.

Then, as if to keep her from exploring that misery again, her mind replays her father's last statement. *He's had almost every treatment, but nothing's worked.*

And now she hears it. *Almost every treatment.*

Almost.

And suddenly she knows it isn't comfort that he's come for.

"Leeza," he says, wiping at his tears. He coughs, clears his throat, coughs again. "I know this is a lot to ask." He takes a deep breath, lets it out slowly. "And I didn't want to spring it on you so soon. I thought I had more time, a few days at least." He continues to look at the water and she can tell he's avoiding her eyes. "But the hospital called after I saw you this morning. Liam's condition is worsening. He needs a bone marrow transplant as soon as possible."

Angry tears now burn Leeza's eyes. "You said you wanted to get to know me," she says, her voice flat and hollow.

But he hasn't heard her. "Neither I nor his mother is a suitable match. His brothers aren't, either. Of course, they have a different father than Liam does, but we were hoping . . ." He pauses, takes another deep breath. "He's been on the bone marrow registry from the beginning but . . ." He coughs again, and the sound is like choking.

"You said you wanted to make up for all the years you lost," she says, each word tearing at her.

And it's now that he turns to her. "You might be a match, Leeza. You're our last hope."

Leeza lets those two words—*last hope*—ricochet around inside her skull, remembering the times her mother used them as she and Jack considered one treatment after another for Ellen. But Leeza has learned there is no such thing as *last hope.* There is only hope, and then it's gone.

"You'd like him, Leeza," her father continues. "He's got a great sense of humour. Even as sick as he's been—" He stops abruptly as though his throat has clicked shut, cutting off the words, and she can hear the effort it takes for him to push out the next ones as he turns again to the water. "He's only *eight*, for Christ's sake. It isn't fair!" And then he's crying again.

"Fair," she says, the word like lead in her mouth.

If he's heard her, he gives no indication of it, seemingly unaware of the effect his words have had on her. "If you're a match," he says, his voice hoarse, distorted, "they can harvest your bone marrow here in Halifax. Our doctor already checked with the hospital." He pauses. "I won't lie to you, Leeza. It can be painful, how they take the marrow—"

"I don't believe you."

He turns to her again as if seeing her for the first time. "Why would I lie about something like this?"

"Not that," she says, struggling against the quaver in her voice. "I can't believe what you're asking me to do. Not after Ellen. She was your daughter. You didn't even *call*!"

She sees his face crease but she presses on. "All those mornings I woke up to hear her sobbing in the next room after she'd found more hair on her pillow. All those days I held her hand while she moaned in that hospital bed, begging for more pain medication. All those nights I held her head while she puked into a basin, too weak to even cry anymore. You didn't even call." The quaver overcomes her and her voice breaks, but she struggles through it, pulling herself to her feet. "You know what isn't fair? That you didn't get to hear her when she *begged* us again and again to let her *die*." Leeza sobs, the harsh sound seal-like there beside the ocean, and she turns toward the path. "*That's* what isn't fair."

"Leeza, please listen to me."

She doesn't look back. Instead, she concentrates on putting one foot in front of the other, moving away from this person who is and will never be her father.

"Leeza!" he shouts.

But now she is running.

"My God, Leeza," Carly says softly. "I don't know what to say."

Leeza blows her nose again, then looks down at the tissues in her hands, now a wad nearly the size of one of the billiard balls on the third-floor pool table. She looks up at Carly. "I just needed to tell someone," she says.

Carly nods. "On the one hand, he's an asshole showing up after all these years because he has no one else to turn to. Do you think he even sees the irony in it? The fact that it's cancer, I mean?"

Leeza shrugs. "What about the other hand?"

"He's a father," she says simply. "A father who loves his son."

And that, Leeza realizes, is the part that hurts most. Not just that he came to her under the pretense of getting to know her better, of making up for lost time. That was bad enough. What's worse is knowing that he loves his son more than he ever loved either of his daughters. After all this time, after all the years that have passed, that realization shouldn't cut so deeply. But it does.

"So what are you going to do?" Carly asks.

"Well, for starters, I'm not telling my mother."

The staff lounge rings with Carly's sudden laughter. Diane Morrison's overprotective, controlling nature was common knowledge among the rehab's staff when Leeza was a patient here. Soon, surprising even herself, Leeza is grinning along with the nurse.

When Carly stops laughing, she says, "You're right not to tell her now. This is *your* decision, not hers. You can tell her after you've made it."

They sit for a moment in a comfortable silence. Already, Leeza feels a little better. Carly has that effect on people. "What do *you* think?" she asks the nurse. "Should I go ahead with it?"

Carly shakes her head. "I can't tell you what to do, Leeza."

"That's not what I mean. I just want to know what someone else might do in this situation."

Carly smiles. "Honey, I'm pretty sure there aren't too many people who've been in a situation like this. Or anything close to it." She pauses for a moment, her eyes narrowing. "I can think of someone, though, who might bring an interesting perspective to it."

"Who?"

"Reef Kennedy."

Any mirth Leeza might have enjoyed moments ago is suddenly gone. "That's not funny, Carly."

"I didn't mean it to be."

"Then why bring him up?"

Carly glances at her watch. Apparently satisfied that she still has a few minutes before her shift begins, she says, "He came to see me this morning."

It takes Leeza a moment to respond. "More court-ordered volunteering?" She hates the pettiness in her voice, but she feels entitled. *More* than entitled.

Carly frowns. "He came to my home, Leeza."

"I hope you counted your silverware when he left."

There is no mistaking the disapproval in Carly's eyes. "That's a little harsh, don't you think?"

"Yeah, well, it's been a pretty harsh day." Leeza gets up. "Look, thanks for listening to me, Carly. I appreciate it. I'll let you know what I decide." She turns toward the door.

"Leeza?"

Not this again, Leeza thinks, her hand already on the doorknob. *How much is a person expected to take in one day?* "What?"

"He still cares for you."

"Right. Maybe almost as much as my father does." She says *father* like it's a different F-word.

"Honey, they're nowhere *near* the same."

Leeza turns to Carly. "That's where you're wrong. I saw him on the news and they asked him about me. He couldn't even be bothered to comment."

Just then her cell rings and she pulls it out of her pocket, sighing when she sees the caller's name on the display. But this time she answers it. *Anything to end this conversation.* "Hi," she says.

"It's about *time* you picked up," says Brett. "DID YOU TRY AISLE SEVEN?" There is muffled conversation, clearly HomeHardwareSpeak, and then Brett returns. "You know I called, right?"

"I know."

She hears a low chuckle over the line. "So I'm assuming that you were *occupied*, huh? I SAID AISLE *SEVEN*!"

"Yes. I was occupied."

"So what'd he say?"

Leeza frowns. Does Brett know about her father somehow? "I don't want to get into it right now."

"NO, ON THE RIGHT! Okay, at least tell me if you're gonna see him again."

"I haven't made up my mind."

"YOUR *OTHER* RIGHT! Cripes, Leeza. After all this you're playing hard to get?"

Leeza frowns. "What on *earth* are you talking about?"

"*Reef*, of course. Who else?"

Leeza clicks off the phone. "Did you put her up to this?" she asks Carly.

"Put who up to what?"

"That was Brett. Wondering if I'd seen Reef."

Carly flushes. "He asked for her number. I gave it to him."

"What *is* this with everybody and Reef?"

The phone rings again and this time Leeza punches the Talk button savagely. "No, I haven't seen him," she says crisply. "And no, I don't *want* to see him. Now stop calling about this, okay?"

Before she can press End, though, she hears a tinny scream emanate from the receiver. And if the astonished look on Carly's face is any indication, it can be heard from across the room. Leeza waits for the scream to end and then gingerly puts the phone to her ear. "*What* are you yelling about?"

"Look," mutters Brett, "I just humiliated myself by screeching in the paint department. If you hang up on me again after I've tried to reach you all day, I swear I'm gonna march out of this store, jump in my car, drive to Halifax, and kick your ass! You got that?"

"What are you *talking* about?"

"Did you get my messages?"

"I've been busy," Leeza replies.

"*Please* don't tell me coursework." Before Leeza can respond, Brett continues, "Reef called me earlier. He loves you, Leeza. Even after all this time."

The knuckles of Leeza's fingers around the phone gleam whitely through her skin. "I don't know what you and Carly have been smoking, but I know *exactly* how Reef feels about me. I saw him on the news."

"Great, huh?"

It's all Leeza can do to keep from hanging up. If not for the aforementioned ass-kicking, she probably would, but Brett isn't one to make idle threats. "No," she says simply. "It was not great."

There is sudden silence, and Leeza hopes a Home Hardware customer has finally run Brett to ground. But no. "He said he's thought of you every day for the past two *years*, Leeza. What *more* do you want?"

He's thought of me every day? "What are you talking about?"

There is another silence. "Look, your phone is Web-enabled, right?"

"Yes."

"I'm gonna forward you a couple links to videos you need to see. My mom just sent me the second one a few minutes ago, but I haven't had a chance to watch all of it yet. We're having a big sale on semi-gloss. My shattered nerves!" As if to emphasize that point, she says, "YEAH, YEAH, I'LL BE RIGHT WITH YOU." Then, "You hear me, Leeza?"

"I heard you."

"Check out those links *now*, okay? I also sent you Reef's cell number. I think you'll want it after you see those videos. I'll talk to you later, okay? I want to hear what you—KEEP YOUR SHIRT ON! THE WORLD WON'T END IF YOU DON'T FIND PAINTER'S TAPE THIS SECOND." And then the call ends.

"What was *that* all about?" asks Carly.

Leeza presses keys on her phone, bringing up her e-mail. "Some things she wants me to see on the Internet."

"Mind if I watch, too? She sounded pretty intense about it."

"Brett was *born* intense," says Leeza, and Carly laughs. "You can watch if you want. You sure you have time?"

"Honey, I'll *make* time."

CHAPTER 27

"WHAT'S WRONG?" ASKS BIGGER ON THE PHONE. "YOU SOUND pissed."

"Long story," says Reef, Catherine Powell's angry face still etched in his mind. He'd been aimlessly wandering the downtown core since leaving Matheson, trying to walk off the shame and the bitterness that clung to him and clouded his thinking. He had to get his head straight if he was going to figure out what to do about Decker, but the walking hadn't worked so he'd pulled out his phone and called Bigger, surprised when his friend picked up on the first ring. "You guys ain't workin' today?" he asks.

"Nah, we called in sick. After last night, no way we coulda stood in the sun all day rakin' hot asphalt." Reef imagines the jackhammers ratcheting in their heads—Bigger and Jink can put back a pile of booze, and Bigger confirms their intake last night was no exception. "After the party broke up, Jink 'n' me went bar-hoppin'. Sometime after who-knows-how-many beers," he moans, "someone challenged Jink to do shooters, and that asshole roped me into it. Don't have a *clue* who won."

"Look," says Reef, "I was wonderin' if you 'n' Jink could come pick me up. I got somethin' I need to do."

"Yeah, sure, but it might be a while 'fore we get there."

"Where are you?"

Reef hears Bigger give an exaggerated sigh. "We might as well gone to work 'cause Jink 'n' me been spendin' our sick-day trampin' through parkin' lots. Right now we're in the lot behind—"

Reef hears Jink curse in the background. "Gimme that goddamn phone!" he snarls. A moment later, Reef hears, "It's as much *his* fault as mine."

"What's goin' on?" asks Reef.

"Somebody sent us home in a cab last night, and we can't remember where we left Beauty. We already been to the bars we *think* we went to, and now we're checkin' out some 'a the others." He lowers his voice. "I'm gettin' worried somebody mighta stole her."

Reef hears a sudden bray of laughter through the earpiece, then Bigger's voice: "No one in their right mind woulda stole *that* piece 'a shit, you idiot."

Jink erupts in an explosion of profanity and then Bigger comes back on the phone.

"Look, Reef, why don't you head over to Zeus's place? We'll meet you there once we find that hunk 'a rollin' scrap metal."

"And if you don't?"

"If we don't, we got a brand new reason to party."

Reef hears another snarled response from Jink in the background and then the call ends.

* * *

"It's open!"

Entering the apartment, Reef finds Zeus in pretty much the same place he was last time: lying on the sofa, his arm and leg propped up on pillows, his scratcher resting on his cast. The floor is littered with clothes and empty beer cans and, like before, an animated program flickers across the flat-screen, this one an old *Road Runner* cartoon from a hundred years ago. "Thought you'd be on a plane by now," says Zeus.

"Change in plans." Reef drops his jacket and backpack on the only chair not covered with junk, then goes to stand by the window. "Okay if I crash for a bit? Bigger 'n' Jink are gonna meet me here."

"Fill your boots." Zeus takes a hit off the joint, holds it in his lungs as long as he can, then releases it almost reluctantly, the smoke streaming from his nostrils like twin contrails. On the flat-screen, Wile E. Coyote is duped by the Road Runner for the zillionth time, but Zeus chuckles anyway. His glassy eyes suggest this isn't his first joint today.

Reef looks out the window and sees a pickup rumble past, the same make and model Frank drives. Except he doesn't. Not anymore.

Grief wells up in him again as he stands at the window realizing once more that he'll never see his friend again. It's been less than forty-eight hours since he learned of Frank's death, and until this moment some small part of him has refused to believe it, has steadfastly clung to the idea that he'll wake up soon and all this will have been a dream. A nightmare.

But it isn't. Frank's gone.

And everything he worked so hard for will soon be gone, too. Roland Decker has made damn sure of that.

What's worse is that Decker has used Reef to make it happen.

Used him to help tear down everything his friend stood for, fought for.

Reef turns to see Wile E. clinging to a boulder that hurtles earthward while the Road Runner watches gleefully from a cliff edge, and he feels a sudden kinship for the cartoon coyote plummeting toward the canyon floor below. He clenches his jaws, swallows hard to keep from cursing Decker again, and glances at his watch.

"You okay, man?" Zeus asks. "You seem . . . I dunno . . . tight."

Reef shrugs. "I'm good."

"You sure? Looks like you could use somethin' to take the edge off." Zeus waggles the joint. "Wanna make a business transaction?"

Reef looks at it for a long moment, imagining Frank's disappointment at his even *thinking* about using again. In the two years since he's done drugs of any kind, he hasn't missed them like he thought he would, hasn't longed for the muffled serenity they bring, the temporary escape they promise.

Until now.

After his appearance at the courthouse, he can't imagine being a bigger disappointment to Frank—or anybody else, for that matter—than he already is. What had Catherine Powell called him? Frank's biggest mistake. So what does he have to lose? Besides, smoking a joint is *nothing* compared to the payback he intends to inflict on Decker. Now *that's* going to be trouble. "What the hell," he mutters. "Yeah."

Zeus tells him the price of an ounce.

"A joint's all I need," says Reef.

"Consider it a goin'-away gift," Zeus says, pointing to a scarred wooden box on the wide pine board that serves as a coffee table. Its legs are cement blocks, and Reef sees white particles on the floor beside them, probably bits of the leg cast that have connected with the concrete at various points. No surprise there. Even when unencumbered by fibreglass, Zeus is a walking accident.

Reef reaches for the box, opening it to find several rows of joints packed neatly inside. He takes one out and holds it up to his nose. Definitely primo. "Thanks," he says.

"Here." Zeus tosses him a lighter.

Reef puts the whole joint in his mouth, moistening it to slow the burn. As he pulls it out, the taste of the paper and the marijuana unleashes a dozen memories, most of them involving Bigger and Jink. He momentarily wonders when they'll get here—he talked to them nearly an hour ago—but suddenly Reef doesn't see time as a problem. He's got a joint to keep him occupied, and he plans to make the most of it.

Flicking the lighter, he hears Frank's voice in his head: *People who respect themselves don't need to put drugs or alcohol into their bodies to keep from feeling the things they can't face.* Reef scowls. He has no intention of not facing what he's feeling. In fact, he plans to *embrace* it. The joint will just take the edge off, give him some breathing room while he decides exactly what he's going to do.

One thing's for sure—he's going to make Decker regret what he's done. *How* is a little less clear at the moment. Reef knows he'll probably just get one opportunity, so he wants to make it count. And a joint can't help but make the whole planning process more pleasant.

He flicks the lighter again. *Respect yourself.* Not easy to do when everyone keeps calling you a low-life.

During the past two years, he's worked hard to put behind him all the actions that earned him that name from store clerks, bus drivers, police officers, even foster parents. *Low-life.*

He's worked hard to become the kind of person who does

the right thing, who can hold his head up even after everything he's done. Even the most terrible thing, that day on the Park Street overpass.

He's worked hard to honour his commitments, to be accountable, to build a life where he could maybe give back a little of the good he's gotten. The good he got from Frank.

And in less than twenty minutes in that courtroom, all that was stripped away. What had Frank's sister said afterward? *You've tarnished his name and everything he worked so hard for.* Well, she was right about that. He *has* tarnished Frank's name. But he's had help. From Roland Bernard Decker.

He flicks the lighter a third time, watches the flame lick the end of the joint, hears the soft sizzle of the paper as the marijuana catches fire, glows red as he sucks deeply. *You should be ashamed of yourself!* He is. And he's counting on this joint to take that feeling away, at least for a little while.

The buzz is almost immediate. Not only is the stuff primo, the fact that he hasn't toked in two years has made his brain an ideal receptor. He holds his breath, releasing the sweet smoke at the last possible moment. Coughs, flicks at something on his tongue, then takes another hit.

"Good stuff, huh?" asks Zeus, grinning.

"The best," Reef replies, his voice hoarse from the smoke.

But the shame is still there, every bit as strong as before. Maybe stronger.

"What's up?" asks Bigger as he eyes the remains of the joint in Reef's fingers. Jink, too, is staring at it from the doorway. They glance at each other, sharing a look.

"Found Beauty?" drawls Reef, getting to his feet. He sways slightly, his face now hot as though the heat in his chest has travelled north, the anger from before lacking its knife edge. It's more of a pulse now. And he's hungry.

"Had her parked behind a Dumpster," explains Jink. "Didn't see it the first time we checked."

"She okay?" Reef asks.

"Yeah. Why?"

"Dunno. You sound like somethin's wrong." He takes a final puff, then pokes the remains of the joint into an empty beer can on the makeshift coffee table.

"*You* okay?" asks Bigger.

"I'm great," says Reef.

"Matheson don't think so."

Reef's face darkens. "When were you talkin' to *him*?"

"He called us," says Bigger. "He's worried about you. He's afraid you're gonna do somethin' stupid."

Reef snorts. "Too late. Did plenty 'a that already."

"He said there was a hearin', said it didn't go so good," offers Jink. "Tough break."

Reef shakes his head. "Nothin' broken yet. Soon will be, though."

Bigger steps forward. "Look, man, how about we get you somethin' to eat?"

"I'd like to, but there ain't time. Got things to do."

"Matheson says you didn't eat much today."

"*Matheson* says, huh? What about what *I* say?"

Now Jink moves forward. "Take it easy, okay?"

"I'm takin' it any way I can get it," Reef replies. Beside him, Zeus raises his good hand and high-fives him.

"Listen, buddy," says Bigger, "you don't wanna screw things up for yourself."

Reef scowls. "Already did. You're lookin' at Public Enemy Number One now." Except that *enemy* comes out sounding like *enema* and he laughs.

"That's not the way Matheson sees it."

Reef's laughter dies in his throat. "*Forget* Matheson!" he growls. "Look, I called you guys 'cause I thought you might wanna join me in a little fun. Like old times."

"Fun?" echoes Bigger.

"Got a score to settle. *Big* time."

"That ain't such a good idea," says Jink.

Reef stares at him. "You two turn into a couple 'a pussies since I left?"

"You don't wanna do this," warns Bigger.

"That's where you're wrong, Big. I *do* wanna do this." He looks at them with narrowed eyes. "You *with* me?"

Jink takes another step. "I think you'd better cool off, okay?"

Reef stares at him. "What's goin' on here? What's *with* you two?"

"Yeah," says Zeus from the sofa. "What's *with* you guys?"

"Shut your hole, Zeus!" grunts Bigger. He turns to Reef. "You're better 'n this, buddy," he says.

"That's where you're wrong. Turns out I'm—" Reef searches for the adjective. "—reprehensible! *There's* a word you don't hear every day, right?"

"Man," says Jink, "any word with more 'n four letters is over *my* head. Forget about it, okay?"

"Yeah," agrees Bigger. "Whoever said that don't know you. Not like we do."

Reef shakes his head. "No, she pretty much nailed it. I screwed up. Because 'a me, they're probably gonna shut down North Hills. Everything Frank worked for, *gone* 'cause 'a me."

"That's bullshit," says Bigger.

"No, I mean it. Remember how you drove me to see Leeza? Somebody took a picture of us there."

"So what?" says Jink.

The frown on Bigger's face shows that he, at least, understands. "The restrainin' order."

"They accused me 'a *stalkin'* her," Reef continues. "Hell, the judge might even recommend the cops lay charges for it. But there's more. A *lot* more. Nothin' I did, really, but they made it *look* that way."

"They?" chorus Jink and Bigger.

"Decker 'n' his lawyer."

"Decker. That's the guy from the funeral, right?" asks Jink. "The guy those reporters were hot for?"

Reef nods. "Wants to get elected and is willin' to do anything to make it happen. Includin' draggin' Frank and North Hills through the muck. And I gave Decker everything he needed to do it." He retrieves his jacket and backpack from the chair, slinging both over his shoulder. "Payback's gonna be a *bitch*!" He moves toward the door. "You guys with me or what?"

Bigger glances at Jink. "Sure, buddy," he says. "We're with you."

But they aren't. Reef sees this as soon as they get him in the car. Jink doesn't even ask him where to go, just starts driving.

"Downtown's the *other* way, Jink."

"Reef," says Bigger, "you're not thinkin' straight."

"Look, you chickenshits," he snarls, "I got nothin' to *lose*! If you'd been at the hearin', you'd know that."

Bigger shakes his head. "Matheson don't see it that way."

And now Reef knows where they're heading. To Matheson's house. Just then his cell rings, and he doesn't even bother to look at the display, knows it's probably Matheson calling. The rage he felt outside the courtroom returns in waves, and he jabs the power button, shutting off the phone. "Matheson can go straight to hell!" he roars. "I'm goin' head-to-head with Decker, okay? Ever since he started this, he's been hidin' behind reporters and lawyers. It's time for him to man up."

"Can't help you," says Bigger.

"I thought I could *count* on you guys!"

"You *can*," says Jink. "We're keepin' you from doin' somethin' you're gonna regret."

"Stop the car."

"Look, Reef—"

"Stop the goddamn car!" Reef swings open his rear door, which caroms off a garbage can standing by the curb, sending it flying.

"Aw, man!" shouts Jink, and Reef can see his buddy's weakness in his rear-view reflection. His beloved Beauty.

"If you don't wanna lose the whole door, pull over!" He hears the squeal of old brake pads against worn drums and the car slows.

"Jink!" growls Bigger.

"You think you can talk sense into him when he's like this? Nuh-uh." Jink pulls the car over to the curb.

"Thanks for *nothin'*, assholes!" And then Reef is on the sidewalk, his jacket in one hand, his backpack thumping against his shoulder as he runs.

CHAPTER 28

LEEZA HITS REDIAL ONCE AGAIN BUT, LIKE THE LAST SEVEN TIMES, she hears the same automated recording: "We're sorry, but the person you are trying to call has the phone turned off." Frustrated, she stabs the End key, resisting the temptation to make sure the number is the same one Brett gave her. Having checked those digits three times already, she knows her error wasn't misdialing. The mistake she made was not going to that funeral yesterday.

Walking down Quinpool Road on her way to Connaught Avenue, Leeza is in no hurry to get home, and not because she'll have to face her mother after taking the car and leaving it at the shopping centre. Her mind is still reeling, still trying to process what she and Carly saw on her cellphone in the rehab's staff lounge. Even on that small screen, the image of Reef had leaped out at her as he'd spoken to the crowd of reporters outside the church.

She clicks her phone's Web browser now and once more pulls up the first of the two videos Brett sent her, grateful for the shade the buildings throw across the sidewalk. The heat hasn't let up all day but she ignores it as she fast-forwards the video, then presses the phone to her ear, listening to Reef's words above the sounds of the traffic:

"Two years ago, I almost killed an innocent girl. I gotta carry that with me for the rest 'a my life. There isn't a day that I don't think of her, don't wish I could take back the terrible thing I did to her. I also don't want to cause her any more unhappiness, so I got nothin' to say about her. She deserves to be left alone. Today isn't a day for campaignin'. And it isn't a day for invadin' someone's privacy, either. What today is about is honourin' Frank Colville, a man who made a difference."

She had been confused about the campaigning comment until Carly told her about Roland Decker, the man her mother said was promising to get tough on youth crime. Carly's tone suggested she didn't share Diane Morrison's admiration for the man, whom Leeza remembered seeing on the newscast her mother had recorded for her. The newscast that had distorted Reef's words by omitting everything else he'd said. *There isn't a day that I don't think of her, don't wish I could take back the terrible thing I did to her.*

Those words tug at her now even more than they did in the rehab lounge: *There isn't a day that I don't think of her . . .* Just as there hasn't been a day during the past two years when she hasn't thought of him. First with anger, of course, and heartache at the discovery of his betrayal. And then something more, something different after learning from Brett about the life Reef had led, a life that had brought him first to the Park Street overpass and then to the Halifax Rehabilitation Centre. And to her.

There isn't a day that I don't think of her . . .

It was the second video that Brett had sent, though, that drove home the truth, the intensity of those words. It showed Roland Decker speaking to reporters outside the provincial courthouse earlier that afternoon, talking about a hearing that would decide the fate of North Hills Group Home. Leeza clicks on that video again now, listens as Decker responds to a question from reporters: "Judge West has promised a decision about North Hills within the next twenty-four hours."

Several hands wave on the screen and Decker points to a man Leeza recognizes from the newscast. "Yes, Mr. Peterson?"

"That seems like a very short time, Mr. Decker, shorter than it usually takes for a judge to bring down a decision. Would you care to comment on why you think Judge West is willing to offer his ruling so soon?"

Decker's smiling face suddenly becomes solemn. "I can't speak for the judge, of course, but I'm sure he's aware of how serious the public views both of the issues addressed by the application I've made to the court."

Other reporters shout questions, but Decker nods only at Peterson, who asks, "And what *are* these issues, Mr. Decker?"

"Ineffective government spending, for one," Decker replies. "I'm here to make sure we don't continue to throw away good money after bad. The other issue, of course, is youth crime. Specifically, making sure that the young people who commit these crimes are held accountable for their actions. During the past two weeks, for example, Halifax citizens on three separate occasions have been assaulted and robbed in broad daylight by two young men. If there were tougher penalties for crimes perpetrated by young people, they wouldn't be so quick to commit them and they'd be even less likely to reoffend."

A young female reporter standing at Decker's immediate right shouts, "Would you care to respond to the suggestion that your effort to shut down North Hills Group Home is nothing more than an attempt to garner more support for your election campaign?"

Decker's face on the screen registers indignation. "People who make such statements are sorely ignorant of the facts that prompted my application to close that facility."

"Mr. Decker," interjects Peterson, "can you share some of these facts now?"

"I'd be happy to." Decker beams, and then turns to address the rest of the group. "Just a few minutes ago, a young man named Chad Kennedy stormed out of this courthouse. Many of you here heard Kennedy admit to the media yesterday that he was the young offender who nearly killed a teenage girl two years ago. In the months following that act, the court issued an injunction to keep him away from his victim. However, during today's hearing, my attorney, Martin Sheppard, presented evidence that Kennedy violated that court order twice during the past twenty-four hours."

"What form of evidence?" asks Peterson.

"A photograph of him sitting in a car outside the young woman's home and another showing him following her through a mall."

"Did he threaten her either of those times?" asks the female reporter.

Decker looks at her with exaggerated sadness. "Does he have to *harm* her again before we recognize the significance of his actions? That he *violated* a court order? And why *shouldn't* he? Two years ago, he got a slap on the wrist after nearly killing her— twelve months at North Hills Group Home." He pauses, no doubt for effect. "It's easy to see how much good *that* did."

Leeza clicks off the video, unwilling to listen to more of the man's comments that, to her mind, sound scripted and rehearsed. Instead, she thinks about what Carly just told her, how Reef has been living in Alberta for a year, which explains why their paths have never crossed again.

Until today, when she wasn't even aware of it.

She lets her mind imagine those two moments captured in Decker's photographs—photographs that were obviously taken by someone that creep hired.

Reef sitting in a car outside her house.

Reef following her in the shopping centre.

There isn't a day that I don't think of her . . .

Again she retrieves the number that Brett gave her, unconsciously crossing her fingers as she presses Talk. But again there is only that automated recording, which she clicks off in mid-sentence.

She knows now that she's too late. Airlines make passengers turn their cellphones off. Reef is on a plane back to Calgary.

Brushing at sudden tears, she's surprised to see she's reached Connaught Avenue already, and she crosses on the green and turns right despite her reluctance to go home. How she dreads her mother's interrogation about her father, dreads the self-satisfied look on her face, her pitying, self-righteous I-told-you-so response to learning why Scott Hemming has reappeared after all these years. *At least,* thinks Leeza, *I get to prove her wrong about Reef, that he's not the monster she thinks he is.*

As she approaches her house now, Leeza imagines Reef sitting in front of it after the funeral, and her heart lurches in her chest. She suddenly can't bear the thought of him waiting outside on the street, probably remembering at the same time the last words she ever said to him, how she'd cried *Go away!* as he told her how sorry he was. She can't bear the thought of him walking unseen behind her in the mall, all the while remembering her screaming at Brett, *He did this to me!*

Why hadn't he spoken to her in the mall, called out her name?

But she can guess the answer to that question—the restraining order that her mother had gotten a judge to sign. The restraining order her mother had renewed last year. The restraining order that Decker had accused Reef of violating. But he hadn't. Not really.

And how she wishes now that he had.

As with so many things in her life, it's too late now to make a difference, but that restraining order is toast. She's no longer a minor incapable of rescinding it. This is *her* life, by God, not her mother's.

And that thought now gives her strength as she braces for the inevitable questions about her father. Yes, she'd been deceived by the man, believed his lie that he only wanted to get to know her, never thought for a moment he might have an ulterior motive. But she's an *adult* now, and it's time she started acting like one. She has a *right* to make her own mistakes, a *right* to see whomever she wants whenever she wants to.

She just wishes it hadn't taken her so long to realize it.

The set of her jaw reflecting the strength of this new resolve, she begins to hurry along the sidewalk, and she is only metres from her driveway when she sees them. Two young men. Staring at her.

What had Decker said on that video? *Halifax citizens on three separate occasions have been assaulted and robbed in broad daylight by two young men.* And hadn't her mother spoken about a mugging yesterday only a few blocks from here?

She tries to shrug that thought away, but fear clutches at her nonetheless. She will have to walk by them to reach her house.

At least she has only a few dollars on her and the cellphone in her hand, which she slips into her jeans pocket. Besides, surely they won't try anything here, not in front of all these homes. But she hears her mother's voice again: *In broad* daylight, *no less! Two thugs bold as brass.*

Leeza considers crossing the street, but the closest intersection is several houses beyond her and she'd be crazy to brave traffic without a crosswalk during the beginning of rush hour. And she doesn't want to turn around, moving farther from the safety of her home.

She draws a deep breath. *You're overreacting,* she thinks. Despite the way the men study her as she walks toward them, they could have a very good reason for standing there on the sidewalk in front of her house. As if waiting.

As she approaches, one of them—a hulking brute of a man—mutters something to the other.

And then they grab her.

CHAPTER 29

"YOU GOT SOME ID?" ASKS THE MAN AT THE CASH REGISTER.
Reef can almost hear the people lined up behind him heave a collective sigh. Everyone's in a hurry. Having already put down the money, he pulls out his wallet again and shows the cashier his driver's licence.

The man squints at it over the counter. "Alberta, huh?" he says, frowning. "You got some Nova Scotia ID?"

The buzz Reef got at Zeus's is slipping away, which is why he's here in this liquor store now buying booze. Picking up a bottle of Captain Morgan moments ago, he remembered the last time he drank rum, even though it was more than two years ago. He'd snagged a bottle off a bum he'd rolled on his way to The Pit with Bigger and Jink, and the three of them had downed it as they walked to the abandoned downtown hotel they often hung out at. Reef remembers it clearly because it was later that same day when he stood on the Park Street overpass and threw the stone that changed everything.

But it didn't, not really. Not in Halifax, anyway. He's still the guy everyone suspects the worst of. *Expects* the worst of. Like stalking Leeza, whom he would never harm again in a million years. Like working with Alexi Sukorov, drug dealer and pimp.

And now there's this guy behind the counter suspecting him of trying to pass off a fake ID. On a day when absolutely everything has gone wrong, it's galling enough to be asked for identification, but hearing this man imply that he's falsified a driver's licence sears him like a branding iron, releasing fresh rage, hot and pulsing. Before he's even aware of what he's doing, Reef reaches across the counter and grabs the guy by the shirt, hauling him close. His mouth a centimetre from the astonished man's face, he snarls, "Take the goddamn money before I shove it up your ass!"

A startled cry from behind him makes him turn, and he sees a wide-eyed woman in a yellow dress clutching a bottle of wine in front of her as if for protection. And behind her are other women and men, all of them drawing back, holding their purchases like ridiculous glass shields. This is all it takes to bring him back to himself. "Sorry," Reef mutters, releasing the man, whose rolling eyes bulge white.

But it's too late. Reef hears a door open near the back of the store, voices low and urgent spilling out, and he knows there are people in security uniforms coming for him.

He flees.

CHAPTER 30

"LET ME *GO!*" LEEZA CRIES AS HUGE HANDS ENCIRCLE HER WRISTS, tugging her toward the curb where a car is waiting. Realizing the two men intend to force her inside, she opens her mouth to shriek, but another hand, this one even larger than those on her wrists, clamps across it, cutting off her screams. Panic claws at her and she tries kicking anything within reach, but her cross-trainers glance uselessly off legs slabbed with muscle as she is half-carried, half-dragged forward. A part of her still capable of rational thought sees vehicles passing and wonders, *Why doesn't someone help me?* Instead, though, drivers wave at her, smiling, and a few even honk their horns.

And then she sees why—signs crudely lettered on cardboard propped in the car's windows: "Suprize!" and "Happy Brithday!", the misspellings no doubt oddly endearing to the drivers who wave at the trio of supposed friends.

Terror grips Leeza as the bigger of the two men opens the back door and forces her inside, his huge body filling the space behind her. With the second man moving toward the driver's door, Leeza finally has an opportunity to scream, and she seizes it.

"For Christ's sake," snarls the brute in the back seat, his huge arms wrapped viselike around her, "settle down!"

The man behind the wheel turns to look at her over the seat, and the sight of his features—a broken nose, sloping forehead, and a snake tattoo wrapped around his neck—turns her legs to water. "We're not gonna *hurt* you, okay?" he says, and she can see he's missing teeth.

"What do you *want?*" she manages to say, her voice a strangled squeak. She knows she can't escape the grip that the bigger man has on her, but maybe if she gets them talking, she can distract them long enough to make a break for it.

"We need your help," says the brute beside her. "Reef's in trouble."

"You know, there are easier ways to ask a girl for help," says Leeza, her heart rate returning to normal as the car cruises south along Connaught. When she'd finally realized who the two men were, she was afraid her mother might phone the police if she spied her daughter sitting in a beat-up Buick with such "colourful" strangers, so she'd encouraged them to put some distance between them and her house as quickly as possible.

The guy in the back seat beside her, Bigger Something, grins as he pulls the crude signs from the windows and drops them at his feet. "Yeah, but it'd take a helluva lotta splainin' to get a girl into a car with a guy as ugly as *him*," he says, nodding at the one called Jink, who flips him the finger. "The *main* reason, though," he continues, "is we wasn't sure what you'd do if we just told you we was here about Reef. We couldn't take the chance 'a you turnin' us down, and there's nobody else he'll listen to right now."

"It's okay," she says. "I *want* to help."

"Good," says the guy named Jink. "We just thought, you know, the last time you two was together . . ." His voice trails off meaningfully.

Leeza looks out the window, feeling her face redden. "I've had time to . . ." She isn't sure how to finish the thought, so she doesn't. "You could've just told me your names. I would've remembered you. Reef talked a lot about you that summer."

"He did, huh?" says Jink. "Nothin' good, I bet."

Leeza grins shyly. "Nothing too bad. Most of it just made me laugh." Both of them scowl and, afraid she's offended them, she changes the subject. "You said he was in trouble."

Bigger nods. "I don't know if you heard about his friend Frank Colville—"

"The man killed in that car accident."

"Reef's had a rough time since he came back yesterday," says Jink, bringing the car to a halt at Jubilee Road, the brakes complaining. He signals left at the three-way stop and then eases the car forward in a wide arc.

"Frank was a big part of Reef's life," Leeza says, then realizes those are Brett's words, the ones her friend said to her on the phone yesterday when she'd called about the funeral. And, once again, Leeza wishes she had gone.

"Yeah, but it's more than just that," Jink tells her. "Some prick's tryin' to shut down North Hills. That's the place where—"

"I figure she knows about North Hills," breathes Bigger.

"Yeah, right," Jink replies. "'Course you do."

"You're talking about Roland Decker," says Leeza.

"You heard 'a him, huh? Total asshole." Now it's *his* turn to redden. "Pardon my French."

"From what I've seen of him," says Leeza, remembering Brett's second video, "your French is pretty accurate."

Jink nods. "The guy grandstands for reporters every chance he gets, and he's makin' Reef out to be a real loser, like he's North Hills's biggest failure. We came by your house yesterday—"

"I know," Leeza interrupts. "I remember the car now."

"*Car!*" Bigger snorts, and Leeza senses that the Buick is a point of contention between them.

Jink ignores him. "Decker says Reef broke the law 'cause 'a that court order your old lady got—"

"*Christ*, Jink," murmurs Bigger, and Leeza can see he's the one who's embarrassed now.

"I know about that," she says. "I saw Decker talking about it on a news video. But the thing is, I didn't even *see* Reef."

"Doesn't matter," says Bigger. "He still broke the law."

"And it's not just the court order," adds Jink. "Reef ever mention a guy named Greg Matheson?"

"The name sounds familiar," says Leeza. "Who is he?"

"Used to be Reef's social worker. Matheson called us and said Decker's doin' a real smear job on him. Says Reef's hangin' with criminals."

Leeza's eyes widen. "You don't believe that, do you?"

Jink shakes his head. "It's bullshit, but Decker says he's got evidence Reef's been meetin' in Calgary with some big-time heavy named Sook—" He pauses. "Sack—"

"Sukorov," says Bigger.

"Yeah," says Jink. "Him."

Leeza is incredulous. "How can Decker *lie* like that?"

"Matheson says it's the truth."

Leeza's jaw drops. "But why would—?"

"Matheson thinks Reef's been tryin' to keep Sukorov from gettin' his hooks into some street kids out there," explains Bigger. "That's why Reef went to see him."

"So," Leeza begins, "all Reef has to do is explain—"

"Matheson says he won't," interrupts Jink.

"Why not?"

"He don't want reporters hasslin' the kids."

Leeza nods. Having seen that reporter—was his name Peterson?—in action on the newscast her mother recorded, she can understand why Reef would want to protect his friends from that kind of attention. But Reef doesn't have a choice. "So we get him to change his mind, right?" she asks. "Make him prove Decker's wrong?" She sees Bigger exchange a look with Jink in the mirror, and she suddenly knows there's something else, something more they haven't told her. "What's wrong?"

"Reef's had enough," Bigger says quietly.

"What do you mean?"

"He's mad. And I don't just mean pissed. The last time I saw him *this* mad . . ." He looks out the window.

"What?" When he doesn't reply, she lays a hand on Bigger's enormous arm. "Tell me."

But it's Jink who answers. "He threw a rock off an overpass."

Leeza's head still reels from the rest of what Reef's buddies have told her, how Reef smoked up that afternoon for the first time in more than two years, how he nearly leaped from this very car before Jink could pull over, how he cut through backyards so Jink couldn't follow him in the Buick. Bigger called Matheson then, told him what happened, but the social worker felt as helpless as they did. All three knew Reef was ready to blow, ready to make Roland Decker pay for using North Hills as a political pressure point, but short of calling the police—which Decker would only use to his advantage later—they had no way of stopping him.

But then Bigger had thought of Leeza.

"What do you think *I* can do?" she asks now.

"When we came by your house yesterday," says Bigger, "we saw how he looked at you."

"Yeah," says Jink from the front seat. "It's like—" He pauses, searching for words. "It's like he was drownin' and you was somethin' to hang on to."

Bigger's eyes widen and Leeza expects him to make a crack about the comment, but he doesn't. Instead, he nods. "Jink's right. That's *just* like how it was, Leeza. Reef's been with lots 'a girls before—"

"*Jesus!*" growls Jink. "Way to *sell* the guy, Big!"

Bigger grins sheepishly. "Look, he's been around, okay? But you're the first girl he ever . . ." He shrugs. "You're inside him, you know? Even after all this time. And if anyone can make him listen, can keep him from bouncin' Decker's head off the pavement or whatever else he's got in mind for that sonuvabitch, it's you. We just gotta find him first."

Instead of her head, it's Leeza's heart that's reeling now. Racing, actually. Just as it had a few minutes ago when she thought she was being assaulted by these strangers. *Can* she make Reef listen? *Can* she make him hear her when he's as furious, as *incensed* as the day he nearly killed her? She thinks of that day now, remembers the moment she approached the overpass in her mother's Subaru, remembers how she raised her hand to wave at the faceless young man on the bridge who she thought was waving at her, remembers the precise second her world exploded. She should. For months she relived that nightmare every time she fell asleep. And she continued to dream it from time to time for months after that. She *still* dreams it occasionally when she gets overtired or her leg gives her trouble. But the dream is different now. The young man on the bridge has a face, dark and handsome, and now when she waves to him, he waves back. As if beckoning.

Like he was drownin' and you was somethin' to hang on to.

She turns toward the window so they can't see the tears in her eyes. "I think I know where he might be."

CHAPTER 31

REEF SITS ON THE BENCH IN THE HALIFAX PUBLIC GARDENS, BRINGS the bottle of rum to his lips again, and takes a long swallow of the dark liquid. Not Captain Morgan, though. At the second liquor store he went to, he picked up the first bottle he saw, eager to get out of the place as soon as he could. So it's Bacardi this time. Not that it matters—the taste isn't important. It burns just as hot as The Captain when it goes down. And it's the burn he wants, the burn he needs, the feeling of liquid fire matching the coals already blazing in his chest.

He's gotten several looks from people wandering the paths of the Gardens in the afternoon sunshine. Not that he's surprised. You don't see many young men drinking in public straight from a liquor bottle, and certainly not without a bag or something else wrapped around it. If he was smart, he'd have poured the rum into a Coke can before he came here.

But he's *not* smart. He's certainly proved *that* in the last forty-eight hours. He was a fool to come back. More than that, he was a fool to believe he could ever really be the person Frank thought he saw in him. Frank didn't *really* know him, not like his grandfather did. *Dummy. Numbskull. Idiot. You are what you are, right?* he thinks, taking another swallow of the rum, enjoying the way it scorches his throat, scalds his chest, blisters his belly.

"You can't drink that here."

Reef turns and sees a man who looks to be in his early twenties, a little overweight, wearing a uniform with "Halifax Regional Municipality" printed across it. Reef looks at him for a moment, then raises the bottle again and takes another swallow. Slow. Deliberate. Feeding the fire.

"I said you can't drink that here," the man repeats. He carries a garbage bag and one of those sticks with a sharp end for jabbing trash, and he looks a little like one of those characters on prime-time comedies, the loser who peaked in gym class and never finished high school.

Of course, the guy might just as easily be a university student working a summer job, but something about him makes Reef doubt that. Something about the indifferent look in his eyes and the way he stands with his weight on one hip, the trash-jabber hanging from his hand like a fallen flag, that makes him look defeated.

And suddenly Reef knows his story, or thinks he does: court-appointed community service, and the soft edges of the guy suggest a string of unpaid parking tickets. No. More likely he was caught spraying graffiti on a downtown building, his desire to leave a mark, some proof of his passing, outweighing common sense. Reef understands that desire, probably more now than ever before.

"I said—" the guy begins for the third time.

"Fuck off."

The man stares at him, then seems to notice the fire in Reef's eyes. He shrugs and walks away, and Reef knows he won't return. Court-appointed community service isn't worth the hassle.

Looking out across the groomed lawns and immaculate flower beds, Reef remembers all the times he visited the Public Gardens during his own community service two years ago. Not that he *had* to. He liked bringing Leeza here. The second day they were together, he'd offered to take her to the Gardens before buying her lunch at Dairy Queen on the corner of South Park and Spring Garden Road. Despite all the years he'd lived in Halifax, he'd only been to the Gardens a few times, and on those occasions only to buy or sell drugs. He'd always been on the lookout for undercover cops so he'd never paid much attention to the place, and he was surprised that day two years ago to see how beautiful the Gardens were. Leeza loved being there. She hadn't been outdoors for weeks, not since the accident that she wouldn't talk to him about, and although the joggling of her wheelchair on the gravel walkways was clearly uncomfortable for her, she never once complained. They returned to the Gardens often that summer. Each time, he'd park her wheelchair beside this same bench and they'd sit watching the activity unfolding around them: birds darting about the flowers and trees, men and women eating lunches perched on laps or briefcases, couples strolling hand in hand along the paths, parents pushing carriages with sleeping infants, kids surreptitiously feeding bits of bread to the ducks on the pond despite the "Please do not feed the ducks" signs posted everywhere. Leeza never tired of it, nor did he tire of taking her there. Sitting on this bench with Leeza parked in her wheelchair beside him, he had never known such contentment, was truly happy for the first time since before his grandmother died.

That happiness eludes him now, his vision blurring suddenly, a fist-sized lump crowding his throat. *Christ!* How can the girl still have this hold on him after two years? He raises the bottle to his lips again and takes long swallows, trying to force those feelings aside. It's a different emotion that he longs for now, and the burning rum fuels it, fans it.

No matter what he does, he'll never be good enough for someone like Leeza. He'll always be the felon, the thug, the badass no one can trust. And it's people like Roland Decker who will always make sure everyone else knows it.

Roland Decker.

Reef replays in his mind the confrontation in the churchyard yesterday, the newscast he saw last night at Matheson's, those first moments in the courtroom today. That smug, self-serving sonuvabitch! *Well*, he thinks, taking another swallow of the rum, *it's about time Roland Decker found out just how much of a badass Reef Kennedy can be.*

He gets up, swaying as he waits for the world to come into focus again. Although there's still rum left, he tosses the bottle toward the garbage can to the right of the bench, but the bottle clips the edge of the metal bin, ricocheting away. If it had landed on the grass, it probably wouldn't have broken. Instead, it hits a rock and shatters.

Why not? thinks Reef. *I fuck up everything else.*

For a brief moment, he nearly stoops to pick up the glass, but then he thinks of the guy in the uniform, figures he'll likely be the one who has to clean it up. And he'll know it was Reef who left it there. For some reason, this pleases him, this leaving a mark. *His* mark. But it will pale compared to what he intends to leave behind when he's finished with Roland Decker.

Call it community service.

He *does* stoop, though, but not for the broken bottle. Instead, he tugs at the rock that shattered it, prying it from the grass. When it's finally free, it's bigger than he thought it would be. But not bigger than he needs.

Wrapping it in his jacket, he moves unsteadily toward the park exit, stumbling once and nearly going to his knees. The people he passes step back, give him plenty of room. Clearly, they know trouble when they see it coming.

CHAPTER 32

"YOU SURE?" ASKS JINK, GUIDING THE BUICK TOWARD THE CURB. "You really think he's here?"

Bigger is equally skeptical. "Reef never was a guy to hang out in a park," he says. "A parking *lot*, maybe."

Leeza nods. "The Reef I knew loved the Public Gardens. He brought me here all the time."

As though choreographed, Bigger and Jink give simultaneous shrugs while Beauty eases to a stop a few metres from the Summer Street entrance. They'd had to circle the park twice before a spot opened up, and Jink ignored the horns that blared behind him as he'd waited for a young couple to buckle in their two small children, then load a double stroller into the trunk of their Toyota before finally pulling out of the space.

When he shuts the Buick off, the motor continues noisily for a few seconds, its loud knocking drawing the attention of people on the sidewalk. "Needs a tune-up," Jink says to Leeza.

"Needs a tomb*stone*," mutters Bigger as the motor gives a final heave, followed by a tremendous backfire that echoes all along the street. One pedestrian runs for cover as if imagining snipers.

Ignoring their banter, Leeza is already out of the car and heading toward the park entrance. Once inside the wrought-iron gate, she is suddenly conscious of people stepping aside to let her pass. But then she realizes it's Bigger and Jink they're making room for, their imposing bodies hard on her heels. Two toddlers just inside the park stare open-mouthed at them, and Leeza notices their mothers pull them close as the trio passes. Glancing behind her, she's not surprised at these reactions. It was, after all, barely twenty minutes ago that she'd been terrified at the mere sight of them.

"You think we should split up?" Bigger asks Leeza. "There's a lot 'a ground to cover."

"If he's here," she replies, "I think I know where he'd be." She turns right, taking the path leading toward the statue honouring the Citizen Soldiers of the South African Campaign, all the while hearing Bigger's and Jink's heavy footfalls behind her.

But he isn't there. Approaching what she'd come to think of that summer as "their bench," Leeza sees no sign of him, and she gives a frustrated cry.

"There's lots 'a other places he could be in here," offers Jink. "What about the other side 'a the pond? Or behind that thing?" He points to the bandstand.

Leeza shakes her head. "This is where we sat every time," she says. "Every time." She shakes her head again. "He's not here."

"Hey! Isn't that his backpack?" asks Bigger, bending down and retrieving a nylon bag from under the bench.

"Yeah," Jink agrees. "That's his, all right. Maybe he's here after all."

For a moment, Leeza's heart leaps. But then the moment ends and she gives a soft moan.

"What's wrong?" asks Jink.

She points to the broken rum bottle on the ground near where the backpack had been, the shards of glass evidence of a violent end. But it isn't the ruined bottle that catches her attention. It isn't the insects buzzing around the remains of the rum that draw her eyes to the grass. It's the nearly circular hole in the ground where a rock lay only a short time ago, a glistening worm at its centre still struggling to evade the sudden sun.

CHAPTER 33

REEF STARES STRAIGHT AHEAD, THE CHANGING DIGITAL NUMBER above the door as red as the heat in his chest. He is only dimly aware that the other four people sharing the elevator with him have moved to one side, putting what little distance is possible between him and them. He ignores them, focusing instead on the number that transforms from two to three, from three to four. When the elevator makes its first stop on the fifth floor, everyone else gets off, although two other numbers besides the one he pressed still glow on the panel by the door. The tenth floor is the one he wants. According to the large directory in the lobby, that's where Roland Decker's office is located.

On the fifth, no one else gets on despite two men waiting there. They glance at Reef, then at each other, both turning and busying themselves with their briefcases. They might have been waiting for an elevator going down, but having seen his reflection in the mirrored panels surrounding his elevator's interior, Reef suspects otherwise. The small space probably reeks of booze, but it's his appearance that's no doubt making everyone uneasy. The blazing eyes, the dark scowl, the bulge beneath the jacket in his arms. Glancing at the video camera above his head, he wouldn't be surprised if someone sitting at a monitor is calling Security right now, but he doesn't care. His visit to the Parker Building isn't going to take long.

The door whispers shut again and he is alone.

At first, he was at a loss about where to go, how to direct the rage that was building inside him. Even when he'd finished prying the rock from the ground, he still had no idea how to find the man he was looking for. The phone book he'd looked through in the booth across the street from the Public Gardens had lots of Deckers but no Roland, who was likely unlisted. Besides, it wasn't yet five o'clock, so Decker would probably be at work when he wasn't ruining lives.

And then he remembered Decker's response on the witness stand to Sheppard's question about his occupation: *I'm a financial analyst for the investment firm Stoffler, Weinberg, and Grant.* Reef had no trouble whatsoever finding that listing. Framed in a large yellow square on the page, it even included the company's logo, a mountain with a sun rising behind it. Apparently, Stoffler, Weinberg, and Grant promised memorable new days for the people whose money they invested, which was, in a way, fitting. As he'd hailed a taxi, Reef had expected that Decker would remember this particular day for a very long time.

The elevator stops on eight, though the person who pressed that number has already gotten off, but Reef is suddenly grateful for the delay—after all that rum, he needs to take a leak. When the door opens, he steps out and crosses to a floor plan mounted on the wall opposite the bank of elevators, a red arrow proclaiming "You Are Here." Scanning it for the nearest washroom, he sees there are two men's facilities on this side of the building, the closest one on his right, so he turns in that direction. Glancing at his watch, he knows he'll have to hurry—it's getting close to the end of the workday.

And he has no intention of letting Decker slip through his fingers.

CHAPTER 34

AS THE THREE HURRY BACK TO BEAUTY, LEEZA HEARS TWO BARS OF
an urban beat she recognizes from MuchMusic, and she watches
as Bigger pulls out his ringing cell.

"Yeah?" he says into the phone, never breaking stride. He
listens for a moment, then grins. "That's fuckin' great!" he
exclaims, then shoots an apologetic look at Leeza. He continues to listen, and then he frowns. "Yeah," he says into the cell,
"we're still lookin'. We got that girl with us, Leeza. We're at the
Public Gardens, but Reef's already been here and gone. You got
any ideas?" He listens again. "We'll try there next, and we'll let
you know." He clicks off his phone, turns to the others. "Good
news," he says.

"About goddamn time," mutters Jink. Then he, too, looks
sheepishly at Leeza. "Who was that?"

"Matheson. The judge made his decision about North Hills."

"That was fast," offers Jink.

"*Too* fast," says Leeza. "That can't be good."

They both look at Bigger.

"Matheson didn't have time to go into everything on the phone, but someone contacted Decker's judge and told him about all the community work Reef's been doin' in Calgary, and a cop out there vouched for him, too. The judge turned down his application. North Hills ain't gonna close."

"That's terrific!" exclaims Leeza, but her excitement is short-lived. "Reef doesn't know, does he?"

Bigger shakes his head. "He's got his cell turned off."

Leeza thinks of the rock and a soft moan escapes her. "Then he's still planning to make Decker pay, isn't he."

Bigger nods. "There's more. Decker's lawyer probably already contacted Decker with the news."

"I don't get it," says Jink. "Why's *that* a problem?"

Bigger frowns. "Matheson says Decker's tied his whole campaign to North Hills. He *needs* Reef to be the jerk he's been tellin' all those reporters about the past couple days. Matheson figures—"

"He figures," Leeza finishes for him, "that Decker's only hope now is for Reef to prove him right. Reef will just be playing into Decker's hands if he confronts him and makes a big scene."

Bigger nods and sudden realization spreads across Jink's face. "Christ!" he growls. "Decker'll probably have his own camera crew there."

"No *probably* about it," says Bigger as all three reach the car. "Matheson told me where Decker works." He gives the others the downtown address. "Matheson's already on his way, but he says we're closer. We need to get there as soon as we can."

They climb into the car and Jink jabs his key into the ignition, twists it, but the Buick barely turns over.

"You gotta be *kiddin'* me!" growls Bigger.

"Give her a minute," says Jink.

"We don't *got* a minute!" Bigger roars. "Try it again!"

But this time there isn't even a click.

Leeza recognizes a dead battery when she hears it. She opens her door.

"What are you doin'?" Bigger asks her, but she doesn't stop to answer.

She runs.

CHAPTER 35

IT'S ONLY WHEN REEF STEPS OUT OF THE WASHROOM THAT HE REALIZES
he doesn't have his backpack with him. *"Fuck!"*

A young woman passing him in the corridor visibly starts, then turns and gives him an anxious look, but he ignores her, trying to remember where he was the last time he had it.

The Public Gardens.

He shrugs. *Maybe that community service guy found it,* he thinks. If he did, he'll still have it, probably consider it payment for having to clean up the glass. Life is all about payback, right? Reef can return to the Gardens when he's finished here. Right now, though, he has some payback of his own to dish out. To Roland Decker.

He returns to the bank of elevators and presses the Up button. Waits.

It's no surprise that they're so slow. Two of the building's four elevators are being serviced, something he saw on a sign in the lobby. Looking at the row of numbers above the two remaining elevators, he sees that the one he rode up in is now headed down and passing the eighth floor without stopping. The other elevator has halted on the second floor. Then the "2" winks out and "3" lights up. And stays lit.

His patience like a guitar string wound far too taut, Reef drums the fingers of his free hand against his leg. His other hand, the one holding the jacket, squeezes the rock beneath it.

He waits.

The "3" winks out and "4" lights up briefly, followed by "5." Which stays lit.

He resists the urge to curse again. Instead, he turns and scans the "You Are Here" floor plan, forcing his eyes to focus. Finds what he's looking for. Staggers down the corridor to his left.

CHAPTER 36

HER FEET POUNDING THE SIDEWALK, LEEZA IS GLAD SHE'S KEPT IN
shape. She's run five blocks and, despite her earlier run from
Point Pleasant and her long walk home from the rehab, her
breathing is still even, her body having settled into that rhythm
she loves, a seemingly effortless confluence of arms and legs and
lungs all functioning with a single purpose, to move her forward.

But one thing is different this time—she wishes she were
wearing shorts. To hell with what anyone might think of her
scars, she longs for the feel of air moving over her skin, wicking
away the sweat now pooling in the folds and creases of her jeans.

She sees the Parker Building at last, only half a block away,
and she's glad she didn't hail a taxi. Traffic is snarled downtown,
the result of an accident at the intersection of Barrington and
Blowers that she passed only moments ago. Even if Bigger and
Jink were able to get the car started, she suspects they're grid-
locked somewhere far behind her. She summons a final burst of
speed and arrives at the building's entrance, taking the steps two
at a time and slowing only for the large revolving door.

Once inside, she looks for the elevators—the social worker told Bigger that Decker's office is on the tenth floor—and finds them easily. Then groans when she sees a sandwich sign in front of two apologizing for their being shut down for maintenance. The third elevator is on the fifth floor, and the doors of the fourth are just closing. "Hold it, please!" she calls, but the doors slide shut before anyone inside can react.

Jabbing the Up button, she sees the elevator is heading toward the underground parking levels. She glances again toward the other elevator and sees the "5" still glowing on the panel above it. Frustrated, she wills it to change. It doesn't. "Come *on!*" she mutters as a man carrying a briefcase passes her, stopping at a desk to her right. "Excuse me," she hears him say to a woman seated behind it. She wears a blue uniform, a silver badge on her chest with "Security" engraved on it.

"Yes, sir?" the uniformed woman replies.

"Um, er . . ." The man with the briefcase looks uncomfortable. "There's, uh, something I think you should know."

Leeza grimaces as the "5" darkens and the "6" lights up.

"I just saw a guy on the elevator," she hears the man say. "Recognized him from the news."

Leeza turns toward them as the woman asks, "What about him?"

"He's got a record," continues the man. "Violent offender, I think."

"And you're telling me this because . . . ?"

"I, uh . . ." The man shrugs awkwardly. "I'm pretty sure he was drunk. And he looked pissed. *Really* pissed."

Leeza turns again to the panels above the elevators, feeling her frustration give way to panic, and she whirls around, scanning the lobby. Her eyes finally register the sign on their second pass, and she sprints forward, praying she isn't too late.

CHAPTER 37

THE SOUNDS OF HIS FOOTSTEPS IN THE STAIRWELL REMIND REEF OF something, echoing as much against his memory as the painted concrete walls he passes. At first he thinks they resemble the sounds that he, Bigger, and Jink used to make on the staircase in The Pit. They went there often before he got sent to North Hills, climbing to the top floor of the abandoned hotel, where they'd sit at the broken windows of what used to be the presidential suite. Jink and Bigger thought Reef liked it there because of the privacy it offered—they were free to enjoy with little interruption whatever booze or drugs they'd stolen or scrounged enough money to buy. The Pit was Party Central and even the cops didn't do much more than cruise past from time to time and flash their lights or give their siren a blurp or two.

But that was only part of the reason Reef liked it so much. The other part had to do with The Pit's view of Citadel Hill, where his grandmother used to take him before the cancer got so bad that Social Services took him away from her and put him in the first of his foster homes. Facing the Citadel from the presidential suite, Reef would imagine himself there with her again, would remember the two of them being as impressed by the licence plates on the cars carrying tourists as they were by the panoramic views the fortress offered of the harbour and the Atlantic Ocean beyond. In those days when he was still Chad Kennedy and the price of gas hadn't gone through the roof, it wasn't unusual to see plates from Ontario or Manitoba and even a few from the United States. Once, Nan pointed out a car from California and she'd marvelled at that, astonished someone could just get in a car and cross a whole continent. His grandfather's ancient Dodge Dart could barely cross the city without breaking down, and the last time it happened, the old man had everlastingly beat the shit out of it with a lug wrench.

And now Reef knows what the sounds on these stairs of the Parker Building remind him of—his grandfather's footsteps in the stairwell of their tenement on Gottingen Street, the one they'd moved into just before the stroke that killed him. Reef used to dread those footsteps, fear like an electric current zithering through him whenever he heard the first tread. He knew he'd be guilty of *something* the minute his grandfather opened the door, even if it was just breathing, so it was a blessing—or whatever passed for a blessing in a Gottingen Street tenement—that his grandfather had gone first. The cancer had found Nan before that but it hadn't told her yet, and she'd held it off as long as she could.

Reef listens to his footsteps now, and he thinks of the person he turned into following his grandmother's death. Or maybe he'd always been that person, the low-life his grandfather cursed daily, and it just took Nan's funeral to set him free.

Frank Colville hadn't believed that, though. Had even convinced Reef that people could change. But Frank was wrong.

Reef has the rum in his belly and the rock wrapped in his jacket to prove it. Not to mention the rage to do something with both.

I'm just glad he isn't here today to see his biggest mistake, having faith in the likes of you.

For the first time since he learned of the accident that killed him, Reef, too, is glad that Frank isn't here.

CHAPTER 38

DESPITE THE SHAPE SHE'S IN, THE STAIRS ARE KILLING HER.
Leeza's thighs throb, the pain reminding her of how she'd felt on the treadmill that Valerie Harris, her physiotherapist, had put her on at the rehab. Val had pushed her hard each day, forced her to grind out one more step, two more steps, and she can almost hear the diminutive brunette now: *You can do it, Leeza!* she'd coax, urge, coerce, demand. And she was right. Leeza *could* do it, despite the tortured response of her left leg and pelvis, broken in several places and held together with a network of metal rods. And the reason she *could* do it had a lot to do with the good-looking guy who would be waiting for her in her room afterwards. The guy whose face lit up each time he saw her, who always seemed as reluctant to leave as she was to see him go. The guy she was racing up these stairs to find now.

It's like he was drownin' and you was somethin' to hang on to.

Leeza knows now that *she* had been drowning, too, floundering long before that rock struck her windshield. And though she will never think of that accident as a blessing, will never be thankful for the horror that was her healing, she can finally appreciate that things happen for reasons far beyond her understanding.

You was somethin' to hang on to.

Lifting her leaden legs, the sounds of her footsteps echoing off those painted concrete walls, she prays she will be in time, prays she can be that something now.

CHAPTER 39

REEF TURNS ANOTHER SWITCHBACK IN THE STAIRWELL AND SEES above him the door he's been looking for. The door with the "10" on it. He grips the rock beneath his jacket, draws strength from it as he climbs those final steps.

And then he's there.

Opening the door, he finds himself in a long corridor, and he pauses for a moment considering his options, surprised by the number of offices he sees. There are more than a dozen doors stretching to his left and his right.

"May I help you?"

Reef pivots to see a guy only a few years older than him wearing what is clearly an expensive suit and carrying a large black portfolio. As Reef turns, the rum makes his head swim, and he momentarily leans back against the frame of the stairwell door.

"You all right?" the guy asks.

Reef ignores the question. "I'm lookin' for Roland Decker. You know where his office is?"

The guy's nose wrinkles and he steps backward, frowning. He's obviously smelled the liquor on Reef's breath.

"I got somethin' for him," says Reef. "His office is on this floor, right?"

The guy looks skeptical. "Is it something he ordered?"

Reef flashes him a broad smile. "Oh, it's somethin' he's been askin' for all day. Took me this long to finally get here."

"Does he know you're coming?"

Reef smiles again. "I hope not. I want it to be a surprise."

"So Roland knows you?" the guy asks.

"Him and me," says Reef, "we go way back." *All the way back to yesterday.*

The guy turns and points. "That way. Third door on the right." He glances at his watch. "You'd better hurry, though. Most of the offices on this floor close in a few minutes."

"Thanks," says Reef. "I wouldn't wanna miss him." He thinks of the rock under his jacket and suddenly laughs aloud at his own words.

The guy gives him a strange look, then walks away.

Directly across from Reef, a door opens and a woman comes out, one hand holding several file folders, the other a cellphone pressed to her ear. Clearly rushed, she barely glances at Reef as she breezes past. " . . . can't make it to your recital after all, honey," she says, her tone apologetic, "but I'm proud of you, okay? You can tell me all about it when . . ."

Reef watches her disappear around a corner, but as her voice trails off, another takes its place, this one echoing along the corridors of his memory, resurrecting in his head an afternoon two years ago. Much like now, he was seething with rage. He was on a bus heading downtown because Jink lay in intensive care hooked up to tubes and machines, hovering between life and death after a savage beating by Rowdy Brewster and his crew. Reef had no plan, no idea how he'd even get within fifty feet of the gangbanger, but he was determined to make Rowdy pay for what he'd done. Bigger sat beside him wanting payback as much as Reef did, but he had doubts about what the two of them could do. Reef didn't want to listen to doubts, though. He just wanted to fight, to feel his fists connect with faces that laughed when those sons 'a bitches kept kicking the shit out of Jink long after he'd lost consciousness.

But two stops from their destination, Reef saw a little kid staring at him on that bus, then suddenly saw himself through that kid's eyes. And for the very first time, he understood what Frank had been trying to show him during his weeks at North Hills. For the very first time, he saw where anger had always taken him, saw the nothing it always left him with.

He surprised Bigger when he suddenly stood up, surprised him even more when he led his huge friend off the bus, telling him they'd let the police handle Rowdy Brewster. He found a pay phone and called Frank to come get them, and they didn't have to wait long. But watching Frank's pickup pull over to the curb, Reef had hung his head. He knew what was coming. He'd broken North Hills's restriction about going someplace without permission and he braced himself for his punishment—he'd be heading to River-view Correctional Institute for the remainder of his sentence. So he was unprepared for the response he got when he climbed into the truck. *I'm glad you called,* said Frank. *I'm proud of you, Reef.*

I'm proud of you.

Reef swallows thickly in that Parker Building corridor. Wipes the heel of his free hand over both eyes. Feels the anger leave him like air released from a tethered balloon. Whatever he has come here to do, whatever crazy, half-formed act of retribution he intended, it no longer matters. Regardless of what Decker has done, retribution serves no purpose. *You've tarnished his name and everything he worked so hard for*, Frank's sister said to him. Probably. But he doesn't have to make it worse. He feels the weight of the rock and knows it's nothing compared to the burden of shame he would feel afterwards. He shakes his head, then turns and puts his hand against the stairwell door to push it open.

"Kennedy."

Reef twists and, over his shoulder, sees Roland Decker in the corridor, behind him the guy in the expensive suit who no longer carries the portfolio. Now he has something else in his hand. And he looks nervous.

"I hear you wanted to see me," says Decker.

Reef shakes his head. "Not anymore."

Before he can open the door, though, he hears Decker's voice again. Louder this time. "You're not *stalking* me, are you?"

Reef hears the emphasis on the word, clenches his jaw. "Watch yourself, Decker," he mutters at the door.

"That sounds like a *threat*, Kennedy."

Reef turns and sees Decker move toward him smiling, his teeth astonishingly white as he passes through a rectangle of sunshine pouring from an open doorway. "Did you come here to *threaten* me?" he asks.

"I don't make threats," Reef replies, reaching into his pocket and gripping the small round stone from Crystal Crescent Beach, concentrating on the feel of its smooth surface beneath the fingers of his right hand. And then he sees what the guy behind Decker has in *his* hand, what he's pointing at both of them now. A cellphone, its video feature no doubt recording everything.

"That's not what Judge West heard," says Decker, stopping an arm's length from Reef. "Your verbal attack on my attorney, Martin Sheppard, almost earned you a contempt-of-court ruling. You called him a son of a bitch, didn't you?"

Reef knows what Decker is doing, goading him for the sake of the camera, but still the heat flares in his chest. "Not Sheppard," he breathes. "You."

Decker seems delighted by this. "*Me*," he says, the word more an affirmation than a question. "Did you come here to verbally abuse me some more?"

"You're not worth it."

"And yet here you are," says Decker. "I'm sure it's no coincidence that you've come looking for me after your behaviour in court today." He leans forward slightly, sniffs. "You've been *drinking*, haven't you? Are you *drunk*, Kennedy?" The sudden smile on his face reminds Reef of the Road Runner watching from the cliff edge as Wile E. Coyote plummets toward the canyon floor.

Reef squeezes the stone in his pocket, turns away again, puts his shoulder against the stairwell door. He's leaving.

"Did they teach you that at North Hills, Kennedy? Was that part of the program there?" There is no mistaking the sneer in Decker's voice.

Reef freezes.

"Yes," continues Decker smugly, "you're a shining example of the impact of our current legislation on young criminals, aren't you."

Reef feels his teeth grind together, feels the heat in his chest char the base of his neck, feels it spread, flooding his face, his arms, his hands. Staring at the door, he breathes through his mouth, struggling to keep from turning around. *I'm proud of you, Reef.* He grips the smooth stone in his pocket even tighter.

"How's it feel to get away with a crime?" Decker asks. "I'm curious. And I'm sure a lot of other people would like to hear the answer to that question, too. What's it like to nearly kill someone and then do time at Club North?"

Reef's fingers release the small smooth stone. He turns.

Decker takes a sudden step back, clearly no longer as confident as he was. He glances at the young man behind him, no doubt checking to see that the phone is still recording everything. What he also sees are a dozen other people now standing in the corridor, having come out of other offices to see what's going on. Decker puts his shoulders back, stands taller. Turning to Reef, he clears his throat, and when he speaks his voice is louder. "When are you going to admit that programs like the one at North Hills are not only a waste of taxpayers' money but dangerous to the welfare of every law-abiding citizen? When are you going to stop pretending your rehabilitation was anything more than a get-out-of-jail-free card, a sham? Showing up here drunk, stalking me like your other victim, threatening me at my place of work, you've proven to everyone here you're nothing less than a menace to society!"

Reef is no longer aware of the heat coursing through his body. He *is* the heat, a blast furnace fusing the air around him, searing the seconds, melting the moment that's unfolding now. The blood-rush in his ears drowns out the office sounds on either side of him, the words murmured by the gathering crowd, the beating of his own heart. He sees Decker's lips moving but no longer hears the accusations that fill the corridor, piling up like thick, dark ash. It's the phone that he focuses on, the phone in the hand of the guy with the expensive suit, the phone held high overhead waiting for his response.

Reef will not disappoint.

He grips the rock beneath his jacket, the rock he thought he brought here to smash a window or break a door. Now, though, he understands its truer target, which offers something far more satisfying than shattered glass, far more sustaining than splintered wood.

Reef feels the muscles in his arm tense, coil, readying themselves for release.

Then he feels something else entirely: a hand on his arm.

Hears something above the blood-rush: a voice. Urgent, pleading. "Reef, don't."

He turns toward the voice, sure that he's mistaken, certain that he's imagined the person he thinks he's heard.

But he hasn't.

"Leeza?"

Panting, the girl in the doorway is red-faced, too, and she says nothing. Instead, she reaches up, places her hand gently on his cheek. It feels cool against the fire in his face.

He wants to say more, wants to tell her he's sorry, that he's been so sorry for such a long, long time, but his voice catches in his throat and his vision blurs.

She raises her other hand, wipes at the tears now rivering down his face, then nods as if she already knows. "Let me save *you* this time," she whispers.

CHAPTER 40

LEEZA CAN'T STOP LOOKING AT HIM. SHE KNOWS HE'S EMBARRASSED now, self-conscious about the rum that's finally wearing off, but she loves seeing what happens to him each time he catches her staring, loves the way his brow furrows for a second, followed by a grin that tugs at the corner of his mouth and spreads across his face. He looks away then and she watches as the side of his neck reddens, waits for him to turn to her again. And he always does.

Despite his obvious embarrassment, he hasn't let go of her since she first appeared in that stairwell doorway more than an hour ago, his hand gripping hers as though he's afraid she'll disappear. She knows that she, too, should be self-conscious since her clothes probably reek with sweat after her long run to the Parker Building, but she doesn't give a damn. He's holding her hand and nothing else matters.

Sitting at Starbucks on the corner of Barrington and Sack-ville—he's on his third cup of coffee while she nurses a bottle of water—she's aware of two young women sitting a few tables away who've been looking in their direction since they sat down. An hour ago, Leeza would have assumed they recognized Reef from the news, but now she's not so sure. The guy sitting across from her, his right hand holding her left on the table's smooth surface, really has no idea how good-looking he is, has no idea the number of people—most of them women but a couple of men, too—who have looked at him long and appreciatively, openly admiring his thick dark hair, chiselled face, powerful shoulders and arms. He seems oblivious to everyone around him. Except her.

He'd told her over his first cup of coffee that he didn't believe she was real when she appeared in the corridor, thought his mind was playing tricks on him, fabricating what he most wanted to see. He said he finally knew he wasn't imagining her when she turned to Roland Decker and called him a slimy bastard. He'd never heard her swear before, not once in all the weeks they'd spent together at the rehab, and he knew even the rum couldn't have conjured the curses he heard as she told Decker he should be ashamed of himself.

She was surprised herself at how she'd behaved in that Parker Building corridor. Running up those stairs, she'd had no idea what she was going to do if she managed to find Reef, but just as she reached the tenth-floor landing, she could hear through the door what Decker was saying, could tell what he was trying to do. As she yanked the door open, she'd fully expected to see the camera crew that Bigger and Jink had anticipated and was, in fact, disappointed to find only a cellphone aimed in their direction. She was going to shut that son of a bitch up once and for all, and she would've preferred to have what she was going to say filmed in high definition.

"What you did," Reef says to her now, his long fingers curling around hers, and she can tell he's reliving those moments again, too. "You were awesome."

She flushes, looks down at his hand over hers, loving the heat of it. "I don't know about that."

But he reaches across the table with his other hand, touches her lips gently with his index finger, stops her. "Awesome," he repeats softly, his voice suddenly husky, and she sees in his eyes that this isn't just a word he's saying, sees how much he means it.

It's her turn to look away now and, as she does, her mind replays the expression on Decker's face when she told him who she was, that she was the girl Reef had nearly killed. Clearly astonished, Decker had tried to talk over her then but she'd kept going, her voice gaining strength as she continued, assuring him that, yes, Reef Kennedy had paid the price of that act in ways Decker's small mind could never *begin* to imagine. And Reef was a different person now, a *better* person, all because of Judge Hilary Thomas's ruling that put him in the care of Frank Colville at North Hills and required him to perform community service. Decker had begun backing away by then, trying to distance himself from her, and he'd even put his hand up to block the phone that was still recording everything, but the young man who was holding it stepped around him. There were other phones pointed at them by then, held high by people in the growing group of spectators.

Finally, Decker darted into an office and slammed the door behind him, and there was a second or two of silence as Leeza glared at it. But then the corridor erupted with applause, and Leeza turned to see among the crowd two men wearing blue uniforms and security badges. They were clapping, too.

It had taken a while for her to get Reef out of the building. By the time they'd ridden the elevator down to the lobby, a news crew was coming in, and Leeza got her high-definition moment after all. She was glad to have a chance to edit her earlier comments, but she repeated her initial assessment of Decker nonetheless. There really wasn't a more fitting description than "slimy bastard." She knew it would probably be cut from whatever remarks appeared on TV—or, at the very least, bleeped—but it gave her a lot of satisfaction saying it. Twice.

Then she'd brought Reef here, bought him coffee and herself a bottle of water, and they'd talked about the events of the past two days, then about their lives during the past two years. About almost everything. There is only one thing neither has mentioned.

Until this moment.

"I've thought of you every day since . . ." Reef tells her now, his voice still husky. "Every day." It's the first he's alluded to their time before, and she can tell how hard it is for him. "I wish—" he begins.

But she doesn't want to hear it, reaches across and puts her index finger on his lips as he had to hers.

They sit looking at each other for a moment, and then Reef nods. Lifting his right hand from hers on the table, he holds it out to her. "Hi. I'm Reef Kennedy," he says.

She smiles, takes his hand in hers and shakes it. "I've heard a lot about you," she tells him. Later, she will think that this could have been exactly the wrong thing to say, but it's the first thing out of her mouth.

And it's not wrong at all. He smiles at her, and it's nothing like the grins she's seen on his face during the past hour. This is all teeth and crinkled eyes, and then he's laughing out loud.

And then she's laughing, too. Hard. For the first time in a very long while. She can't remember the last time she roared like this with no holding back, gusty whoops drawing wide-eyed looks from everyone in the coffee shop. It feels completely foreign to her—and unbelievably good.

In the middle of all that laughter, Reef's phone rings. Leeza can guess who it is, and she's right.

"Yeah, Big," Reef says, still chuckling when he answers it. "I think we're ready now. Thanks, man."

She'd convinced Reef to call Bigger and Jink when they'd left the Parker Building to tell them what happened, that everything was all right. Jink had finally gotten the Buick going again, thanks to a Good Samaritan with a set of jumper cables, and he'd offered to pick up the two right away. But Leeza had taken the phone and asked if she and Reef could have an hour alone together first, and Jink had said no problem, he'd give them a call in a while. Handing the phone back to Reef, Leeza had marvelled that two people she'd been so afraid of earlier that afternoon could have turned out to be such great guys. It was the girl-in-the-beer-T-shirt thing all over again.

"They'll be here in a couple minutes," Reef tells her. "That all right with you?"

She nods and the two stand, making their way toward the exit.

After the air conditioning in Starbucks, the heat outside hits them like a fist, and once again Leeza wishes she were wearing shorts, makes her mind up in that moment to buy a dozen pairs tomorrow. Right now, though, there's something else she wants to do, *needs* to do. Standing on the sidewalk, squinting her eyes against the sun that streams down Sackville, Leeza puts her hand on Reef's arm, amazed all over again at the coiled strength she feels beneath her fingers.

He looks down at her. "You okay?" he asks, concern lining his forehead, and she can tell he's thinking about her leg.

She nods. "More than okay," she says as she reaches up, and his eyes widen as she places her hands on either side of his face, drawing him down to her.

She envisioned this kiss countless times in the weeks after she first met him, wondered before falling asleep each night in the rehab what it would feel like, what he would taste like. Imagined being held against his broad chest, gently crushed by his muscled arms.

But he'd never touched her except to help her in and out of her wheelchair, and she'd assumed he didn't feel the same way toward her. It hadn't surprised her, of course. By then, she'd accepted the fact that no one could possibly find her desirable, not with her body now spoiled by surgeries, scars on her skin and her soul.

But that didn't stop her from visualizing this kiss in the dark and in her dreams. Even afterwards, when she'd discovered who Reef was and her mother had thrown him out of their lives forever, she'd sometimes wake up at night trembling, having imagined his body moving against hers, and she'd force the corner of her pillow into her mouth to keep from sobbing.

However vivid, her imagination has not prepared her for this moment, for this kiss. Leeza feels things leaving her. Traffic sounds. The smells of hot pavement and engine exhaust. The air around her body. All gone. Her knees buckle as something turns inside her, turns and releases, and those powerful arms are doing more than embracing her now. They're keeping her from falling, supporting her until she wills strength into her legs again.

Her heart pounding, she looks up and sees everything she's feeling mirrored in his eyes.

"My God," he whispers. It's all he tells her, but it's all she needs to hear.

Suddenly a horn blares, and they turn to see Jink's ancient Buick labouring toward them down Barrington, Bigger leaning out the passenger window hooting and whistling as the car rattles up to the curb.

Leeza can tell that Reef is as reluctant to let her go as she is to pull away. Their fingers still entwined, they look once more into each other's eyes as they step forward, moving toward Beauty.

EPILOGUE

REEF STILL CAN'T GET USED TO SITTING IN THE SAME ROOM AS DIANE Morrison. Every so often he feels her eyes on him but he knows that if he glances up from his magazine, she'll only look away. As unnerving as he finds this, at least she isn't screaming at him this time.

Leeza had asked Jink and Bigger to drop them off at her house following their hour together at Starbucks a week ago, and the meeting with her mother had been a disaster. Diane was already reeling from having watched Leeza defend Reef on a Channel Nine newscast, and when she saw Reef standing in her doorway, Diane's shock had ratcheted into rage. Leeza's stepfather did all he could to keep her from physically attacking him as she screamed, "I'll see you in *hell* before I allow you to step one foot inside this house!" and he'd given Leeza his car keys and told her that she and Reef should go stay with friends while he tried to calm her mother down.

Jack, who left a few minutes ago to get coffee for all three of them, has been great. He's the one who finally convinced Diane to meet with Reef today. *Insisted* on it, actually. Leeza tells him that her stepfather has always been easygoing, never one to put his foot down about anything, but he dug in his heels over that, even threatened to move out of the house if Diane didn't do as he asked. Leeza isn't sure Jack would have followed through on that threat, but she loves him all the more for making it, proof that a guy doesn't have to father a child to be a great dad. More than once, Reef has thought that Frank Colville would've liked Jack Morrison a lot.

Technically, Diane has honoured Jack's wishes. She is, indeed, sitting in the same room as Reef, but she refuses to speak to him, has responded with stony silence each time he's tried to talk with her. So he's given up. Now he just wishes Leeza's stepfather would hurry back. Odds are, though, that he won't return any time soon. Reef knows about Jack's almost pathological aversion to hospitals, how he can't stand to hang around them any longer than he has to.

At least the procedure facing Leeza this time isn't life-threatening. It was supposed to have begun an hour ago but there's been a delay getting an operating room. Timetabling surgeries in a hospital this size, he muses, probably isn't much different than forecasting Nova Scotia weather. A case in point is the drizzle and fog that obstruct the view of Halifax Harbour now, despite the Weather Network's continued assurance the city will see sun today.

Reef tosses the magazine onto the table he got it from, then gets up and moves to the window. Looking down, he isn't surprised to see what looks like Beauty sitting at the far end of the hospital parking lot. He'd told Bigger and Jink on the phone from Calgary last night not to bother coming, that he'd call them when it was over and tell them how everything turned out, but they're here anyway. It makes no sense at all for them to miss a day's pay to wait in a beat-up Buick for who knows how long. At the very least, they could be relaxing at the Lord Nelson Hotel with their feet up watching pay-per-view on an enormous flat-screen that's just going to waste. The Mathesons had invited Reef to stay with them while he's in town, but he booked a room instead because he wanted to be close to the hospital today, and the Lord Nelson is only a few minutes' walk from here.

Reef reaches into his pocket for his cell and brings up Jink's number on the screen. His buddies avoid entering hospitals— they've lost too many friends to accidents and drug overdoses— but he can arrange to meet them in the parking lot and give them his room key. Looking down at Beauty, though, he doesn't press Talk. Instead, he returns the phone to his pocket knowing full well that neither Jink nor Bigger will take him up on his offer. Despite what he might say to try to convince them to leave, they'll continue to wait right where they are, and it has very little to do with him.

It's Leeza.

They've checked up on her every day since Reef flew back to Alberta last week, making sure she's okay, seeing if there's anything she needs. They even called and offered to take her to an Ultimate Cage Fight match at the Forum last night to get her mind off what's happening today and, much to Reef's surprise, she went. And loved it. She called him from the Forum as he was waiting in Calgary Airport for the red-eye to Halifax, and he could hear Bigger and Jink in the background laughing over how wound up she was as she described it to him over the phone.

Both of his buddies tell him all the time how lucky he is. Jink saved on his cellphone the news clip of her calling Roland Decker a slimy bastard, and he and Bigger laugh like loons every time they watch it. "The girl has guts," Jink says again and again, admiration in his voice. "You're one lucky guy."

But they don't need to tell him this. He knows.

He wishes Frank had met her, wishes his friend had had the chance to see the two of them together now. Finally. More than anything, though, he wishes his grandmother could have known her, could see how happy he's been these past seven days. Back in Calgary working on the condo complex, he's caught himself whistling and, a couple of times, even singing songs he hasn't thought of in years. The guys on his crew razz him mercilessly about it, and all he can do is grin.

As crazy as it sounds, he thinks his grandmother knows all about Leeza, is sure somehow that Nan was there that afternoon at the Parker Building, that she stood with the rest of the crowd in the corridor and watched as Leeza made media mincemeat out of Roland Bernard Decker. And whenever his mind returns to that afternoon and paints pictures of that moment, Reef sees Frank standing there with Nan, both of them cheering Leeza on.

As for the past week, things have turned out far better than he could have hoped. He even got a phone call from Frank's sister, who apologized over and over for what she'd said to him. He thanked her, told her no hard feelings, said that Decker had done such a great job of smearing him that it was no wonder she believed it. He'd even begun to believe it himself.

He almost feels sorry for Decker now. The day after Leeza's interview appeared on TV, Judge Hilary Thomas held a news conference in which she, too, lambasted the man, describing him as a showboating opportunist who had played fast and loose with the Privacy Act, and she was considering recommending defamation charges be brought against him. The following morning, Decker briefly announced he was withdrawing his candidacy "for personal reasons." And for the very first time, he took no questions from reporters, obviously unwilling to face another trouncing like the one Leeza had given him.

Yes, Jink and Bigger are right—the girl has guts. But it isn't what she did last week at the Parker Building that he's thinking about now. It's what she's going to do this morning.

Reef has asked her many times on the phone from Calgary if she's sure she really wants to go through with it. And each time she's said yes, despite the pain the procedure will cause her. But it isn't just the physical trauma Reef knows she has to cope with. After the coma, her multiple surgeries, and the months of rehabilitation she endured following her accident, he can only imagine the courage it has taken her to enter this hospital today so that doctors can insert needle after needle into her hips and extract the bone marrow they're after.

She told him her decision to undergo the procedure the morning after their first night together, which they'd spent at Greg Matheson's house because of her mother's meltdown. The Mathesons were thrilled to have Reef with them again, and they'd been just as welcoming to Leeza. Greg's daughters had taken to her immediately, especially the older one, Taylor, and Reef had had to compete for Leeza's attention before the girls' bedtime finally rolled around.

They'd spent most of that night talking. Leeza was upset when he told her he was flying back to Calgary in the morning, but she'd eventually come to understand why he couldn't stay in Halifax. He couldn't just desert Wayne McLaren, the employer who'd been so good to him. More important, he couldn't turn his back on those street kids, especially not after that threatening call from Sukorov, which worried Leeza when he told her about it. "What if he comes after *you?*" she asked, upset all over again. Moved by her concern, he'd drawn her into his arms and explained that he had no choice. He *had* to go.

But he also couldn't give her up. He had loved her for two years and, now that they were finally together, he couldn't imagine his life without her. She was everything to him, and he'd begged her to come to Calgary.

He was thrilled at how quickly she'd agreed. She said she'd already decided it was time to leave home, and now she knew exactly where she wanted to be. She couldn't come yet, though, she'd said. There were a couple of things she had to do first, one of them finishing her summer course. As soon as it ended, though, she'd be on a plane. She could complete her degree just as easily at the University of Calgary as in Halifax.

Because the Mathesons were asleep by then, Brett was the first one they told. They called her sometime after midnight, and once she was finally awake and coherent, neither needed to be holding the phone to hear her squealed response to their news.

Bigger and Jink, whom they reached at a party, weren't as enthusiastic. After seeing Reef and Leeza together at last, they'd just assumed their buddy would be staying in Halifax, so it was a real surprise for them to hear otherwise. Leeza tried to ease their disappointment by telling them she had tons of Air Miles that were just going to waste and they were welcome to use them whenever they wanted to visit her and Reef in Alberta. Bigger initially refused, making a dozen muttered excuses before finally confessing to a morbid fear of flying, a weakness he knew Jink would ride him about for months. But Reef had finally sold it by describing the blast the four of them would have attending the Calgary Stampede together. "You'd better warn 'em we're comin'," Bigger had finally snorted, "'cause if I'm gettin' on a plane, I plan to see Jink on a bull."

Of course, Reef and Leeza hadn't spent the *entire* night talking. The Mathesons had given Reef a pillow and bedding for their living room sofa and the same to Leeza for the sofa bed downstairs, and although Reef's whole body ached for her, he'd held back, unwilling to rush her into anything she wasn't ready for. So he was surprised when, after they'd made their phone calls, Leeza took his hand and led him downstairs. And she surprised him a second time when she wouldn't let him turn off the lights. "I've kept my body covered for two years," she whispered, then kissed him gently when she saw his face crumple with guilt. "That's not what I meant," she said softly, then told him about her phone conversation with Brett the day before and how, despite all her bravado, even Brett struggled with intimacy sometimes. "You already know me better than anyone else," she told him. "I don't ever want to hide anything from you." He began by tenderly kissing each of her scars and, afterwards, he kissed each of them again.

Standing at the window of the waiting room now, Reef's body responds to the memory of that night and, with considerable effort, he forces his thoughts elsewhere, thinking instead about the morning that followed. As she drove him to the airport, Leeza had grown suddenly quiet, and he was afraid she'd had a change of heart about coming to Calgary. But it wasn't that.

She was thinking about the second thing she had to do.

She told him then about her father, and at first Reef was relieved to learn the guy he'd seen in the food court wasn't a former boyfriend. But when she described her father's efforts to manipulate her, Reef had grown livid. He'd said she owed Scott Hemming nothing, not after the way he'd abandoned her and her sister, and she'd agreed. But she'd decided to go through with it anyway. She wasn't doing it for her father, she said. It had nearly killed her to lose Ellen to cancer, and hadn't Reef experienced the same kind of loss? How could she *not* help someone else fight that disease? Especially when that someone was family, a brother she hoped she'd get to know someday.

Reef had thought she might resent the child their father had chosen over her and Ellen—didn't she have every right to?—but he'd been wrong. "Liam had nothing to do with that," she'd told Reef as she walked him to the airport's security gate. "Just because my father didn't want *our* family doesn't mean I should cut myself off from his." When Reef kissed her goodbye, his heart suddenly seemed bigger than his body as it tried to hold all he felt for her at that moment.

It was, of course, no guarantee that a half-sister would be a sufficient genetic match for the bone marrow transplant, especially since Liam's half-brothers hadn't been suitable donors, but Leeza called her father anyway and met him that same day at the hospital, where they did the tests. It had taken nearly a week for the results to return, and they were better than expected. As soon as he'd learned that the hospital had scheduled the extraction for today, Reef had been on the first flight back.

Looking out at the drizzle making watery veins on the waiting room window, he wishes again that his flight had arrived early enough to allow him to bring Leeza to the hospital. He glances at his watch wondering how much longer it will be until the two-hour procedure begins. He longs to see her again, and twice he has gone to the nurses' station to ask if someone will come get him before they take her to the operating room.

"I suppose you're happy."

Reef turns and sees Diane looking at him, her body rigid with resentment. He reaches into his pocket, gripping the smooth round stone from Crystal Crescent Beach. "About what?" he asks, although he can guess what's coming.

She sniffs. "Everything. She doesn't listen to anything I say anymore. This thing today is a perfect example of that. We were fine until you showed up again."

He sighs. He doesn't want to get into this with her now, doesn't want to risk another screaming match, especially without Jack here to referee. But he also won't back down.

"*You* may have been fine, Mrs. Morrison," he says, returning to his seat. "Leeza wasn't."

Diane's face twists in a sneer. "You think you *know* her? You were together how long? A few *weeks* at that rehab. She was my daughter for nineteen years."

Reef takes a deep breath, releases it slowly. "She's *still* your daughter. And she'll go on *bein'* your daughter if you don't drive her away."

Diane looks down, the fingers of her right hand slowly rotating her wedding ring. "*You* took care of that. She's already bought her ticket, packed up most of what she's taking."

He dislikes this woman, dislikes even more what she did to him two years ago. If not for her restraining order, he and Leeza might have been together long before this. But it's because of those two years that he knows what she's feeling, understands what it's like to contemplate life without Leeza, and he softens. "Did she tell you what she regrets most?" Diane doesn't look up, silently turns and turns the ring, so he continues. "Not havin' you there to help her decorate the apartment."

When he moved into his one-bedroom in Calgary last year, he'd furnished it with a bargain-basement bed, scarred kitchen table, two mismatched chairs, and a futon someone had left at a curb, and he's done little else since then, hasn't even hung a picture. He warned Leeza what to expect, but she'd liked the idea of what she called a "blank canvas." And then her face had fallen as she'd shared with him what he's just told her mother now.

The woman still doesn't look up and, for a moment, he thinks she hasn't heard him. Then, "She said that?" Her voice is small, lacks the sharp edge he has heard in every other exchange.

"Yes," he tells her.

Diane turns her face away. Even from this angle, though, he can see the tremor in her chin.

Reef hears Frank's voice in his head—*Do the right thing*—and wants more than anything to ignore it. He shrugs. "I know she'd like it if you came out sometime, helped her with it. I don't care what the place looks like. I just want Leeza to be happy."

"That's all I've *ever* wanted," she says as if to herself.

"Leeza knows that."

Diane gets up and moves to the door, her back like iron as she scans the hallway. "I think she's making a mistake going out there."

"She knows that, too."

She turns to him and, in her eyes, he sees the anger and resentment he expects, but also something more. Pleading? "She'll have no friends there," she says.

He remembers Greg Matheson telling him how he and Jenny were friends long before they were lovers. "She'll have me."

Diane scoffs at this, then tries another tactic. "You're just *kids!*"

"You weren't much older than Leeza when you married her dad."

"And you know how *that* turned out," she snaps. "But as worthless as that man was," she continues, the hard edge returning, "at least he never tried to *kill* me."

"Mrs. Morrison," he says, gripping the stone harder and struggling to keep the anger from his voice, "I love Leeza. More than I thought I could ever love anyone. I'm not good enough for her, I know that. But I'm gonna do everything I can to be the kind of person she deserves. I don't know what else I can say."

"I think that says it all."

They turn and see Jack holding a cardboard tray with three cups of coffee on it. "May as well drink it while it's hot," he says, defusing the moment. He enters and hands them each a cup, then leads Diane back to her chair, taking a noisy slurp from his own cup as he sits down beside her.

All three sip their coffee, chilly silence piling up like unseen snowdrifts in the waiting room. Mercifully, the ringing of Diane's cell shatters it. Setting her cup on the low table in front of her, she opens her purse and takes out her phone. Seeing the caller's number on the display, though, she scowls and abruptly clicks the ringer off, returning the cell to her purse.

"Who was that?" asks Jack.

"Who do you think?" she replies, her voice venomous.

Jack nods, comprehension in his eyes. "He just wants—"

"I know what he wants," says Diane bitterly. "To find out how soon they'll airlift her bone marrow."

Jack puts down his cup, reaches across and takes both her hands in his. "Diane, he's her father."

"*You're* her father," she says. "Scott was a sperm donor."

He frowns. "What if the situation were reversed? What if Leeza needed marrow from *him*? Or," he continues, "what if Ellen could have been saved by this procedure? You'd have moved mountains to get it."

She pulls away. "What kills me," she says, fury unmistakable on her face and in her voice, "is that he can do all this for his *son* but he turned his back on both his *daughters.*"

Jack nods. "I'm not excusing that. No one can. Maybe it took him this long to figure out what it means to *be* a father. You always said he was self-absorbed."

"What I said was he's a self-centred son of a bitch."

As much as he dislikes her, Reef can't help grinning into his cup at the woman's bluntness. It's oddly heartening to know there's another person she hates as much as him.

"Scott never wanted to grow up," continues Diane, her voice like acid. "I didn't realize it until after we were married, but he was the eternal teenager. In hindsight, I don't think he ever really *wanted* kids. Father's Day was just another Sunday on the calendar for him. When he divorced me, he divorced the girls, too. To be honest, I'm surprised he *had* another child."

Jack shrugs. "People can change, Diane," he says, and he looks at Reef and smiles.

"What surprises me more," she says, her voice even harsher, "is that he didn't run off when the boy got sick."

"Maybe that's what it took to wake him up."

She turns to her husband, astonishment creasing her face. "I don't know how you can possibly defend him, Jack."

"I'm not. I just think nothing good ever comes from holding on to what gives us grief. Scott has to live with the choices he's made. And so do we." He reaches into her purse and pulls out the cell. "Okay?" he asks.

She glowers at him but he clicks the phone on anyway, retrieves the last incoming number, and presses Talk. "Hello," he says after a moment. "Scott, this is Jack Morrison. I'm at the hospital with Diane and Leeza's boyfriend, Reef. I'm putting you on speakerphone, okay?" He presses another button on the keypad and then sets the phone on the table. "You called a moment ago?" he asks.

"Yes," says Hemming. "I just wanted to know if they've begun the extraction yet."

"Not yet," Jack replies, then explains about the delay with the operating room. "It shouldn't be long now, though. How about I call you as soon as it starts?"

"I'd really appreciate that," Hemming says. There is a moment's silence. Then, "You said Diane is there with you?"

Reef sees the woman glance at the phone as if looking at roadkill.

"Yes," says Jack.

"Hello, Diane."

"Scott." She could as easily be hocking up phlegm.

"It's been a long time," he says.

"Not long enough."

There is a sound on the other end of the line, and Reef imagines the man clearing his throat. "How's Leeza doing?"

Diane doesn't miss a beat. "That's a question you should have asked two years ago."

There is another pause, longer this time. Finally, "I deserve that," he says, his words barely audible.

"What you *deserve*—"

"Diane," interrupts Jack softly, his voice like a hand in a glove. Then he speaks louder. "Leeza's fine, Scott. A little apprehensive, like all of us here, but fine. How's your boy doing?"

"He's—" Seconds pass and Reef thinks he can hear Hemming struggling through the silence, forcing his next words. "—not good. It's taking so much out of him. He's trying to be brave, but—" There are only breathing sounds coming from the phone now. Or sounds that might be sobs muffled by a hand over the mouthpiece.

All three of them stare at the phone on that waiting room table as if seeing the tormented man on the other end of the line. Even Diane looks stricken. She is the first to speak and, when she does, Reef hears more mother than martyr in her voice.

"You have to be strong for him," she says. "You can't let him see you like this."

There are more of the same sounds, and there is no question now that they're sobs. "I'm trying," he finally offers, his voice like gravel.

"You have to try harder, Scott." Surprisingly, Reef senses no admonition in her words, and he suddenly imagines this woman gripping her dying daughter's hand, suddenly appreciates what it must have cost her to be unceasingly stoic until the end. "You have to try harder," she repeats, more softly this time.

After a long, difficult moment, Hemming speaks again. "Look, Diane," he says, his voice a fraction firmer, "I can't thank you enough for allowing Leeza to do this—"

"I didn't," interrupts Diane. "Leeza's an adult. She makes her own decisions."

Reef can't help but wonder whose benefit she's saying this for. Surely not his. Perhaps it's as much for herself as anyone else.

"Excuse me. They're ready now."

All three turn to a woman in the doorway, her dark green scrubs a dramatic contrast to the room's pale walls. "If you'd like to see her before she goes to the OR, this is your chance."

The phone call forgotten, they all stand and Diane takes a step toward the door, but Jack puts his hand on her arm, shakes his head. She frowns, opens her mouth to speak, but he glares at her and something seems to pass between them. She looks at him a moment longer, then nods grudgingly at Reef.

"Thanks," he tells her. Putting down his coffee, he follows the nurse out.

He doesn't have far to go. Turning a corner, he sees Leeza lying on a narrow, wheeled bed in the hallway by the elevators, another nurse by her side. When he reaches her, he takes her hand, squeezing it as he leans down, presses his lips to hers. And just like every other time she has kissed him, his head swims. "You look beautiful," he murmurs when it's over.

She makes a face. "Yeah, hospital green's definitely my colour." Then she grows serious. "You must be exhausted after working yesterday and then flying all night."

"I'm okay," he says. "It's you I'm worried about."

She strokes his arm absently with her other hand, clearly unaware of the effect her fingertips have on him, making his pulse race. "I'll be fine," she says. "Really." And once more he's overwhelmed by her courage.

Just then a man in a white uniform approaches and speaks softly to the scrub nurse. She sighs and turns to them. "Looks like you'll have to wait a while longer, Leeza. They need your OR for an emergency. A man with a heart attack."

Leeza nods. "I understand."

"We'll take you back upstairs until they're ready for you, okay?"

Leeza looks at Reef, concern in her eyes. "There's no reason for you to wait around here. This could take hours. You should go to your hotel and get some sleep."

"Mm," he says noncommittally.

"I mean it," she tells him. "Or go *do* something. See a movie, maybe. You could hang out with Bigger and Jink. They said they'd be around today."

"Don't worry about me." He leans down and kisses her

again, lingering momentarily in the warm swirl of her. "I love you," he says, his voice ragged with emotion.

"I love you, too," she tells him, her eyes like twin moons. "Now go."

He watches them take her, standing motionless until the elevator closes and the light above the door winks out, then turns and heads back to the waiting room where he'll remain. No matter how long it takes.

AUTHOR'S NOTE

IN MY AUTHOR'S NOTE AT THE END OF *THE FIRST STONE*, I APOLOGIZED to readers for taking liberties with the judicial system for the purposes of that story, and I offer the same apology for *The Fifth Rule*. Although I distorted the hearing process, I'm grateful to Crown attorney Lloyd Lombard for helping me achieve some semblance of realism.

Speaking of *The First Stone*, I'd like to acknowledge the many readers who have responded so enthusiastically to that story. I have received more letters and e-mails from readers of that novel than responses to any other book I've written, and most of them offer essentially the same comment: "I loved the story, but I *hated* the ending." Most readers tell me they wanted Reef and Leeza to get together in the novel's final chapter and, as I was writing *The First Stone*, I intended for this to happen. But as I worked on the scenes involving Leeza's injuries and subsequent healing process, I researched rehabilitation facilities and saw first-hand the suffering that people with Leeza's injuries endure each day as they work to regain the mobility they've lost. The more research I did, the more I realized that it simply wasn't realistic for Leeza to forgive Reef so quickly for what he had done to her—considerable time would have to pass in order for that to happen. Countless readers have begged me to write a sequel to tie up that storyline, and I've responded to every request the same way: "I'm not a sequel kind of guy—there are so many stories I want to write that I can't imagine re-entering a world I've already created." All that changed, however, with the death of a close friend.

It's no secret that writers write best when they write about what they know, and I often begin the process of creating a character with a real person in mind. As I develop my characters further, of course, they move away from the model and take on lives of their own, but their genesis is invariably my relationship with an actual person. This was certainly true of Frank Colville in *The First Stone*, whom I modelled after one of my closest friends, Frank Pecora. Like Frank in the novel, Frank Pecora once worked with youths in the penal system, and he later became a teacher whose caring nature and commitment to social justice not only guided his professional experience but were hallmarks of his personal life, too. For instance, many years after his own sons were grown, he chose to become a Big Brother to a boy whose father was killed in a tragic accident, just one example of how Frank made a difference every moment he lived.

When Frank passed away, I delivered the eulogy at his funeral—one of the most difficult things I've ever done. That experience resonated with me long afterwards until I began to wonder what Reef might say if Frank Colville died and he were to speak at his friend's funeral. I was working on another novel at the time and, when I finally finished it, I found myself writing that funeral scene, which occurs more than two years after the event on the overpass in *The First Stone*. I stood beside Reef in the pulpit, listened as he described the extent of his loss, watched as he struggled to find words that would adequately sum up a person whose impact he would feel forever. It was both the easiest and toughest scene I'd ever written and, once I finished it, I realized Reef had more to tell me, more to show me. The rest of the novel unfolded pretty much on its own—in fact, I've never written a novel so fast. I hope I haven't disappointed readers who have their own ideas about what happened after *The First Stone* ended. For me, it's been a joy returning to characters I've loved, so it appears I'm a "sequel kind of guy" after all.

As always, I want to thank the incredible team at Harper-Collins—in particular, my supremely talented editor, Lynne Missen, for her patience, guidance, and good humour as I resurrected Reef and Leeza. Lynne has edited all but one of my young adult novels, including *The First Stone*, and there is no person I trust more with a story than her.

Finally, I would like to thank the many teachers, librarians, and booksellers who have championed *The First Stone*. Although its profanity can be problematic, especially when the book is shared in classrooms—sorry, but I just couldn't get Reef and his buddies to use words like "Gosh!" and "Darn!"—I am grateful that so many people have been able to look beyond that language and accept the reality it characterizes. I hope readers of *The Fifth Rule* are able to do the same.